HEAT SIGNATURE

BY THE SAME AUTHOR

Dive
Glow in the Dark

HEAT SIGNATURE

A NOVEL

LISA TEASLEY

BLOOMSBURY

Published by Bloomsbury USA, New York
Distributed to the trade by Holtzbrinck Publishers

All papers used by Bloomsbury USA are natural,
recyclable products made from wood grown in well-managed
forests. The manufacturing processes conform to the
environmental regulations of the country of origin.

Library of Congress Cataloging-in-Publication Data

Teasley, Lisa, 1962–
Heat signature: a novel / Lisa Teasley.—1st U.S. ed. p. cm.
ISBN-13: 978-1-59691-101-7 (pbk.)
ISBN-10: 1-59691-101-8 (pbk.)
1. Mothers—Death—Fiction. 2. Murder—Fiction. 3. California—Fiction. I. Title.
PS3620.E43H43 2006
813'. 6—dc22
2005026838

First U.S. Edition 2006

1 3 5 7 9 10 8 6 4 2

Typeset by Hewer Text UK Ltd, Edinburgh
Printed in the United States of America by Quebecor World, Fairfield

For my Dad

0

The Fowl and the Pussycat

They weigh in the cocks. With virgin voyeur rush, Sam stands third row from the pit. Stroking the flat half moon of his thumbnail, he eyes the baby oil gloss of the black bird though the red is the favorite. The big-boned handler faces his prize fowl. He pulls on his left sun-scorched earlobe for luck, as he is missing a chunk of his right. Sam touches his own soft brown ear. He looks around the filthy warehouse for Haley and wonders how much longer she'll take with the drinks. Just above him in the makeshift stands, a young drunk couple rubs against one another. Sam's nose prickles with shame before the sneeze. He watches their pierced tongues whip like lizards, and their closed eyes flutter. Pretending not to be envious, Sam grabs the back of his hot neck, stares over their heads, then turns back around.

Outside, the California desert shantytown sags with heat. It is a dense, early August evening. Every direction Sam peers, lurid faces obscure his view. Beer, mildew, and meth sweat fuse the air. He sneezes again and wipes with the back of his hand. He squeezes his temples, feels a headache come on like fever.

They bring out the lean, dark chocolate–feathered cock they'll use for bait. One of these birds will be killed right in front of him. Sam can't help thinking of his mother. Sixteen years has passed since he last saw her in the flesh. Now a man, he may as well be a child; the pain is just as hot and fresh. In two days her murderer will be out on parole. Sam holds his wide creased forehead, the only feature suggesting his age, thirty-one, and vocation of concern, nurse. His nearly defined arms are folded, clammy palms cradle his elbows the way he would Haley's hip. He draws out the self-pity moment. Caressing the pinch of elbow, he soothes the dry ash spot just over the funny bone. He doesn't know he locks ankles, rocks himself to sleep in this same rhythm every night in bed whether with Haley, his cat, or alone.

Here at the cockfights waiting on a girlfriend his mother may have been kind not to judge, Sam thinks of any opportunity for escape. He calls to her in his head, waits for a response, but she only speaks in his dreams. The low rumbling around the ring reverberates. As he tries listening, tries feeling his mother's presence in places he knows she never would have been, his stomach rolls and tightens with disbelief. He could never accept that she brought on her own death.

Excitement rises in the warehouse. Sam's hairs stiffen. The strong, dank must smothers. It is the rank high of gambling. The alchemic thrill of money, violence, and strange bodies packed close together. "Fools," he says under his breath.

At last Haley returns as the handlers secure the blades to the steel spurs of each bird. Towering over Sam in her zebra-striped heels and frank, brief clothes of pink and peach tones, she holds a bag of nuts. Her longneck beer is already open and drooling. She pulls the can of soda from her big denim bag, heavy with a fat September *Vogue*. The strap indents her bony shoulder.

"Here," she says, her voice husky. Sam's furrowed brow forms a hood. He concentrates on the cocks so hard he could claim he doesn't hear her. She lays the cold can against her forehead, both glisten with sweat. She leans against him. Sam stares at the pit until she shoves the soda at him. Her blunt, chin-length orange hair glows, casting a science fiction amber hue to the tan of her otherwise white skin.

"You should have bet on the red one," she says.

"I should have bet on the black one," Sam answers. He pops open the can, catching the overflow fizz with his tongue. It stings with a cut when the bulky guy on his left bumps into him. Sam tastes the iron of blood and waits for an apology that doesn't happen.

"Look at Dad," she says, shaking her head, flaring her nostrils. "Just look at him." Her painted-purple lips go tight. Sam nods, but with disgust examines up and down his neighbor who does a tweaker two-step. He puts his arm around Haley, she half-smiles and gulps her beer.

The cocks face off in the center of the ring. He wishes he could hear a word anyone else but Haley was saying.

"Don't you see him?" she whispers, pointing with her bottle at one of the two white handlers from the Inland Empire. "Look at that face. Look at that gnarly, maniacal, *insane* look on his face. Bet he blew as much coke up the bird's nose as his." She shakes her head again. Sam feels the goose bumps rise and dot her arm; he lets go.

"All I see is a burnt leathery desert rat, like the rest of 'em," Sam says, shrugging in emphasis of his own bad posture and sloppy, ill-fitting, extra-large pants and T. "He's not so bad."

"Yeah, well, wait until it's *his* cock out there. I don't think I can take this. Maybe we should just go."

From the audience comes a high-pitched squeal. The tweaker throws his hands out, knocking into Sam again. He can't make out what's happening behind the flying dust and flurry of feathers. The crouching official jumps to his feet. Avoiding the blades, the deft handlers grab back their cocks, readying for a second round.

"What happened?" Sam asks. "What are they saying?"

"Who knows," she says.

"But you've been to so many of these."

"I'm not watching, Sam. I'm ready to go." She downs the rest of her beer and drops the bottle to the ground. Sam glances at it there, glares at her, then picks it up.

Silence hovers over the ring as the cocks advance toward one another. Their eyes bead hard with hate, the hackles stand on end. The red one hurls itself against the black, who lowers its head, but not quick enough. The neck rolls back. Black feathers float among red like a slow motion action painting. Blood soaks the pit. The red's spur strikes the black breast; Sam thinks he hears the rattle from its lung. Both birds panting, the black cock falls, legs jerking, the beak spurting. The crowd cheers.

"Now you know how I feel," Haley says, clutching Sam's arm. She lets go and heads for the exit. Sam looks once at the dead cock. The handler, with his winner, milks the rabid crowd, some delirium high, others sick with losing.

Haley's father prepares his fowl. It's not coke but rum and pepper that he's given the bird, Sam hears the tweaker say, but doesn't ask how he knows. Sam has only met Haley's father twice, and watches him at the pit once more. If he concentrates he can see how the father could have spawned her. The way the lazy top lip covets the bottom, never touching. No way to get his attention from so far to say good-bye—a courtesy Haley would never offer—Sam meekly makes his way out to find her.

She already stands next to the "convertible shoebox," her name for his '88 red Chrysler LeBaron. Her bag sits on the trunk as she attempts to light her cigarette. She squints, deepening premature crow's feet. With distinct femininity, she cups the flame from the wind.

"Well?" she says, blowing the smoke out in front of her. She waves her slim hand. "What did I tell you, is it nasty or what?"

"I'm still leaving at the end of the week, Haley," Sam says. He unlocks the passenger door, though he doesn't open it for her.

"Did I say anything about that?" She grunts, pushes her lower

4

jaw forward, and jerks open the squeaky door at the same time he does. "Did I bring you here for pity? Or did I bring my boyfriend to see what I grew up against?" She stares him down from across the hood of the car.

He focuses on her with pronounced patience until she gets in, and sighs heavily. Irritated, she gets right back out since her purse still sits on the trunk. Once inside the car again, the door squeals as she slams it shut.

"Shall I take you home?" Sam asks. Shy, he looks at her, makes pillows of his lips. When she doesn't react, he impatiently yanks at the neck of his worn, brown T-shirt.

"No, I wanna come home with you," she says, softening. She puts her head on his shoulder. He slackens it, she rolls off.

"It's not like I don't have the cat."

"She won't bother me."

"Allergies magically disappeared?" He looks at her for one flash as if everything gone wrong in his life up to now is her fault. He holds that thought until he can make himself let it go, and starts the car. The engine purrs, spits, and coughs. She laughs, raffish with girlish rings. His mother used to laugh with her girlfriends like that, but even more so, her regal head back, full abandon.

Sam backs up between two badly parked trucks, his right arm rounding the back of Haley's seat. As he takes the car out of reverse and it jumps into gear, she makes a clucking sound, tonguing the roof of her mouth, tick tock, like the car could explode any second. When he crosses the railroad tracks and is free from the hectic lot, he laughs with her, maintaining a distant lover's amicableness for the forty-minute ride home.

A weak warm wind kicks. Salty sediment moves in hops and skips, spotted by Sam's headlights as he climbs the turnoff. The air falls still again. As he floors it up the washboard road just rocky enough to knock out the occasional oil pan, dirt rolls in spirals behind them all the way to the house he shares with his adoptive father, Joe. As they pass Joe's handmade UPS box, the front end scrapes the drive as he pulls up to the garage that serves as Joe's overflow storage of extra fittings for the pipes business. PVC, rubber, and metal stack the entrance of their environmentally sensitive home, insulated with cans of salt. A solar-paneled dome crowns the off but charming construction of wood and tin set against the northeast hillside of Joshua Tree National Park.

Sam and Haley exit the car. Their footsteps crunch loudly on desert sand, echoing like a Western. Zeke, their closest neighbor by an acre, leaves Joe's garage through the open door. Freckled, sun-scarred, with the appearance of too much rouge, Zeke is dressed for the desert's top speed on his parked Suzuki Hayabusa 1300. A red-tailed hawk sails overhead, disturbing his balance as he hops off the porch.

"He-eey," Zeke draws out, and knocks knuckles with Sam. "Caught your barrel rolls, man, that car is a miracle. Thought you were gone already." He looks him straight in the eye.

"Nah, I'm taking off Monday."

Zeke clears his throat. "You see geezer's wheelchair Joe's been working on? They brought it in couple hours ago. Can you believe he wants his spoon collection welded onto it?" Zeke opens wide his scoop-shaped eyes.

"What's Joe doing that for?" Sam asks.

"Don't deny your old man a little creativity. It's *crazy* looking, you gotta go check it. Art, dude."

"Zeke?" Haley asks, putting out one hand, holding her hair back from her face with the other. As the wind returns gentle as a fan, her nipples push out of her tight peach top.

"Sorry, man. This is Zeke, Zeke, Haley."

"I can't *believe* I haven't met you all this time. What's it been? Two years?" Haley asks, tilting her head, face soft and porch-lit.

"Oh, I've seen *you*, Diamond Girl," Zeke says, wicked smile. "You're a great dancer." He winks, taking in the length of her body. He does a second once-over of appreciation for her solid hip-to-toe leg of diamond tattoos.

"I don't dance anymore. I work in an office." The hot wind lashes out, and Haley moves two steps forward with it. "Whoa."

"It's kinda early for Santa Anas," Zeke says. "But that's all we need with the fires blazing."

"That's far from us, man," Sam says.

"I met your sister," Haley says. "I've run into her quite a few times, she's very cool. Sam never told me, she used to be in that show—"

"That's well before your time, isn't it?" Zeke interrupts.

"I'm older than you think," she says, her smile curving higher on one side.

"But look at you, baby," Zeke says, nodding with approval. Sam tries to retain an indifferent expression.

"Your sister was gorgeous back then! What were you doing, beating them all off with bats?" she asks, getting too loud for Sam's taste. He shifts his weight.

"All before my time as well."

"So what do you do?"

"Oh, this and that," Zeke says, juts his chin in the air, then looks at Sam.

"Anyway, tell your sister I said hi. I like her boyfriend, too."

"Andrew, the snob limey wanker. He still resents Paige for choosing Twentynine Palms over posh Palm Springs."

"Well tell her I said hello, anyway," Haley shouts over the new whip of the howling wind.

"She's up in Mendocino, they're leeching off his parents."

"I thought this place was her house." She motions toward the imposing modern monstrosity with its own street name, Twilight, which forks off from Sam and Joe's road.

"One of three. And I'm the house sitter, what can I say?" He nods to Sam, who is already two feet closer to his porch. "I'm off, bro."

"Catch you later."

"Will I see you before you leave?"

"I'm around," Sam says.

"Very good." Zeke nods, takes Haley hand, and kisses it.

She watches Zeke slink off, as Sam continues to the front door.

"I'm gonna go say hello to Joe," Haley calls to Sam, who keeps walking.

Appearing at the side of the house is Charlene, fat and calico with nose, tail, and feet dipped in white like she'd stepped in snow. With confrontational, surprised, and ice blue eyes, she yowls and brushes against Sam's ankle. He bends down to pick her up. Sam turns around to see Haley hasn't made a single step toward Joe's shop. She stands there with a pleading stare, the wind pushing her one way as she resists, keeping her distance from the cat.

Sam takes Haley's hand, leads her through the corridor, and notices the hall cabinet of his mother's document collection is shut. This is odd to him since the door gets stuck, and they have lived with it ajar for ten years without bothering to fix it. He tries the knob, and it easily opens.

"What is your problem?" she asks, eyeing his dropped bottom lip and knit brows.

He quickly closes it up again. "Nothing."

Sam still holds the cat with one arm; Haley pulls on his free one, now leading him to his bedroom. He turns his attention to her and away from his mother, surprised to feel again a virgin's anticipation and dread.

"He's letting me into his room," she says, pushing open the door, her voice high-pitched in sarcasm.

"You've been here at least ten times."

8

"Right. In *two years*."

She looks around, her hands on tight pink-skirted, happy hips swaying to the growing swirl of sound outside. Charlene jumps from Sam's arms, Haley makes exaggerated space for her to get by. She shakes her head, unbuttons the pale peach top he would now like to rip off, and she throws it at him. It hits him in the face; he smiles.

"Come to mama," she says, unzipping her skirt and wiggling out of it, keeping her zebra-striped heels on. He slips his finger in between her thighs, she is not as wet as he would like, nor is he as hard. With so much emphasis on the height and heat of their very first time, all of the following have felt like embers outing to ash.

"You can't run from all of this, you know," she says in her party girl-used voice, lying naked in bed, sheen of sweat like a mustache above her lip. She is looking down between her small, mango-shaped breasts, tweezing a single stray hair with her long, elaborately painted fingernails. Sam rolls from his side to his back, looks up at the low ceiling.

"You can't run. Do you hear me?"

"I'm not running. I just need to think. I just want to get out on the road."

She moves onto another hair, flakes off a bit of drying come.

"I know it's painful, Sam." She meets his eyes, and he looks away.

Since he could never emotionally connect with patients whose body products he's handled, he can't stand these kinds of intimacies with a woman, when she is comfortable enough to make a double-chin in going for the hairs on her chest, or even spitting the toothpaste from her mouth.

He looks at her again, knowing she has just read his mind. There is a curl of indignity on her lips. It strikes him that she looks a great deal like a picture of his real father, the one he used to moon at as an adolescent. His mother, named for the month July, used to tell him his father was not a bad person but for her own reasons—which he had to respect—she couldn't remain in touch.

"You never talk about him getting out of prison, and you know you need to."

"Don't bring up his name in here."

"I *didn't*. But you have to accept that you did all you could."

"Drop it, Haley, would you?"

"Okay!" She holds up both hands. Her nails–a palm tree scene on fuchsia—catch her attention. She admires them as if he should do the same with her. "I'm not gonna get all worked up with you tonight."

She gets up out of bed, standing first on top of it like a stage, the long, bare, tan leg looking like an odd mistake next to the ornately inked, diamondback snake–like skin of the other. The sight of her shaven muff, flaking pearl necklace, and the amp of her anger gets him hard again. She hops down, landing graceful as an acrobat. But Charlene slips through the cat door on the back wall, jumps up on the bed, tries to nuzzle the underside of Sam's knee, and Haley sneezes from where she stands.

"I can't sleep here," she protests, now shutting herself in his clean, lemony ammonia–smelling bathroom. "I'm not wanted here, anyway," she whines from behind the shut door.

It's true that tonight he wants to be alone with his dreams. His mother is long due a visit, and he's convinced she is trying to tell him something. She hasn't come in months, and he wonders if it's because he hasn't been accessible enough. On the road, she could have him all to herself. He picks up fat, fluffy Charlene, cradling her in his arms before getting dressed to drop Haley home to her isolated shack twenty-five minutes northwest in Pioneertown. She'll beg him to stay over, but he won't.

1

Sam's July

July Brown was a native Los Angeles feminist who wore polka dots and other busy patterns. Tall, dark, gamine, and gregarious, upon graduation she denied her education, spoke in spates of slurred consonants and musical dissonance. A teetotaler, philosopher, and guitar player (with a secret desire to write hit songs in Nashville), July liked hanging in bars afternoons with the pros while still unemployed. She picked up her pattern of speech during this extended period of bluesy twang.

Moving two hours south to the whiter, military-centered, and more conservative city slowly stripped her of the African way of language as music. By the time of wide computerization in 1987, she worked downtown overlooking the bay in the San Diego County office as a data entry clerk. Updating from paper and microfiche, she peered over frameless, rectangular reading glasses while keying in a thousand marriage licenses daily. When she wasn't pushing Sam on homework—of which he was always well ahead—July spent evenings with Ed, a Native American, descendant of the Kumeyaay tribe, who binged on candy and soured most of her gatherings.

Young Sam got along with Ed, trusting in his laconic, straightforward manner. Few readily approved of July and Ed's on-again, off-again union, since at that time in San Diego the few African Americans there stuck together. Tongues clucked when

Ed walked Sam in unison stride from school to the corner store for ice cream. Some gave July the notion she deserved the hurt of that final break with the sugar addict. This inspired her valiant effort to speedily mend. She truly loved Ed, but was done being prone to heartbreak. She felt the ever-longing Sam deserved more. She had already denied him his history—his natural and willing father.

A late bloomer even well after Sam's birth when she was twenty-seven, July didn't fill out her dresses until she hit forty. Few considered her sexy until after her first night with the modestly industrious and content Joe Braxton, the man Sam still lives with and calls his dad. Her pores opened, the heat off her skin could melt the cream down Sam's cone from across the room. Never embarrassed by his mother, her new man equally fascinated Sam. Joe was the first Muslim July had ever met, and without proselytizing or overt machismo he led her body and mind to health. July then took up with Joe full-time, and the tiny overbearing community embraced them as an acceptable, magnetic couple.

July carried herself away creating a colorful house of non-blending hues. She cooked the most adventurous newspaper recipes, and to ward off any potential jealousy of her new enthusiasms, coddled her son's nurturing tendencies. Though still working in a building of records, deeds, and death certificates, July frequented garage and estate sales, collecting original documents with increasing fervor: family Bibles with lineages, wanted posters, indentured servant and slave contracts. Without the least bit of embarrassment, she read tarot with talent for the ever-expanding circle of friends in her aquamarine dining room of framed sports heroes and political icons. The year she was murdered, July drew The Hanged Man as her Growth Card. Believers always said she expected her killer, and had practically set a place for him at the table.

No one knew what she was doing near the lighthouse that day. Especially not Joe, when she called him on the pay phone. She told him she had abandoned her car some blocks away from the Cabrillo National Monument due to an inexplicable bout of dizziness. As her lies accumulated, he didn't take it to heart, and was much too slow in picking her up. Half an hour later, he found only her car.

Days before Sam turned fifteen, the police caught the culprit of her obscene and gruesome murder. This man was also her rapist, which Sam didn't learn until he read the news-in-brief that was nameless except for the arresting officer. He stopped growing shortly after. At five foot ten he was an inch shy of what his beloved mother had been.

Sam's new status as orphan made him all the more adorable and tragic to July's closest girlfriends. Two of them would have taken in the boy with the roast-pecan brown skin and Japanimation-huge, deep set, rum-colored eyes framed by the worried forehead. But Joe put up a fight through the legal route of adoption, and July's estranged mother never answered the court papers sent to her last address in Portland, Oregon. (The city adoption agency found more about July's past than the district attorney's office, which failed to turn up even her real birth certificate.) Joe had been with July for not quite a year and wasn't overly taken with her son, but after her death he came to worship her. Sam was old enough to express a good opinion about where he should go, but never having a father in the first place left him wont to lean on most anyone. Trustworthy, though wavering in faith, Joe would certainly do.

Already savvy of this weakness in himself—never choosing what he wanted, but rather what chose him—Sam soon latched on to the idea of giving for getting. He supposed this would not only win him recovery from pain, but also the superhero strength it required. Sitting on his favorite sandstone cliff under a snarled and twisted torrey pine in the national park, he admired the view of agaves, chaparrals, sage, and his newfound courage. Right then and there, he vowed to become a nurse, and not long after, July came to visit in his dreams. She sat at the foot of his bed, without speaking.

A year ahead in school since second grade, at the age of sixteen Sam went against the advice of a school counselor who had expected more of him; he enrolled in the nursing program for his BSN at California State University, Los Angeles. Joe made the move with Sam to LA, resetting up his pipefitting business, which fortunately relied on shipping rather than walk-in. Joe's warehouse of welded, recycled joints and hubs was on the outskirts of downtown near Sam's school, but they lived forty minutes away in "the creative city" of West Hollywood. The Spanish-style apartment had its original art deco green and black tile, and it sorely reminded them of July. They couldn't help but imagine all of her loving dashes clashing about the place.

At first Sam was somewhat relieved to be lost in the larger, spread out city, which he didn't even know was July's birthplace, though she came to him more often there. Joe left for work before Sam got out of bed. He thought if he could prolong his dreams, he would be able to embrace the details of her, rather than just the feeling. It was rare that Sam and Joe ate meals together; they passed one another in the bathroom hallway, where on occasion Joe played up the humor of his nudist tendencies. Their continuing hushed mourning never gave rise into words until the epidemic arrival of Nordic rats. The pests imitated the downtown LA traffic, running boldly in droves across the telephone lines at twilight. Sam bought Joe a birthday cat, and though her trophies were many, she caused a brief period of yelling matches. Joe was seeing an elusive woman, Charlene, who (after the ever-building grief over July) nearly did him in. Joe never cared for the cat, and watched it take shape as guilt, but Sam grew all the more attached. To rub in Joe's mistake of falling for any woman after his mother, Sam changed the pet's name from Cat to Charlene.

Sophomore year, Sam kept focus on studies, though he managed to move from girl to girl without conscience. He used his sensitive, melancholy look as magnet. After his first degrading and short experience with sex, where the girl, numb on coke, asked him to "ram and ram" it harder, Sam never admitted to himself a new determination to take pride in his prowess. An equal opportunity dater, black, white, Latina, Asian, fat, thin, short, medium, or tall, he envisioned each one to be everything she wasn't, and so fell in love with none. Considering himself damaged goods, he thought he did them service by not sticking around. Disturbing to him still was that each girl had a stranger word system than the last. Whether in speech pattern or lovesick letters, they were alarming and individual, and this only served to further justify his fleeing every one of them. Two more years of this and upon graduation, Sam soon followed Joe, who relocated once again for an affordable mortgage in the high desert military town of Twentynine Palms, near the postcard views of Joshua Tree. There they found a taste for hot summers, cold winters, and too brief a wildflower spring and clear, crisp air fall. Sam and Joe grew closer there, but July visited less and less.

Sam's first nursing job was at the naval hospital in this new baffling world of the combat center, where he met his command sponsor, the married, ginger-haired, and plainspoken Tallulah Larkin. She was mesmerizing to him, and it was then Sam became mindful of reincarnation. He went around staring at every baby in hopeful recognition of his mother. He was convinced that God might try again, this time around making her an icon of devotion. Tallulah shared his beliefs of the afterlife, as well as his afternoons of sex with punishment. Whether following *Kama Sutra*, tied up, dressed as a woman or an infant, Sam soon tired of new roles and left her. Tallulah put up a strident fight to no avail. She burned the bridge in asking him to rape her in costume as a Blood or a Crip. His disappointment was profound, and Sam re-evaluated his assumption that he really came close to feeling with her. He ended up thinking of her as the magus.

Not long after he was honored at the hospital as Civilian of the Quarter, Sam met the young and interestingly unstable chaplain, Abel Kozinski, who was fresh from divinity school, following gambling and kibbutz. Abel's betting days over, he nevertheless taught Sam card tricks and poker. They ate snacks for dinner together; they spent hours making light of tragedy. They watched sitcoms and, on occasion, rented foreign films, over which Sam spent more energy guessing whether the words and gestures fit the subtitles.

Abel consoled the dying at the Hi-Desert Medical Center, which he convinced Sam was a less stifling place of employment. Hospitals always in need of nurses, Sam had no trouble getting a job there. He was seeing Abel so much he looked upon him as a brother, and Sam felt Abel—who was estranged from his own sibling—did so likewise.

It was Abel who brought Sam to the strip bar, den of the magi, where he took up with Haley. She had long, pomegranate red hair. Her skin was pale, unriddled by the desert, and he was transfixed by the intricate patterns on her leg of solid turquoise and navy diamond tattoos. She moved at first as if she couldn't claim the stage, but then with a naughty fairy's brusqueness, pulled off an arabesque before gyrating with the pole. She seemed both ridiculous and enigmatic, particularly after the one black girl who was luscious, unstudied, and precise. He tipped Haley with a day's pay and bought her a drink instead of taking the lap dance. He was moved by her eyes, strange, morose, but celestial. And because her name was Haley, he fell over himself trying to impress her with what he knew about Halley's Comet. She puckered like an imp with her painted purple lips and pointed out the difference in spelling and pronunciation. When Sam brought up further confusion over Hale-Bopp, she cocked her head. A loop of thick red hair framed her eye, and she cleared him up on the particulars she knew well of both comet and cult. Sam clapped his hands together then opened them in surrender. With true tenderness, she kissed his worried forehead.

On their first proper date at the local barbecue house on Highway 62, he found out she was just as motherless. She blamed her four years of hard partying on her parents, and attributed the nine of sobriety to a higher power, which troubled him just as much. At this point, Sam had never figured to what or whom he could assign responsibility for his fate. His life was somewhere out there in the dark of the future. Haley wiped the corner of her upturned mouth of sauce when she finished the story he had only half listened to.

He stared into his baby back ribs, made a trail with his finger through the pork and beans, imagining all the ways the two of them would be tied for life, and all the various methods he—or July—could try to get her to leave him.

2

The Brothers Grim

Sunday morning, Joe stands at the griddle over sweet potato pancakes. He's got his dirty, threadbare, baby blue hospital slippers on that Sam long ago brought home for him. A burgundy striped cotton robe opens up to the tight white and charcoal gray naps on his chest. At sixty-seven, he is still a healthy golden sultry brown, his hair thick, insolent and a touch too long. Barely lined, age moles like beauty marks splatter his Dizzy Gillespie cheeks. He flips the CD-sized buttermilk cakes, yawns over the fumes, and smiles high with hunger. He pretends to be unaware of Sam behind him, but Sam knows that he knows he is there.

"How can you stand it with your robe on in this heat?"

"You got company up in here, don't you?"

"Haley's gone, I took her home last night."

"In that case, then," he says with his gravel voice, taking the pancakes off the griddle, pouring more batter, and letting his robe drop to the floor. The torn blue slippers make his nakedness all the more saucy and vexing to Sam as Joe wiggles his balls for reaction.

"Ah man, put it back on," Sam says, throwing up his hands, going for the coffee pot at the corner of the full copper counter-top.

"How were the cockfights?"

"Sickening."

"You lost," Joe laughs bawdily, flipping more cakes.

With a dainty fingertip securing the fail-safe lid, Sam pours himself a tall beer glass of coffee. He opens the antique fifties turquoise fridge, scratches his head—also in need of a comb, cut, and shape—shoulders stooped, he searches for the whip cream.

"I don't gamble." Sam responds late and in disgust at Joe's still naked behind.

"Good. Neither do I." He turns his back on the stove. "So d'you see the chair, yet?"

"No."

"That cat Dawson and his scrawny wife brought his wheel-chair and crazy spoon collection over—"

"I'll go check it out before I leave," Sam interrupts, holding the small carton of whip cream, now scratching at the back of his waist under the pinstriped boxers' elastic.

"Thought you had nothing today. Saw you were already packed."

"I am. Just a got a few errands, one in Palm Desert . . ." Sam sits down at the junky dining table, opening up the paper, pulling out the travel section first.

With his stout index finger, Joe pushes in a nostril, a loud, gunk-filled inhale, then hacks into the stainless steel sink. He puts a stack of pancakes on two plates, crowned with melting pats of butter, sets it down in front of Sam, who doesn't look up from the paper. To set down the milk and maple syrup, Joe pushes aside old *TV Guides*, bills, washers, finish nails, and a brand new box of cat food. Sam cracks his knuckles, looks up at Joe, still naked, and Joe looks right back at him and sits down.

"So you got a plan, son?" He clasps his fingers, waits. "You got a plan?"

Sam eyeballs Joe then the messy table. "Don't get serious on me, now, please." With finality, he scoots back his chair to fetch them forks. When he returns, Joe has torn into pancakes, stuffing bites in with syrupy fingers. They sit and eat in silence together.

"All I'm asking is where you going?" he returns to the subject with a mouthful.

"Up the coast, I told you a hundred times." Sam roughly wipes his generous mouth with a paper towel.

"I thought you weren't sure of where your mother said to go."

"North."

"North, where?"

"I don't know."

"For how long?"

"How can I know, Joe?"

"But, work—"

Sam interrupts. "When I run out of money, I'll hook up with the Travel Nurses company—"

"Easy as that?" Joe interrupts him. "Don't understand why you don't just do it *now*."

"I don't want to deal with any calls on the road for a while, I just want to stay open."

"If it's really your mother talking to you, she can reach you whether you're relaxing or you're working."

Sam looks up at him from under the heavy canopy of his brows, then back down at the paper.

"You going back to San Diego?"

"Why would I do that?" Sam snaps.

"Don't know." Joe closes his eyes, shakes his head slowly as if tuning into a mournful choir. "There ain't *nothing* we can do about it." His face goes bad berry sour, tongue curling snakelike and ready behind his teeth. "Would kill him myself." Spit spurts with the *k* sound.

Sam stands, taking his plate with him, just as the phone rings. He lets the machine pick up. He won't directly look at Joe, who has his face in his hands, though he is right there in Sam's peripheral vision. Watching Joe's pain makes it all the harder.

"It's Kayla, Sam, pick up," says the young, nasal voice, crackling in and out with cell phone roaming. "Abel's in trouble . . . where are you?"

Sam trips over himself to grab the phone. "Hey, what's going on?"

"You're there, thank God."

"What is it?" Sam asks with urgency.

"Abel's having a nervous breakdown or something—"

The machine still on, her voice echoes in feedback, cutting in and out. Joe turns around, wipes the tears from his eyes, and looks Sam up and down. Sam hits STOP on the machine.

"Where are you?"

"I'm in Taos with that guy."

"Taos? Don't you think that's all it is?" Sam's tone quickens in anger.

"Yes and no. I mean . . . this has been coming for a while, and you know it, Sam. Just go to him. Please. Who knows what he might do."

Sam writes down her phone number, while Joe hacks again at the sink. He stares at Sam, waiting for the story. Sam hangs up, looks at Joe with guilt, but Abel obviously needs him more. Joe turns around. Leaving the dirty dishes stacked, he picks up his robe and walks out, patches of ash dry skin and dark spots on the backs of his legs.

Seven minutes away in the middle of Abel's bungalow, Sam stands stunned by the overturned chair, broken window, and molded food stench.

"Jay?" Abel calls from the bathroom.

"No, it's me!" Sam answers, stepping over trash, following Abel's voice to the bathroom doorway. "Since when do you smoke?"

Abel raises one lazy eye, inhales, fingers straight up, cigarette drooping like a junkie's. Sam eyes the incredible length of Abel's dick, wondering why he came to be so slighted in this area. *It's not in the size but how you use it*, he thinks, now staring at the dark circles under Abel's eyes.

"What's happening around here, man? The place is a *mess*."

"Kayla call you?" Abel asks.

"What's going on here, A?"

"She tell you how she was sitting with her legs wide open?" More alertly he sits in the tub, now squeezing the cigarette between his fingers. "Did she?" he snaps.

"When?"

"You were here, oh, *you were here*," Abel says, shaking his head, his voice guttural. "It may have been a while ago, as you've sure forgotten about your friend, but you were here for her—"

"She was wearing shorts or something, wasn't she?" Sam cuts him off.

"But *still*," he snarls. He drops the butt of his cigarette in the murky bath water. "She's gone. Just like that. Just like our rights, one, two, three, up in a puff." Abel blows on the end of his finger as if it were a gun. He looks up at Sam, smiles with brevity, then his expression blurs, slowly sharpening into anger. "Will you hand me that towel?"

Sam looks around: dirty washcloths, beer bottles, candy wrappers, ash on the floor, turned over products on the shelves. No towel in sight. He shrugs. "I don't see one anywhere, man. Don't you ever clean up anything around here?"

Abel stands, his bony knee a bruise of rose purple bloom, the scant black hairs on his white body lying slick to his scared skin. The penis still long and defiant. Abel looks up at Sam, the fat lid over the lazy eye an appealing but sick violet like his knee. He kicks the inside of the tub as if his containment was its fault; the splash licks high in retaliation. "Fuck," Abel says, biting down, his jaws spreading.

"Oh, so, no, no problem. Today's my day for butt naked men," Sam says, nodding.

"You're a nurse, you can take it." Abel spanks the fat of Sam's bicep, shakes his head and body like a dog. He grabs Sam's wrists. Sam unlocks himself from Abel's grasp, turns him around, takes him by the shoulders, leads him out of the bathroom, and finds a towel on the bed.

"So what's going on here, man? What's up with the broken window and the upside down furniture?"

"I was robbed," Abel says, stomps once like a child.

"That was months ago."

"That was last week," he raises his voice. "And where were you? You don't answer your phone anymore, Princess? And off you go to Kabbalah knows where."

"Robbed *again*?"

Abel falls over trying to put one leg into the jeans handed to him, so Sam helps him back up, but Abel starts crying.

"Hush," Sam says, not realizing it's exactly the way July did to him.

"I don't want my brother to see me like this," Abel snorts, wiping his nose with the shirt he hasn't yet put on.

"He's not here, is he?"

"Kayla called him."

"She called *me*," Sam says, pulling him up to lead him into the kitchen. "And we're going to get you something to eat. We should probably get you out of here."

"No!" Abel exclaims, grimacing. "Didn't you hear about the murder that just happened?"

"The Marines in the burning car?"

"Yes," Abel says, smacking his tongue as if tasting something almost as delicious as it is revolting.

23

"That was last week. And you're not a Marine, so why worry about it?"

"My robbery was last week."

"There wasn't no robbery here last week. That happened *months* ago. You been living with your windows broken all this time, man? It's a wonder there's anything left up in here. Come on, A, sit down." Sam pulls a chair out from the surreal, shiny, and round oak wood dining table. "So what, you polish this thing and ignore everything else?" He looks at Abel, who drops down in performance to the chair. Sam takes the T-shirt from Abel's hands and throws it at his face. "Put it on, *now.*"

Sam finds eggs and mustard in the fridge, pita bread in the cupboard, and sausage in the freezer that he dunks in a bowl of hot water in the sink.

"You're leaving, aren't you?" Abel asks, narrowing his dark eyes then scratching through the top of his wet hair. He lets the shirt drop to the floor, puts his foot on it, using it like a mop.

"You know that, man," Sam sighs, whipping the eggs with a fork, stopping to pick out bits of the shell that fell in. "It's work that's getting to you. Don't blame it on her, man. That shit gets tiring, doesn't it? Consoling the dying?"

Abel picks a booger from his nose, flicks it in Sam's direction, though he is at least eight feet away.

"Go put some music on in this sorry rat's house before I leave you here to finish these eggs yourself." Sam turns down the fire; Abel obeys. Cat Stevens is already in the player, he presses PLAY. Sam looks up at Abel, standing there pale, thin, and haunted, pinching his top lip together as if trying to stop the blood flow. "Now get back over here, man, and sit down."

"Abel?" The call comes from outside the broken living room window.

"Shit. I told you she called my brother. When he comes inside, just hit him hard across the face with the cast iron pan."

24

"Abel, sit back down and shut up," Sam says, putting the eggs on the plate. The front door opens, Sam looks up at the balding, fortyish IT outsourcer, Jay, whom he has only seen pictures of. He has the look of arrogance and denial, no matter the situation.

"What do we have here?" Jay asks, hands open with false compassion.

"You can just turn the hell around and get out of here," Abel says with a much younger and rubbery voice.

"You're a *wreck*," Jay says, his nose flaring with disgust. "What happened here?" He looks at Sam. "Are you Kayla's brother?"

"If he were, he would kick your ass," Abel hisses.

"*What?*" Jay screws up his face, revealing dentistry's latest, perfect, white teeth. Sam cuts the moldy corner off the pita bread, puts it next to the eggs. He maintains an oblivious expression.

"You fucked her too, didn't you?" Abel says, spittle in the corner of his mouth.

"What *are* you talking about?"

"Have they even *met*, A?" Sam asks, putting the plate on the table, and yanking Abel by the arm to sit him down.

"You fucked her," Abel says, pointing at his brother with the fork Sam placed in his hand. Sam stands there looking as if he wants to slap him.

"Such language from a man of the cloth," Jay sneers, pulling his chin into his neck. "That was ten years ago, another girl, another time. What happened to you? You are literally out of your mind, she wasn't kidding." Jay shakes his head. "When are you going to move out of this trashy, depressing, jarhead hole? And what's with this music? Aren't you embarrassed by it?" He turns to Sam.

"Abel borrowed this from my father." Sam scuffs the floor with the heel of his shoe, folds his arms with challenge.

"Really?" Jay nods and folds his arms, as well. "You'd think he'd want to hear his precious Paganini. Music to go crazy by.

You know this boy here actually used to be quite the gambler, just like his hero." He points at Abel now with his thumb. Abel reaches up to grab it, but too slowly. "He thinks he used to be a Jew, as well, and let me tell you my brother, he still is."

"I'm outta here," Sam says, hands up in brief surrender.

"No," Abel says, putting a forkful of food in his mouth, as if to prove his devotion. "Don't go," he adds hoarsely, some of the egg falling out. He swallows hard, and stands up, smashing the table with his open hand. "Jay, get the fuck out of my house. Now."

"He was a blue baby," Jay says, still pointing at Abel. "You know what that is?"

"He's a *nurse*, you asshole," Abel snarls.

"Unless you have a different mother then you're one too," Sam says calmly.

"Then as you know, it was worse for him. He had his blood transfusion while still in the womb. Might explain all this, don't you think?"

Sam shakes his head as if to say, *Enough*.

"Delicate." Jay sighs. "Always delicate. How many times have you fainted?"

"I'm warning you," Abel says with the fork pitched toward his brother.

"He was laid out for a month with food poisoning at kibbutz. He made his dazzling transformation into goy after that. And no one tried to stop you, did they? Mom always let you do whatever the hell you want."

"Like you don't do whatever the fuck you want?" Spit at the back of Abel's throat makes the sound of the words sizzle.

"Tell me why should you have the luxury?" Jay gets in Abel's face, and he puts the fork down.

"You should probably leave," Sam says, getting closer and physically ready to back it up.

"Why should you have the luxury?" he repeats with menace.

"Why should you always be the one to self-indulge? *I* was the one who kept Mom going. *I* was the one who paid for at least half of that school—"

"Where do you get *that*?"

"Because I gave Mom the money that she was giving *you*. You and your gambling debts."

"That's bullshit."

"And now you think that we should all sit back and watch you dramatize a breakdown, ham it all up just to get away from working for *once* in your life, when it is *me* who deserves some time in this world, when it was *me* who supported the both of you when I was really just a child, and when it was *me* who came in on Dad fucking some guy!"

Abel pushes his hand through the broken window. The glass drips in deep brilliant red. Jay backs up as if Abel were going to take a shard to his face. Sam rushes with a T-shirt he tears into a tourniquet.

"I can't *believe* this shit," Jay says under his breath.

"You're going to get him to the hospital, *now*," Sam says. "He's going to need at least ten staples."

"Don't leave me, Sam," Abel starts crying softly again.

Sam takes him by the shoulders to lead him to Jay's car. Jay follows. "I really don't believe this," he says, defeated. "You know, I met this Kayla once. *Once*, with you, Abel, or don't you remember?" Jay talks to Abel's back.

"Unlock the car, man," Sam orders.

The lock clicks open, Sam squints as he opens the passenger door of the black BMW, helps Abel in. With gentleness, Sam assures him he'll be okay. Looking frightened, Jay stands there in front of the car, holding the keys.

"Last night she leaves me a message saying you were losing it." Jay shakes his head, opens his mouth wide, exhales, as if it were to see his breath form in cold air.

But the day is hot, thick, and stark. The desert opens with space and fear, Sam thinks to himself, though he's home and usually comforted by it. The heat seems to circle him closer at the head, as always when he feels his mother near, just as he wakes up. Abel is pale, staring at the dashboard.

"And my wife," Jay turns to Sam, showing him the whites of his eyes, "she's out at the nursery, as usual, *interviewing* plants."

"Just get in the car, will you? Get him to the hospital now. Take care of him. I mean it." Sam slams the driver's door on Jay for emphasis, and he watches them drive off.

In Sam's more horrific nightmares, he is not July's son. He is a spectator at the scene of the murder—exactly as the murderer says he was. But unlike the murderer's relatively emotional and remorseful blurting out of turn to the judge when he maintained that he was not alone (and yet could point no fingers), Sam is made to enjoy it. He never admits this to himself during waking hours. Instead he attempts to clutter his mind with memories of the more particularly exasperating patients, such as the diabetic who was so proud of her thin stool, rolled like wilting lettuce, or the seventeen-year-old with the brain infection, caused by a blood clot during an abortion. It left her in a coma, her body contorted like a frog. He witnessed the desire in some of the male doctors, orderlies, and stewards, which left him with disgust for her, rather than for them.

As the nightmares of July—rather than the rarer sweet dreams—continue haunting him throughout the day, he makes a point of buying some nice perfume or soaps for Haley, and together they take a spa bath in her tiny shack of a house. Two hours after the insane visit with Abel, heat and blood visions of his mother insist. He still attempts escape with oolong, black tea, and honey-scented candles he brought from a Desert Hot Springs New Age store. They now flicker in Haley's bedroom, the black velvet curtains like a womb blocking out the high gold light of desert afternoon.

Haley chatters about Tish, her best friend, who is the one black stripper at the club. Tish never liked Sam, he has always assumed, and he imagines it is because he did not notice her first. But he did. While the other girls dance to the band of the moment or Queens of the Stone Age classics, Tish dances to Marvin Gaye, and the men throw plenty of money down for her on the floor as she walks by. She never picks bills up with her teeth or tits. She has a smile of joy, a self-satisfaction bordering on ecstasy when she's on stage. Otherwise, her lips seem incapable of maintaining the arc of a smile. She appears quiet, discontent, and spiritually malnourished. Like she could not acknowledge any force or possibility outside of the self. He would admire that if he had a personal history considered normal, a more ordinary circumstance, but his situation as it stands—a mother sexually and violently ripped from him during the peak of puberty—he can feel little other than powerless, sorry for himself, and entirely suspicious of God's existence. More to the point, he has dedicated himself to a profession of care and help, all the while trying to figure out what has made him so unworthy.

Right now, Sam might even listen to whatever Haley is saying about Tish if she weren't once more linking the story to her abandonment by her mother. She left when Haley was six, then came back a decade later, befriended her with chivalry, only to take off with Haley's twenty-year-old boyfriend, never to be heard from again. That's when Haley started drinking, sobering up when she became legal, and has stayed clean for the eleven years since.

"They're having a good-bye dinner for me tonight," Sam interrupts, lying on Haley's bed with his arm stretched over his head, his nose close enough to smell his freshly washed pit. "You feel like coming?"

"And hang with all the work folks? No thanks." Haley's lips form a straight line of disappointment. "You weren't listening to me, were you?"

Sam inhales with force through his nose. "You know, now that Abel can't be there, I don't feel like any party either. Sue's the one having it. They're inviting a few other people. The guy that's working on her house—"

"Ray?" Haley props up on her elbow with a forced excitement. "You mean the big, beautiful, butter-haired guy?"

"Yeah, 'the big, beautiful butter-haired' stud."

"You know he *never* comes into the club," Haley says.

"I thought you weren't dancing anymore."

"You know I'm not." She grits her teeth. "Do you *ever* listen? Did I not play hookie from the office today just for you? I must be out of my mind."

"Well, he's married."

"Who?"

"*Ray*," Sam says impatiently. "I met his wife *and* his kid."

"That never stopped them, are you kidding? Look at you. You're still going and I'm not even there!"

"We're not married, Haley."

"And don't I know it."

"Let's not go there, not today."

She puts up her hands. "Of course not. Not today. You had the Brothers Grim, right? It's always about the Priestess."

"Don't call him that."

"Well he calls you Princess."

"That's different. It's a joke."

"Whatever. Point is, no time for me on your last day in town. Why should you, huh? And a party to cap it off. A party you tell me about a half hour before it starts."

Sam looks up at her and is filled with such love it hurts for a moment. Love for her need, and love for his own. Her face breaks

30

into an asymmetrical beauty of insecurity and reassurance, all of this crowned by the flame of her hair. He touches her chin, lifts it with his thumb and index finger.

"Nanodiamonds are forever," he says. With coyness he laughs.

"Forever, heh? Maybe not." Her curious nose wrinkles. "Will you remember you said so as you blaze up the Lost Coast?"

"Will you make love with me, already?" He strokes her bare hip and inkless thigh down to the back of her knee.

"Will you promise to take the tantric sex book with you?"

"Zi-zoomp," Sam says, making a drooping arc for his member with a finger.

"Well," she says sitting up, cupping one breast with her palm, and making a traffic signal with the other. "How many more times are we going to disappoint each other, Sam? Can you do one fucking thing for me?"

"Watch your language," he snaps, then slaps his own face, because again it brings in sharply the image of July.

3

Ernest's July

Few knew in San Diego, if any, that July was married very briefly to Sam's natural father. She didn't have to tell anyone because she moved there from Los Angeles in August 1972, twenty-seven years of age, and three months pregnant. She kept to herself in the cheap decrepit apartment in the southeast of the city for the first year. Later she moved to a better one a few blocks away there in Logan Heights, right next to the Calvary Baptist Church. She never attended service, but its presence was reassuring as it stood for Mother. She remained embarrassed about the marriage because she had been unfaithful. Sam's father had waffled in his affections, seethed in his anger, and stunted her growth. This didn't justify her acts. Guilt droned on in her head, but only she was privy to it.

She thought changing her name would help. Gwendolyn Purvis always sounded so solemn and weighty; her married name, Gwendolyn Griggs, was too housewifey. July Brown seemed unpretentious yet propitious. Fun. Independent. With it.

Up until the seventh month of pregnancy, July played guitar and wrote elastic, bluesy country, unsatisfying songs. She felt she'd failed in elaborating upon the union between Memphis and Nashville. She entertained the idea of taking up the banjo, with intent to emphasize its origins from Africa. She wanted to do her own brand of blue yodel, a Swiss and African falsetto.

The more July thought about the music, the less she played. She picked up the guitar again here and there when Sam was two or three and still delightfully clingy and unadventurous for trouble. He would look at her adoringly and clap hands through it, or he held onto the chair with one hand and shook his butt to the music. But it's doubtful he could remember these sounds today, save in quiet and fleeting interstitials. The guitar case was dusty by the time Joe entered her life, and had she known that he and Sam would give it away, she would have told them all it once meant. She might have even confessed she had been married.

But it wasn't Sam's father who occupied her mind. In the evenings when five- and six-year-old Sam sat on the linoleum floor next to the defunct water radiator in only his flooding teddy bear or tiger-print pajama bottoms, his animated face mooning over his father's picture, July would sit there too, holding her son tight, and secretly obsessing over Ernest Milk.

Ernest briefly taught free jazz guitar to children on Saturday mornings at the Watts Towers Arts Center in Los Angeles. July, still known as Gwen at the time, volunteered her time giving tours of the Towers on weekends. Though this was post–Watts Riots government guilt, community and private donations funded the robust programs; the city wouldn't step in until years later. She took the bus from her mother's apartment in the outskirts of Leimert Park, where she stayed the first time she left Sam's father and their shared car. She sat in on Ernest's classes, admiring his skillful, nimble fingers, and his generous disposition. On occasion he gave her rides home, when it was out of his way. He offered to sell her his broken down blue Chevy Nova that needed a new transmission, which a buddy of his could rebuild for her. The price went from $100 to $50, which she kept refusing. She felt ashamed the morning she accepted it as a gift.

They went together to the garage where his buddy Otis Hamilton worked. Any fool could see how immediately taken

Otis was with her, while Ernest's affections never really reached a height above charity. He made love unselfishly, but it was how he lived with less complication. July knew this, and Otis watched it all with the kind of intensity July couldn't believe Ernest abided, and maybe even appreciated.

"Have you met his wife?" Otis asked testily the day July came on her own to pick up her new car. The dimple in his chin seemed vulgar to her, his eyes had the look of a changeling, penetrating, covetous, but remiss.

"Love is, in some ways, only a measure of brain chemicals," July said, then looked Otis full in the eyes.

"That means no then, I take it." He put the greasy rag in his back pocket, stood with his legs apart, hands on his hips. July then mirrored his position, with her pointed, white comfort shoes, and daisy print yellow dress.

"Aggression and depression are measures of chemical levels as well."

"And where's your husband? Angry, depressed, or still in love?"

"How did you know I was married?" she asked, a crack in her musical voice.

"There's little Ernie doesn't tell me, Gwen," he said, backing away from her to get the keys to the Nova. July looked around wondering why there was no one else at the garage. She stepped her feet together, so that the insteps formed a perfect slim oval. She looked down at her chest to make sure no part of her cleavage showed. She touched the naked band of lighter skin where her wedding ring had been. She tried to visualize herself as an empress. Otis returned, dangling the keys in front of her.

"You're a beautiful woman, but you don't impress me," he said firmly, dropping them into her waiting hand. She stood there mortified that he could affect her so. Her frozen stance couldn't have lasted more than three beats, but inside it was magnified tenfold. She tried to convey an attitude that said he was beneath her. But she knew he was just as smart, difference being he believed he'd long ago lost the chance to apply it in any satisfying way. She couldn't blame him for that. So what came out of her instead was energy pollinated with the fact that they were already somehow intimate. Besides, no one had ever called her beautiful before, and this boost in confidence made her glad that her skin was too dark for the flush in her cheeks to show.

"Otis is a drifter," Ernest said to her in bed one afternoon in her mother's piously decorated apartment. Jesus was a clock, a wall hanging, a figurine; the chair, sofa, and vanity each wore its own shawl.

July rolled onto her stomach, elbow propped, her chin on her knuckles. The raised popcorn design of the bedspread irritated her legs, and she kicked it off. She crossed her ankles up in the air. He caressed her shoulder, moved his hand down the long curve of her back, and placed his hand in ownership on the cheek of her slim rump, so the fingers slid smoothly down the crack. She moved away, now leaning on her side, looked up at him with eyes as big and mink brown as Sam's.

"What are you trippin' on Otis for, anyway? He's runnin' from a lot of things I don't need to know nothin' about. And hypocrite he is, as ain't it always the case, he's got nothin' but church on the mind."

"Well, maybe both of us could use a little church."

"You kiddin' me, woman," he said, sitting up, taking his watch from the faux wood bedside table. "What you need is to get up out of your mother's place and do somethin' with all that education up there in your head."

July grabbed her white blouse with the pearl buttons from off the floor.

"If I was you, that's what I would do. That guitar ain't gonna get you nowhere. Look at me."

He stood up making the room look like a shadow box closing over her head, though keeping her naïve adulteress nudity on display. He steadied himself to put one leg and then the other into his pants, as if he was an old man. In that moment, July decided to get off the Pill and go home to her husband. At twenty-six, she was getting up in years to be childless. She thought in her mother's words. Though her mother was far off in Chicago, running after the last man who showed her any kindness.

4

The Weather Girl

Top down on the freeway and only forty-five minutes alone into his late Monday morning journey for adventure—first stop, Los Angeles—Sam calls KTLA's weather girl, Sheba Moses, and gets her curt, sassy voicemail. He leaves a refreshing, easy message, his voice light and unencumbered. This is in dire contrast to the heavy rumble in his throat as he said good-bye to Joe, who had his glasses on, bent over a best seller of new tax laws. Eyes magnified, Joe looked up at him and wearily waved. Then he was at the window, as Sam pulled off. Thirty-one years old, and still he's never gone longer than a weekend away from the only father he's ever known.

It's been nearly a year since Sam was head nurse on duty during Sheba Moses's emergency appendectomy, cutting short her desert vacation. At first sight, taken by the elegance of her long, caramel hands, the delicacy of her closed eyelids, he promised her he would show her the real beauty of the Mojave, how she could empty herself in the hot, mystic Martian space, lie down and become part of the clean, infinite line of the horizon. She nodded in weakness, smiled, and looked up at him. He thought she recognized him, and in the moment assumed he understood the concept of déjà vu. Was this the woman his mother saw him spending the rest of his life with?

As she slept, he described to her the many ways he would make love to her near the ocotillos and smoke trees. He was never so bold when she was awake, but he told himself that in her dreams she was listening, the way he kept his mind open and ready at night for any messages July might send him.

Feeling sure she would return his call, Sam comes to the dead end of the 10 freeway at Pacific Coast Highway, stops at the Santa Monica Pier, and buys a corndog roped bright yellow with mustard. He sits on a bench, holding the stick like a pinwheel, taking small feminine bites of the fried dough, licking his lips and the corners of his mouth, while watching a family fishing for contaminated perch. When it occurs to Sam that he's on a dock, creeping in is the image of his mother on the phone with Joe for the last time, as he'd described it.

In the arcade bathroom, Sam gets sick with stomach cramps that subside some twenty minutes later once he exits. He spends twelve dollars on an old snowboarding game, still feeling the dizzying headache heat of July's signature haunting. Nightmares in the daytime. It is never calm enough for him to communicate with her, the pain throbs sharp and pungent as her smell the day he came home, at not quite fifteen, and found her gone. The same flowery forest scent she spritzed before leaving the house for the evening is what became for him the smell of desertion.

He could blame Sheba for the memory, as his temper revs up. If she weren't blowing off his call, he wouldn't be here waiting with hideous visions.

He stares at the ocean, the sailboats following one another in a thin line of glistening citrus gold on the water. It is five o'clock; the sky is pixilated with smog and indecision over a hot or cool color palette. Falling off the edge of vulnerability, Sam is just about to dial Haley when the phone rings. It's Sheba, taut and brisk, instructing him where to meet her near work for a quick drink.

After an hour and a half in traffic, his car belching at the stops and starts, he knows he's on Hollywood Boulevard when at the red light he turns to see another convertible, white and slick unlike his own, the driver leaning back with a boastful smile, a blow-up doll propped in the backseat. In front of the Grauman's Chinese, Captain America, in flimsy nylon blue shorts, digs the tights from out of his crack. Superman approaches, slurping an ice cream cone, his hair sprayed stiff into a see-through helmet.

From the parking lot, Sam enters through the back of the Musso and Frank Grill. Down the steps, he stops on the worn wood spot where people have pushed open the French door since 1919. First straightening his pants, he takes a seat at the bar, watches the red-jacketed waiters—none under fifty and most of them much older—which makes him feel at ease. Even the busboys in their bright green jackets are just as seasoned. Sam orders a coffee and looks up at the yellowed pastoral wallpaper of wild peacocks, art deco lighting, and defunct twenties speakers hanging in the corners. He scans the brass-studded burgundy booths for early diner regulars, but he can't get a handle on the customer type here, they seem to be varied, though he is the only black guy in the place, including the help. He admires the octagonal and square leaded glass design of the cabinet doors behind the bar. He puts his cheek near the mahogany veneer counter to get a glance of his hair sticking out a little too much at the sides, and he pats it down.

Twenty minutes late, Sheba walks in catwalk-confident in heels, an elegant, egg yolk–hued gypsy blouse, and fitted, but not skintight, dark denim jeans. Sam pats his own faded camel jean pockets for his keys, feeling classless in an oversized, glib-worded T-shirt and his new, outdated trainers. He touches a sideburn with his thumb just before she kisses the same side of his cheek. She smells like jasmine and vanilla. Her makeup is thick yet finely toned with her skin. He misses the sight of her bare face, as he knew it, and the way she breathed in her sleep. He had wanted the chance to protect her, the way he didn't get to for his mother.

They know Sheba there, and the bartender closes out Sam's bill with a mannered, old-fashioned professionalism. A distracted, near surly waiter escorts them to her favorite table, and in handing Sheba the menu, regains a polite, elegant disposition just short of bootlicking.

"Wow," she says, sighing with drama after ordering a vodka gimlet. "Am I ever light-years from the last time I saw you." She laughs on demand, showing the whites of her eyes over macadamia brown irises.

"You look beautiful," Sam says, meaning it, shaking his head in slow motion.

"SEDITION, NOT FEAR," she reads off his chest. "I didn't figure you the type."

Sam pulls on his shirt, looks down at it, biting the inside of his cheek. "What type do you take me for?"

"Go with the flow." She smiles. "Are you hungry?" she asks, turning her attention to the menu.

"I could surprise you," he says. Her smile spreads wide. "And I am hungry. So what's good here?"

"Meat and potatoes," she says, hitting the table once with a fist. "And they insist on iceberg lettuce here, so don't get your hopes up for any fancy salad."

"Do I look like a salad guy to you?"

"Yes."

"I had a corndog for lunch," he exclaims, as the waiter strolls up with her drink.

"Thank you, thank you," she says, laughs, and takes a sip. "I'll have the filet mignon, medium rare." She touches her throat.

Flustered by pressure for quick choice, Sam looks down at his menu, fighting the urge to lash out at her just a little.

"I'll have the lamb chops, well done. Glass of red, please," he says, snapping it shut.

"Cabernet, Merlot, Pinot Noir, Zinfandel—" the waiter lists with exaggerated patience.

"Cabernet, thank you," he interrupts, looking up at the waiter's swept, kempt hair and soporific expression. He imagines that he is an Evangelical or Scientologist. Sam playfully squints at Sheba, then remembers to take the napkin off the table. He lays it like a kitten in his lap.

She smiles, sighs again like she can't believe her own nerve, and sits up straighter in her seat. "I'm engaged."

Sam looks at her as if she said nothing.

She slowly blinks at him as if her contacts hurt. In the softer light of the restaurant, her closed lids are as thin as the skin of a worm, naked, raw, and pink. What now turns Sam on most is the surprise of natural, subtle gray running through her nape-length, straightened hair when she couldn't be older than thirty-five. It makes him feel safe, like she could take care of him.

"So tell me. What makes you say 'Have a good supper!' after every wrap?" Sam asks, smiling at a second more generous thought; they could have such a wonderful relationship taking care of each other.

"Did you hear what I said?" One brow appears to reach for her nose.

He nods. "After every 'wrap of a segment,' is that how it's put? Tell me what makes you say in the morning like that, 'Have a good *supper*'? It turns me on, I have to tell you."

Her face illuminates with surprise and false modesty. "It was a good luck thing my grandfather used to say."

"Is he gone now?"

"No," she says, now looking uncomfortable. "My grandfather was a great ventriloquist in Vaudeville, you know."

"Really?"

41

"Yes. And my dad, his son, became the first black sports commentator. Ed Dorsey."

"I didn't know that."

"Yes, he was." She takes a long sip of her drink, sits back in her seat. "The governor's fiscal Darwinian approach has left people like my grandfather near destitute. He's really fucked them all over."

Sam loudly clears his throat at the curse word. "And what are you doing to help?"

"Everything I can." She looks at him, taking offense. "My father's not made of money either, you know. How much do you think a retired black sportscaster makes?"

He shrugs.

"How much do you think a *weather girl* makes?"

"More than a nurse." Sam shrugs again.

"Why don't you want to be a doctor, anyway?"

"I prefer not being the one who makes the life or death decisions. I'd rather help someone get well, ease their misery just a little bit."

"I can understand that." She takes a sip of her drink. "You certainly were a great comfort to me," she says, changing her tone with matter-of-fact seduction.

"So, Dorsey . . ." Sam says, trailing off.

She cocks her head as if trying to follow.

"Your father's name is Dorsey, why is yours Moses, then? Were you married?"

"My name used to be Sheila Dorsey. I changed it to Sheba Moses. It came to me in a dream."

"Really," he says, sticking out his bottom lip. "Was it a premonition, a spirit talking to you?"

"Nothing mystical about it, someone called me by that name in the dream and I remembered it when I woke up."

"Okay."

"It was a bit of a fight at the station. But then soon enough I got in front of the camera, and I knew I'd done the right thing."

"You actually look more like a Sheila," Sam says, voice teasing.

"So, I'm engaged, I said." She cocks her head to the other side at him. "Quite a while ago, I told you that."

"Really?" he looks up at her with lazy, heavy-lidded eyes.

"Well, almost engaged."

"Are you engaged or not?"

"He's a location scout, so not in town a helluva lot. Our schedules are totally mismatched."

"Oh."

"He's a heavy smoker too. He tried to quit once." She opens her eyes wide. "My *God*. I'd rather live with a junkie kicking heroin! He was a *monster*, an absolute *evil* creature from the depths of hell. He can smoke himself to death now, for all I care." She shakes her head.

The waiter brings their plates and she doesn't wait for Sam to pick up his utensils before she cuts into her steak, scratching the plate with her knife. He watches her teeth scrape the fork as she takes in the first bite. He would never admit to anyone else how proud he is to know so intimately a television personality.

"How's your steak?"

"Hmn."

"Can I taste it?" he asks, reaching for her wrist so she might feed him. She looks at him as if the motion were too forward, but then she cuts a piece, puts it in his mouth. He watches her lips as he chews it down.

"Could be smoother, huh?" she asks.

"Want to taste mine?"

"No thanks, I should be watching what I eat, anyway. My mother's side of the family has had everything: diabetes, heart disease, cancer, you name it."

43

"How are you?" Sam pushes aside the iceberg lettuce.

"Since the appendicitis, you mean?"

"Yes."

"In the vain and cutthroat world of the news, my health is the least of my worries," she laughs. "I'm fine," she says, flicks her hand. "Why don't you write a letter to the producers saying how much you love the gray in my hair. That might help." She laughs more heartily.

"I didn't notice it."

"You did so," she says, pointing her knife at him. "I saw you staring."

"No, that's not true. But now that you mention it, I must say, it's beautiful."

"Right. Well, I'm not ready to dye my hair. I'm not ready for Botox or a boob job. I'm not going to change anything God's given me. The rest of them at the station? The women? Not one thing they were born with. And the men? What a bunch of pricks. The station manager, *whoo*! I'm telling you. His motherboard is shot. It's amazing who gets a job in this business." She wipes the corner of her mouth, then throws the napkin with force into her lap, as if her situation were its fault.

"A nice long massage is what you need."

"I have one weekly. An amazing woman comes to my house Thursday evenings. Shiatsu trained, some Thai massage experience. Amazing."

"I'm not that bad myself," Sam says, leaning in, hoping to inspire her to quickly finish her dinner.

Sheba's house in Beachwood Canyon has a view of the Hollywood sign from her backyard patio. The pool is small; the roof extends over half of the deep end. Rhododendrons line the yard spotted by soft blue lights. The grass is long, dark, and wet under Sam's bare left foot, which he uses to balance himself as he sits, massaging her lower back while she lies on the wide, striped chaise lounge. Half of his butt is off the cushion.

"Beautiful, warm night," she says in between long pleasurable moans. He presses his thumbs now into either side of her tailbone. Her jeans are unzipped and rolled just to her dimples.

"There couldn't be a more perfect setting for a seduction," he says so low he barely hears his own voice.

"Who's seducing whom, Nurse Brown?"

He lays his palm flat on the small of her back, leans in with his face, and gently blows heat in the space between his thumb and index finger.

"You smell unbelievably delicious. Hmmn, like honeysuckle," she hums. "What is that scent?"

He drags his bottom lip up her spine until it touches the bunching of her blouse. The white bra is already unhooked but distracting enough that he stops unsure he can go on. She turns over and pulls him to her, her kisses not as sweet as he'd imagined. The hungrier they seem, the more intimidated he feels at the idea of pleasing her. He is hard, but less so when she pulls down his pants. She has to help him work it inside of her until he is full-grown. Surprised to last as long as he does, he is embarrassed that he cannot come after her. With charm school gait, she leads him inside the house. Her self-assuredness overcomes any small imperfections in her caramel-smooth skin and long, narrow, pear-shaped body.

Cigarette odor permeates the bedroom, and he suspects she's lying when she insists she lives alone. He wanders past her and the bed into the bathroom, though he doesn't have to urinate. He fights the urge to close the door and masturbate, the idea of wanting her better than having her. Instead, he comes back out, talking himself into being more of a man than he ever has before. Upon witnessing the rapturous flutter of her throat and nostrils, he represses the image of seeing her head covered with a pillow.

He tells himself, as she comes this second time so easily, that he is in fact her sexual awakening.

She falls asleep with her leg thrown over his thigh, and he lies in bed looking up at the ceiling, wishing he could see through to the stars. His mother could appear as a new constellation. He runs his hand through Sheba's hair as she purrs softly in REM. He envies her dreams, devoid of tragedy, loss, and frustrating symbols to be interpreted any number of ways. But North is what he'd made of his mother forming a triangle over her head with her hands.

In the morning, he awakes alone in bed. He crawls into his clothes, finds a pithy note taped to the refrigerator, instructing him on how to lock up behind him. He kisses the piece of paper and puts it in his back pocket, now feeling an icy guilt over Haley circulating in his chest. His clothes seem frumpier in the hard, thin light cutting its way through the window from a foggy mist. He panics for a moment over his car, because it's not where he remembered parking it. He runs outside, only to find it is there at the side of the house, opposite the new but permitted bamboo fence, over which Sheba's neighbors are threatening to sue since its design doesn't jibe with the historic route to the Hollywood sign.

Sam takes his bag out of the trunk, savors a quick shower in the celebrity-lit luxury of his conquest's domain. He sprays just a little of the perfume on the pulse of his wrist, places the bottle back in his bag. For some years he had come to feel so numb, but these days it's instantaneous how his head rushes with mother memory. The self-loathing he can ride out, as long as he recounts her daily I-love-yous. She didn't leave him because she wanted to; she was taken away from him. He sits on Sheba's vanity bench, waiting for the spell of self-pity to pass.

In the mirror is a boy that Joe cares for, and one that Abel trusts. He tries to imagine himself an emperor, as his mother would call him whenever he needed a boost in confidence. He doesn't know who he is; he doesn't know what to feel for himself. He picks up Sheba's lipstick, tempted to draw his outline there on the glass. But he puts it back down, afraid to be a freak.

As Sam backs out of the hilly drive, he notices a dented silver Toyota pulling out up the street. He adjusts his rearview mirror, and the car pulls over to the curb. This couldn't bother him more, already feeling near the height of paranoia after an infidelity and now that his mother's murderer is free.

Feeling suffocated, Sam rolls down the window. He turns his cell phone back on, convincing himself that his mother will watch over him as long as he stays on her intended path.

5

Parallax of the Son

There are no messages on Sam's cell phone as he hits the 101 freeway north out of Los Angeles. Haley disciplines well, he thinks, feeling lonely for her. It has only been a little more than twenty-four hours since he saw her last, and far less since he cheated. The fog burns off ahead, and the day seems full of mean beginning. He concentrates now on the image of the weather girl, nude and supplicant in the sky. Construction signs derail fantasy as he is forced to merge with all of traffic into one lane.

An hour and a half into the ruthless, dull drive, at last the ocean appears on his left in spotted snapshots of blue, unfettered here, fettered there by buildings, billboards, and non-native trees. The sum of these parts takes a subtle swank as he continues. What he'd heard of Santa Barbara seemed fussy to him, but he exits anyway for hunger, pushy with sweet tooth. He parks the shoe box—top still up from his overnight with Sheba Moses—and stops in front of the window of a used bookstore before business hours. He decides he'll return to find a gift for Sheba, something on Vaudeville, black Hollywood, or meteorology. Maybe something for Haley on the cosmos, he remembers her recently mentioning that she's been writing poetry.

Passing all coffeehouse chains, he lucks upon an open door original. Behind the counter is a pale, thin beauty with dyed black curls piled high on her teen head like soapsuds. As he orders an apple Danish, he imagines himself with her in the bathtub. While she takes her time, he contemplates asking her what whiny voice of death sings in the background. Sharply feeling his age, he decides against it, but gets a smile out of her when he grabs the Danish with exaggerated ravenous eyes. If being over thirty wasn't unnerving enough in the moment, on his way to a cluttered corner table he passes a clean mirror capturing the softness of his arms and hint of gut.

He moves the newspaper from the seat. From his window view, he scans across State Street for a gym as he bites into the Danish. The music changes midway to reggae, and he looks around the café, which is empty, then at the girl who pores over papers, elbows on the glass of the counter. It irritates him that she should sense he didn't appreciate the whiny depression sound of choice, and he wants to tell her that he never cared for reggae, but since she isn't paying much attention to him anyway, he would probably only make a fool of himself.

Sitting at the table, he wishes he could speak aloud to his mother without looking crazy—just chat with her until the lonely feeling blows away. He calls Joe, who seems put out to have been taken from his work, so he doesn't bother mentioning his success with the weather girl. Joe wouldn't appreciate the details anyway, and would see Sam as less a man to kiss and tell. He stops himself from calling Haley, since she would be getting ready for work, distracted and heavy with nuance of her abandonment. As if her abandonment was worse than his. So out of the café he walks, aimless and in circles, annoyed to find the streets collecting with white or Latino faces, and no others like his.

It takes an hour to find the right book—he surprises himself in grabbing Neruda's *Twenty Love Poems* and can imagine Sheba laughing when she opens the package. But if he gave it to Haley she could teach him something, as he knows nothing about poetry. "Who could resist Neruda?" The clerk asks, with lips pursed. Perhaps only to add to the murky, lost feeling inside, he decides to stay in town somewhere, but finds quickly that no hole-in-the-walls exist in Santa Barbara. He springs for a nice room a couple blocks from the main street and is delighted to find a fireplace and two large, mission-style armoires, ostentatious and almost satisfying for his buck. He couldn't know that he was conceived in that very hotel, in a different room, during one of its previous incarnations.

A comedian Sam has vaguely heard of is on the corner theater marquee. He enters the open side door to find someone to ask how good she is. The theater seats line the mock street of Spanish apartment complexes at both sides leading to the stage. Some of the façades open to the trompe l'oeil courtyard, balconies above the head with real planter boxes and vines. Curved like a planetarium, the ceiling is painted like the sky at dusk.

"We're not open," a deep, craggy voice booms from below. Sam looks around for it, answering to the air.

"I just came in to ask you if this—"

"We're not open, would you please leave."

"Well, fuck you, then," Sam shouts, his ears hot, scalp prickly. When he is out of the door, all of him itches, and he feels enraged that anybody should have to make him curse like that.

He wanders back down the main drag, resenting himself further for entering the mall. Alienation slogging his brain, it doesn't take him long to find the bar. A few heads turn, their faces register the slightest bit of hostility, then indifference. Sam picks the stool next to the one with the most wizened skin and whitest hair.

The old man stares at him kindly. The skin under his eyes is pronounced, almost separate from the rest of him, shiny, delicate, folded like a baby's. The eyeballs sit in the beautiful folds like clouded toy eggs.

The bartender asks Sam what he wants. He looks at the old

man's three full shot glasses then orders a beer. The bartender slides a bottle to him showman style.

"I was in LA the other day," the man begins in a manner of midconversation. "Healthy young guy parked in a handicapped space, I ask him what he's doing there, he tells me he's wearing a diaper and to go fuck myself." He pats his chest with both hands. "That's LA."

Sam shakes his head. "How'd you know I just came from LA, man?"

"I don't. You're wearing a Lakers shirt," he points at the emblem, raises his brow. "And so who's this guy telling about diapers? I have a medical supply place. I know who needs diapers when I see 'em."

"So do I."

"Your parents wearing diapers, kid?"

"I'm a nurse."

"No kidding."

"No," Sam says plainly, without humor.

"Well, you got me there. I wouldn't have guessed that," the old man says, pressing his pants with his palms, then downing one entire shot.

"What would you have guessed?" Sam asked, smelling the tequila now.

"A career student."

"Really? Now why is that?"

"You have the look of many scholarships."

"I'm not sure how to take that."

"Exactly. But once you are sure about matters as trivial as this, a lot of your problems will go poof." He gestures like a magician, his eyes twinkle, a deep cataract blue.

Sam laughs. "I see. A sage. The hierophant."

The old man waves his right index finger, *tsk tsk*.

"I'm as lost as the rest of them, son, don't you be mistaken."

He touches the rim of his second glass. He goes into himself, Sam can see, but with little effort could be pulled back out. Sam exhales with a puff out of his nostrils. He bears down on his jaw teeth, trying to resist the obvious needs of another human being.

"Lived here long?" Sam asks.

"No, no," the old man says smiling. "My wife had a lead foot. She weaved in and out of traffic like a cornered wolverine. She thought driving was a video game."

Sam nods, a beer bubble rising in his throat.

"She was beautiful though, and smelled like hot biscuits." The old man grunts to clear his voice, then with embarrassing tenderness touches his Adam's apple.

"You lost her. I'm sorry," Sam says, with extra depth.

"To another man." He holds up his dry and veined ring finger, faded as an artifact. "No need to let anyone do you in, son."

"Sometimes it can't be helped." Sam truly smiles for the first time with him.

"Sure it can, like everything else. Sometimes I would have preferred it if either of them were dead. But that's just an illusion as well. Think about it, son. If we didn't know anything about death, we wouldn't die," the old man says, raising both brows, and then his glass.

Sam glares at him with disbelief. "All we have to do is look at the plants and the trees."

The man points to his temple. "Use your head, not your eyes. What do you think you knew about pain until you were told?"

"I didn't have to be told about pain," Sam spits. "My mother was murdered when I was fifteen," he says like a trump, with more distance from it than he's ever felt in his life.

"I'm sorry, son," he says, looking down at his lap. "I see my attempted suicide stories will seem all the less dazzling."

"That's for sure," Sam says, stretching his lips into outraged grimace.

Sam finishes his beer, puts the money down with a healthy tip for the bartender.

"How does she come to you?" the old man rushes out, straightening in his chair.

Sam looks at him with suspicion, rolls his tongue over his top teeth, his lower lip raised to cover it.

"You still see her, don't you?"

Sam clears his throat. "In dreams, sometimes, others it's something else. I've read a bit about visits. You know," he tightens his chin with skepticism. "And it's not the way most people feel it—not at all—that cold spot, that something happening in the room, their loved one talking to them. No, it's not like that. It's this feeling that surrounds me, a kind of heat, you know, where I'm queasy and then it's as if a fever takes over. Almost like an invasion."

"And you're sure it's her."

"Oh yes."

"Did she torture you somehow as a boy?"

"No, no, the opposite," Sam exclaims, indignantly. He looks at the old man wondering if he can really see out of his eyes. "Where would you get that?"

The old man shrugs.

"She could have been a saint, really."

"Lotta people feel that way about their mothers. Look at 'The Virgin,' why is that something to believe? Immaculate Conception? BAH!"

Sam scoots away an inch in his seat from the man.

"That's how they control us, of course. Keep us thinking we're the product of original sin. How could we be worth anything then, tell me? All sex is dirty? All reproduction? Every living creature, every one of them doing it is filthy, then?"

Sam shrugs.

"It's a bunch of hogwash, it is."

53

The old man is quiet for a while, then he takes his pinky finger and cleans his ear with it. The pinky nail is long and yellowed, and what he flicks has an orange hue to it. Disgusted, Sam swallows, looks away. But then, he thinks of his boyhood aquarium with the magic rocks like stalagmites that grow into castles. The old man lifts his third drink.

"When I was about your age, I took time off in the middle of the height of responsibility. I had a kid, a first wife, and parents to bear. I found a book one day, *The Hot Springs of California*, and it struck me right then and there that I was going to do every last damn one of them."

"And so?"

"And so I did."

"And here you are," Sam says, extending his arm to wave across the bar like a showroom salesman.

"Much happened in between, son, or didn't you notice. Forty-one more years of it, to be exact."

Sam nods, raises his index, and motions to the bartender at his empty bottle.

"You're in love with your mother, you know," he says turning to look at him. Sam is quiet for a while, examining the specks on the counter.

"Who isn't, really?" Sam mutters under his breath.

"Ah, not me, son," he slows to a slight intended drawl. "*Not* me." The old man gets off the stool, and Sam is amazed at how small he stands. He digs in his pocket, pulls out an expensive money clip of bills. Painstaking, he counts out the appropriate sum, then grabs Sam's wrist, and opens up his hand. He puts a small string of purple worry beads in it, and closes Sam's hand around them. Sam looks the old man in the eye, swearing that he couldn't possibly see very well.

"Thank you," Sam says, putting the beads in his pocket.

"They're for your mother," the old man says, his back already to Sam, walking with a lot more spring in his step than Sam would have guessed.

Sam is so drunk by the time he reaches the corner of his hotel that he doesn't care to look ahead at the cop cars forming a triangle at the intersection. Neither does he glance at the particulars of the auto accident as he passes by on foot, even when stepping into the middle of the street to avoid the mess. Traffic officers direct the rubberneckers. The loud whistle—which ordinarily would be shrill—makes San feel oddly comforted. Like people should be aware of how dangerous life is. He does glance at a silver Toyota, at least a block and a half from where he stops to feel for the beads in his pocket. They are there. He stares at the Toyota, sweat collecting in his pits. Just when he wants to hear Joe's voice, he remembers he must have left his mobile in the room. The paranoia clots the blood flow, he thinks, his extremities prickle at the early evening cool breeze. As he steps into the driveway of his hotel, he fights the urge to run back out to that car and check it for the dents he spotted in front of Sheba's house. Then he reminds himself there is nothing more pathetic than assuming the world revolves around him. He goes into his craftsman-style, mission-precious room and falls fast asleep, dreaming sweetly of his mother, sitting at the foot of the bed, behind her a painting of the ocean, the frame shapeshifting into the letters NO.

6

Mother's July

July was back home with her husband for two months when she got a small envelope in the mail with no return address—her maiden and married name, Gwen Purvis Griggs, handwritten in childish, looped, and lumpy letters. Off the Pill and queasy with hormonal imbalance, she sat down to open it in her husband's easy chair. When she saw Ernest's face, loving, surrounded by small figures she assumed to be his wife and three children, she called out in fright to no one. She felt stunned and cruelly heckled by these images, and this only multiplied when she looked again in the envelope and saw the note: THINKING OF YOU. GLAD YOU MADE THE RIGHT CHOICE. OR DID YOU?

She stared at the words for a long time before tearing the paper up into bits of confetti. She was newly enraged at Otis Hamilton when she saw the mess she made on the carpet. July stood up too fast with intention of getting the vacuum. Bugs performed lit pirouettes behind her eyes, and she fell back down in the chair, her head banging and overheated. Guilt planted itself at the center like an abscess that would only grow bigger. Had she been thinking more clearly, she might have taken this for a premonition of doom, then dodged its way.

Instead, she made herself rise in new suffering of a migraine. She snatched the photograph and went to her closet to find her mother's muumuu with the violet clematis-patterned pockets. July's mother—whom she only called *Mother* with continued singsong irony in her voice—had asked her to keep the muumuu in remembrance and warning of how fat either of them could get. Mother was always more proud of her many periods of significant weight loss than any accomplishment of July's. It was because of her that July nervously picked at her food, silently calculating calories.

Tell me, what's a black girl going to do with a degree in philosophy?

How far you think you gonna go with no talent and that guitar?

When Mother found out she wasn't invited to witness July's civil service wedding, she didn't seem to care. Her Baptist faith and deep reverence to Christ convinced her she was never to blame for any other's shortsightedness or wrongdoing, particularly her daughter Gwendolyn's.

If Mother had known that July had committed what she would call "double adultery," and in *her* apartment, she would have castigated her in the most vicious ways. And it was out of sudden deference to Mother and morality that July put Ernest's family picture in the muumuu pocket. She ran for aspirin and a tall glass of ice-cold water. Her head throbbed and parted.

Holding one ear closed, she vacuumed up the mess and made an appointment with the family doctor. By the time she hung up the phone, she thought she might be growing a tumor. Coincidently, July's husband came home early. She suspected he had been fired, or worse yet, tipped off on her wrongdoings, but she said nothing. He worked as an insurance agent for the only black-owned company in the city, and lately he hadn't been selling half as many policies. In quiet, they opened cans of chili together; he pulled out leftover Chinese takeout rice from the refrigerator and put it in a pot to warm.

"How was your day?" she asked finally, as they sat at the table in the cheery pink kitchenette.

"I left early. Had a bad headache," he said, not looking at her.

"That's funny, so did I," she said, not too quickly, in a low-key tone.

"Been thinking, Gwen." He put his fork down square in his food. "I'm tired too of all of this fighting we do. I thought we could make some changes when you came back."

"Haven't we?" she asked alarmed.

"Yes, we have."

"Then tell me exactly what you mean, Wayland."

He looked up at her, surprised to hear his name come out of her mouth, because she never seemed to call him anything, as was her intent.

"What do you mean?" she repeated, getting impatient.

"I mean, I think it's time to quit."

"Quit?"

He jerked his head no, as if he was going to get riled up, but he pushed himself away from the table and picked up his plate.

"*What* has gotten into you?" July asked, her mouth still open, her eyes following him. "You're seeing somebody, then."

He dropped his plate full of food into the sink; she jumped at the clang.

"After all this," she said, getting mad, "after *all* I've put up with, you're leaving *me*?"

"I'm not going anywhere. You can stay wherever you want. I'm just saying, I quit. Separate lives under one roof, if you want. I just quit, is it." He brushes off his hands in two claps of dismissal.

When the doctor told July she was six weeks pregnant, she knew it was her husband's, even though they'd only had sex twice since she'd been back. Both times were during their reconciliation trip to Santa Barbara, where July frequently ruined the mood with spats of paranoia. Afraid that her husband would find out she'd cheated, she tried distracting him from the fact she felt sure they were followed. It seemed to her that she succeeded in disinteresting him altogether. Further foiling her husband was the anonymous note, confirming to her that Otis was obsessed—which in some ways she had to admit she rather liked, just as she liked thinking of herself and Ernest as the lovers.

July went to her husband's office to tell him the rabbit died. Right then and there, he changed his tune of estrangement. This pissed her off to think he wanted the baby more than her. During the drive home, she made hasty plans for escape—much like Mother did with her every few years of July's young life.

She emptied the joint account, rationalizing that the sum would add up to only a short period of alimony and child support, had she gone through proper channels. This was 1972, and divorce was always in the papers: Steve McQueen's, Johnny Carson's, and Priscilla Presley's from the King. July was sick of the issue; the very word rang with shame. Still, she wouldn't admit to herself that the stigma bothered her—the assumptions made of folks more ordinary than celebrities, stereotypes she believed to be true, as well. One morning, when July's husband suspected nothing, she packed the car Ernest gave her, and split for San Diego.

From a motel pay phone, she called Mother, who was finally back in LA from Chicago.

"You're a fool, and you always were," Mother said, when July wouldn't tell her from where she was calling. "But don't expect God to look after you."

"I'm taking care of myself," July said, closing her eyes to the glare of the sun and wishing she had the nerve to drive all the way to Nashville.

"I thought you loved that man," Mother said, coughing, having spoken too fast after a drag on her cigarette.

"I did," July said, thinking of Ernest. "I do. But he doesn't love me."

"He never hit you, Gwendolyn," Mother said, her voice lilting in lullaby.

"That's a paltry excuse to stay with anybody."

"I'm not talking about *anybody*. I'm talking about Wayland. I don't understand why you ever went back to him just to leave again. Have you lost all sense? Just look what happens when you give up the church. You lose your mind and you lose the light. Your husband provided for you well, as well as any colored man could these days, and he loves Jesus. That man is saved. And he was your beloved. Now what sense does your leaving him make?"

"A lover is a more divine thing than a beloved, Mother, for he has the god within him."

"Are you a *man*, girl? What the hell are you saying?" she asked angry and out of breath from speaking too fast. "You've got a lover now, too? You better not have had him in my house!"

"I'm hanging up now, Mother."

"Blasphe——" July heard her mother say as she slammed the phone down, feeling better that she'd told anyone off.

7

Fly by Night

.

"Where are you, son?" Joe's voice arrives too measured through Sam's phone earpiece.

"What's wrong?"

"Nothin's wrong, just asking where you are."

"Ragged Point, I think. Or I just passed it. I must be a little way yet from Big Sur. It's beautiful, Joe. The water, the cliffs . . . amazing."

"There somewhere you can pull over?"

"Just tell me what's going on."

"You didn't take your mother's papers with you, did you son?"

"Of course I didn't!"

"Maybe moved them a long time ago, but just can't remember doing it?"

"Do you mean me or you?"

"Either."

"They're not in the hall cabinet where they've always been?"

"Calm down," Joe says, getting ruffled. "Calm down. I'll find 'em."

"Where are they?" Sam asks, feeling a head rush. "What were you looking for them for, anyway? How could they be gone?"

"Shit. Shoulda *never* called you."

"I'm turning around."

"You will *not*." Joe uses his lowest baritone, slow like a dog's growl, meaning business. "Let's get off the phone then. Catch you later. I'll find 'em." Joe hangs up.

Sam doesn't make out the sign he passes, but with recklessness he U-turns for shoulder parking at what turns out to be Jade Cove. He takes the path through a wide-stretching field of tall, stiff grasses and weedlike coastal chaparral, the wind slapping his jacket to static cling against his skin. He is entirely alone, embracing only the company of wild vegetation thriving in fat-grained sandy dirt leading to the marine terrace. His ears feel like seashells, the wind tickling immortal tune. Tempting vertigo, he looks down the steep trail that seems as long as half a mile leading to the bluff and the rocky coves he imagines falling down and dashing his head against. Who would find his body here? With painstaking care, he begins his scale of the hill, at times grabbing onto the prickly bushes that mock his fear in their sturdiness. What if he were followed and shoved? What if he were forever lost in the infinite body of water?

At this point, he cannot look all the way down. He loses balance twice, and slips a few footfalls down the rock and sand. He imagines snakes hissing and baring their fangs. For an eerie, ghoulish moment, he is his mother watching her own nude and lifeless body falling down the cliff. As he picks himself up once more, by an inch he misses stepping on sea fresh dog shit near the branches of sage he must hold before making his last gravitational-forced run down to the beach.

Here at the big breakers there is really no beach to speak of but rocks, midnight blue and deep green schist, that look like volcanic eruption. He hops over the foamed stones and steps perilously up the slickenside of a giant rock, where he sits at the peak, dangling his feet, and looking down at the waves lashing the graywacke and nephrite jade the cove is named for.

Sam's face is so kissed with mist that at first he thinks his sniffling, his cold, runny nose and welling eyes are due to allergy. As the sweat from his climb cools to a sickly chill at his neck, he questions his mental health. He should be enjoying this incredible beauty surrounding, he scolds himself. He should be taking it easy, reading this terrain of spiritual notation instead of feeling afraid of it. If his mother is truly trying to speak to him through pictures of water, he should listen.

What he needs, he decides, is to be around some people, anyone at all to take his mind off the awful lack of warranty in life.

Sam pulls over at the Henry Miller Library, the first sign of homeyness he notices in Big Sur. He stands cloaked by the voluminous pines and oaks, waiting for the silver Toyota that missed its chance at Jade Cove. He may take it by surprise, he exclaims to himself. He still isn't sure that anyone is following him. Close to chalking it up to full-blown paranoia, he feels utterly ridiculous, and comes from around the wide, scabbed trunk. July doesn't seem to be with him now, though she made such a torturous leap through him as he'd climbed down to the coves. She stayed so near in LA and just after his talk with the old man in Santa Barbara. He looks up through the canopy of leaves, again afraid of the beauty, refreshing alarm over Joe's call. What would anyone want with his mother's old documents anyway? The birth and death certificates she'd taken a strange fancy to are surely of no value; he can't imagine the indentured servant and slave contracts amounting to much.

Sam strolls up the mulch path of beehive and computer sculptures. The lawn welcomes with childlike carvings and posts. Past the outdoor woodburning stove and inside the cozy cabin, he pretends to be interested in any of the books there, but he'd already bought one for Sheba—or is it really for Haley?—and didn't particularly want to buy another. More of a small house than library, he scans the shelves of mostly Henry Miller titles, eyes the bathroom, then heads for it. The light streams in muted and thin on pale green erotic tiles, whimsical drawings, bent and peeling postcards. As he stands there dreaming into the old flyers, faded watercolors, and engraved lines of intercourse, he gets the urge to have himself off with visions of Sheba pressed against the wall.

When he opens the door, he's embarrassed to find a woman waiting there, exactly as his mother had once when he was fourteen. July wore a pleasant knowing look on her face, and tried too hard not to make him feel embarrassed. He couldn't help feeling dirty, anyway. The woman before him with his mother's eyes is twice as wide as Sam, at least two hundred pounds, and unintentionally blocking his way. He excuses himself to get by, and she looks up at him, her face only slightly pimpled, rubicund, and sweet. With the thickness of her long, shiny midnight hair, he can't tell if she's Greek, Italian, Iranian, Armenian, Mexican. Neither can he guess by her size and teen-aged complexion if she's in her late twenties, thirties, or forties. Her smile charms him; something about her energy, her vibrations are familiar. He turns to watch her enter the bathroom and close the door.

Uncharacteristic and quick for a woman, he thinks, she is back out by the time he finds what seems like a private room filled with Miller watercolor prints and collector's editions. The clerk enters as well to guard and answer questions, but during all the historical acquainting, the woman with a kind of Hindu goddess light in her eyes looks only at Sam. When the clerk turns to leave, she says, "Don't you feel better?"

"What do you mean?" Sam asks, glancing behind him at the wall as if someone were there.

"You look like you're feeling better."

"Better than when?"

"Better than probably, what, ten minutes ago?"

Her hand repeatedly returns to the safekeeping of her munificent thigh, her gestures stir up mirages of playfully punitive positions he's never tried.

"Am I so obvious?"

"No," she says, smiling, grabbing at the oblong amber beads around her thick neck.

"I mean downer that I am?"

"I don't really believe that's you."

Sam smiles, looking her in the eyes trying to figure out if his mother is trying to talk to him through her. Then he realizes what he's doing. Feeling crazy, he turns to walk out of the door.

"Are you hungry?" she boldly asks, hurrying to accompany him down the steps of the library, neither with a purchase.

"What?" He wants to hear her voice once more and make sure it's not his mother's.

"I said, are you hungry?"

"I could eat," he says, quickly, batting his lashes like a girl, a glint of sun in his eyes.

"Are you from around here?"

"I could be."

She smiles with satisfaction. "Well, have you been to Big Sur before?"

"Can't say I have."

"We should go just up the road to Nepenthe, then. The view is marvelous." She looks down at her feet in strappy, flat, green sandals. Her loose white pants billow like a flag with the cool breeze. She bites her bottom lip. "Then again, I don't live all that far from here in Carmel. It's a bit of a haul, but I'm a mean cook, better than any restaurant you'll find around here, which is saying plenty."

Sam claps once, with awkwardness, opens his hands. He didn't mean to make it that loud. "Well okay, then. You twisted my arm."

65

She lightly scratches the side of her nose, flushes with self-consciousness, amazed at her own audacity. "We're off then."

Back in the car, top down, he is following this stranger, a fat woman in a Lexus. He still imagines himself rather glamorous, and devoid of problems, if only for five minutes. The phone rings again, and he doesn't look to see that it's Haley, but he tells himself he would have answered anyway.

"Hello?"

"Hi babe," she says.

"Hi," he says, leery but missing her.

"So you couldn't call after three days?"

"Two, it's been *two* days."

"This is Wednesday, is it not? Sunday was the last day I saw you."

"Technically, it was Monday morning. But how's about a 'How are you? I miss you'?"

"How about it."

"You're breaking up," he says.

"I hear you perfectly. And I called on a light note, I was feeling really pretty good."

"I'm glad to hear that," he says, looking ahead at the Lexus, and feeling guilty for this stranger rather than for the one he's called his girlfriend for the past two years.

"So, I saw Huell Howser today!" she exclaims, drastically shifting tone. "He said hi to me."

"Really."

"In Hadley's."

"What were you doing there?"

"I'm at the outlets right now, I'm shopping. I'm outside Gucci."

"Why aren't you at work?"

"I'm playing hookie."

66

"You're gonna get fired."

"Why don't you say something like, 'I'm glad you saw Huell Howser today and that he said hi to you, because you love his show.'"

"Okay, I'm glad."

"It's better than me telling you my hours were cut down to part time."

"Why didn't you say so before, Haley? 'Playing hookie'? You lied."

"I'm not lying. They cut my hours, so I walked out for air."

"Now you're shopping and spending money? Does that make sense?"

"It's my birthday in a few days, Sam, or didn't you remember?"

"Yes, I remember," he convinces himself. "So let other people do the spending."

"What *other* people? You? Far away and on some trip without me? Dad in his sick world?"

"You have friends, Haley."

"Yes, well. I'm trying to forget that Tish came in on her roommate the night before last, totally whacked on meth and heroin, and screaming bloody in the bathroom. When she went in she found that she'd cut out her own breast implants."

"*What?*"

"Tish got her to the hospital before she bled to death."

"*What?*"

"She told her after, that she just thought of them as foreign and infested and contaminated, and wanted them out."

"That is so nasty," Sam says, making a face. "So, so *nasty*. I am so *glad* I wasn't on duty."

"You don't work emergency, you shit."

"Why am I a shit?"

"Because you don't understand what I'm saying."

"You're thinking about *implants*?"

"I'm back at the club, Sam, and I hate it. Duh."

"You know what?" Sam says, getting angry now. "This is not, I repeat, *not* going to get me to come back. You hear me? You better learn how to take better care of yourself."

She hangs up on him.

"F—— you too, lady," he says aloud.

As Sam makes a left following the Lexus down Casanova Street, the whole neighborhood smells like a fireplace. He looks at all of the Hansel and Gretel houses, thinking *This is the town that cute built*, signs in front of almost every home with a precious message of ownership. Up ahead, he sees a magnificent tree with roots like talons growing out from the front yard grass, gnarling out onto the sidewalk and bursting through the asphalt in the street. She parks just before it. As she gets out of the car, from this rear view he sees her as fat, and only as fat, wondering what he's doing here. But then she turns around, and motions with her hand toward the house, like a kindergarten teacher telling the kids they're free to play outside. He steps out of his car, thinking he would like to just follow someone's orders.

"Did I tell you my name is Wendy?" she takes his hand, as he walks with her over the bumpy sidewalk. There is a fine spray of perspiration around the front of her hairline.

"Wendy. Sam."

"Sam, watch your step here."

They have to stoop under the grape arbor beckoning him up the path to her solemn blue-shuttered house with stripes of raised wood, wavy glass windows, and an ornate cedar shake roof. He follows her along the round stepping stones, which force him to do a kind of skip all the way to her door. He cannot miss the LOVE IN A MIST sign on the porch, and as she pushes open the front door, he agrees with himself to be equally unabashed by the banner across the fireplace that says WELCOME HOME! scrawled in red letters.

"For my cousin," she says, with her hands on her hips. "Back from Iraq. He only stayed here for a few weeks. I'm his only family. Can I get you some ice tea?"

"Sure," Sam says, wondering where her flirtation has gone.

He follows her into the kitchen, she seems shorter than before reaching up to the cabinet for a glass. The sound of the liquid hitting the bottom to the top, the condensation around it, the smell of lemon, gets him in the mood to romance her.

"Chocolate mint, lemon verbena, and a squeeze of orange," she says, handing it to him. He takes the glass from her hand, lingering there, feeling her warmth against the slippery cold. He licks a small part of the rim, then gulps it down.

"Honey too." Sam smiles at her wickedly, thinking there is actually too much of it.

"Yes, honey." She smiles too. He notices a tiny beauty mark, almost black and infinitesimal, at the corner of her bottom lip. He bends to kiss her there. If he made his way inside of her, would his mother speak through her more clearly? Her mouth tastes faintly stale of Altoids, her smell dusky with a tincture of mineral and cinnamon. They tussle softly with their tongues. Sam runs his hands over her contours, stopping at the friction of elastic at her waist. She guides him into her bedroom, and he is so quickly hard, and throughout the short foreplay so fast in coming, that he worries Wendy will lose her interest before he can find out why July led him there.

With a second chance to satisfy her, he takes time now to meld to her, face, neck, mounds of shoulder, breasts, iridescent and beautiful with more desire. He should taste her this time, he thinks, but the smell of her is so pungent he can't. Feeling

69

innocent and liquid as vanilla, he prolongs his erection, plunging in and holding the sweet absence of torture in his head like a meditation. He waits for her, shy in her shuddering, then she finally lets go, and shouts above their heads. He can come now, but the release takes over him with devastation. She lays her hands gently on his middle back, pinkies touching, and though it shocks him, he just can't help exploding into tears.

"It's okay," she says, his face buried so deep in her chest, the voice sounds like a man's.

"How did you know I wasn't a psycho killer?" he asks, grabbing the seventh piece of tissue from the bedside table, used ones on the floor and on the bed.

She laughs with gusto, he holds on through her shimmy. "What's so funny?"

"You, a psycho killer."

"That's not funny." How could his mother have had a *relationship* with the guy who killed her? Most of her friends had seen Lamb before.

"I guess you still could be." She laughs again, he rolls completely off of her, and she seems glad. She stretches out her arms, still laughing. "I feel good. Everybody needs a good cry. You did it for me," she says, winding down into chuckles.

"Don't you want to know what I do?"

"Not really."

He grabs his heart, as if fatally wounded. She laughs. "Then I don't want to know what you do either."

"Good."

"What were you doing at the library?" he asks.

She laughs, and Sam feels his impatience coming on.

"I read *Big Sur and the Oranges of Hieronymous Bosch* not all that long ago, and I was really moved by his way of thinking."

Sam winks at her, she laughs.

70

"No, it's really a spiritual book, I would say. He talks about 'the task of genuine love.' He poses questions of you, such as how would you order the world if you were given the powers of the Creator, and asks what you desire that you don't already possess."

Sam blinks slowly, hoping she'll give all the way into his mother, let her invade and speak.

"And really, I was just on my way back up from a friend's in Pismo Beach. I stopped in on a whim, never having been, though I've lived so close to it all this time."

"I played Frisbee with a kid in Pismo Beach early this morning! Maybe you saw me," he says, getting excited.

She shakes her head, smiles lazily.

"Where do you hang out here?" he asks, putting his pants on. She frowns.

"I don't hang out, really. Where's to 'hang out' in Carmel?"

"I wouldn't know. Isn't there some hip section of town?"

"Hip? Only hip in Carmel is hip replacements," she laughs, festive again. "Where are you from?"

"The desert. Joshua Tree area." He looks at her like she knows perfectly well where he's from.

"I've never been."

He smiles. "Either you're a desert person, or you're not. There's no in between."

She nods. "I'm a cool, temperate kind of person. But it doesn't surprise me that you live there." She sits up naked in bed, her breasts at once full and flat against the mushy soft flesh over her ribs.

"We should go take a walk at the beach. Fine white sand, soft and deep on the steep hills."

Sam smiles politely. "You want to talk to me there?"

"Yes. Later maybe?" she asks carefully.

He shrugs, still smiling.

71

"You hungry?"

"Starved."

Wendy lays out olives, rosemary bread, goat cheese, and foie gras. As he nibbles on the latter, he finds it perverse, the texture and the slide on his tongue. He glances up at her, hoping she missed his disapproval. She is as pleasant as before. He gazes out the kitchen window to her backyard dwarf fruit trees, and the sunset beginning to blaze just beyond. He remembers his mother picking lemons from the tree, smiling as she squeezed them. The smells of oregano, tomato, and minty lamb rise in Wendy's kitchen. She doesn't talk to him as she cooks, and he feels himself steadily losing his nerve to come out with what he thinks.

Her meal tastes as mean as she had claimed. After dinner they sit in her living room, she pulls out her flute and plays. The timber at first like a bee at his ear until he recognizes the tune, "Light My Fire," and tries not to laugh. The melody much like José Feliciano's version, surprised that he could remember his name, though he pictures Joe's CD collection and finds it unalphabetized in his mind's eye.

He could easily spend the night with her, but her conversation grows annoying and winsome when she describes how she's gotten into Reiki healing. As a nurse, he tells her, he has heard a lot about it, and believes it, sure, but the thought that they are both into making people feel better depresses the hell out of him.

Her eyes are less and less like his mother's. By the time he's had it with waiting for July to speak, he makes up an excuse about having to hurry to a friend's wedding tomorrow, and even resists the urge to add that he is best man. She hugs him good-bye with an overpowering comfort he can't stand.

Back in his car, the chariot, amid cottages in the forest smelling high of seaside night and burning wood, he hopes he can find his

72

way back to the highway. Feeling spooked by the dearth of streetlights, he thinks as he pulls away from the curb: *What if he got into an accident and lost all memory of his past? Life could be perfect then.*

8

Magic's July

Sam was in the church preschool when July was out of work, and hanging out afternoons in a bar. Fired as a result of complaining to a manager about the boss's sexual harassment, July was ultimately glad to be out of the hotel business. It was racist, besides. Collecting unemployment was her rock bottom, she thought, and filled her with the guilt of living off the state. Other than Sam, nothing in her life added up to happiness. She felt worthless having so little direction on the heels of her thirtieth birthday, and here she was a mother, responsible for the well-being of a strident, little person. She ached for the time when Sam was an infant, kept close to her body and away from toddling, disobedient harm. She didn't want to work and be away from Sam ever. Yet, here she was in a bar, while the church ladies watched him. She ordered Coke or club soda, and talked to whatever drunk spun a yarn thick enough to distract her from all she thought wrong of the morning's job interview or of her life in general.

"You're dressed to the nines, Gwen," Otis said loudly, as he walked into her favorite bar carrying a jacket by one finger so that it hung down his back. He sat down next to her. "Bicentennial celebration somewhere?"

"What are you doing here?"

He smiled at her. "I'm here for a friend's wedding. I'm the best man."

74

"You, a best man?"

"I'm doing up his bachelor party. Standing next to him in his hour of need—the whole nine yards."

"You're kidding me."

"I'm not." He clasped his hands, and looked at her features, one by one. "I like your hair. It suits you."

Resisting the urge to pat her short afro, she stared back at him in defiance. "How did you find me, Otis?"

"I wasn't looking, Gwen. Guess it was just luck."

"What kind?"

"That depends on you. In my opinion, it could be magic."

"How could you convince me," she stated instead of asked.

"Love Potion Number Nine."

"What's with the obsession, Otis?"

"You know what's lucky about the number nine, Gwen? Multiply it by any number, and the digits of the answer add up to nine."

"You just figure that out?"

"I just figured out, in this very moment, that we were meant for each other."

"I don't believe this."

"Believe it. Come to the wedding with me."

"And set myself up for a little torture?"

"That's not very nice."

"I'll tell you what's not very nice," she snapped. "Did you send me that note, Otis?"

"What note?"

"You know what I'm talking about," she said getting angrier.

"I'm afraid I don't."

"The one with Ernest's picture, the one with his wife and kids."

Otis laughed until he coughed, covering his mouth with his fist.

"Well, who else could have done it?"

"You ever thought of Ernest's wife?"

July sat there quiet for a moment. Then she looked up at him with Sam's dumbingly beautiful eyes.

"Ernest was a fool to let you go."

July shook her head, thinking of her little boy.

"Your husband too."

She couldn't help her eyes from welling. "Maybe it was good riddance. What kind of woman sits up in a bar in the afternoon talking to a guy like you?"

"Come on now, Gwen, you don't have to disrespect me every time you're feeling a little down on your luck. What did I ever do to you?"

She folded her arms on the counter, wanting to put her head down for a nap.

"Where's the bartender anyway?"

"In the back room, getting drunk." She put her head down.

"How do they make any money?" Otis asked, banging his fist hard on the counter, causing her to get back up.

The bartender came out instantly, swung his thin hips awkwardly to get by two customers and make his way to Otis. His face was purple and mean with despair.

"What do you want?" he barked.

"Gin straight."

A man came in then, put his hands intimately like a brother's on Otis's shoulders; Otis laughed when he turned to look at him.

"Here's the sorry groom now," Otis said to July, who barely looked at his friend.

"This is my cue, then," July said, getting up. "I have to go pick up my boy."

She pulled the silk dress from clinging to her legs; in the bar's low light the pattern of tiny red-beaked white ducks on navy created a shooting star effect.

"See you here tomorrow?" Otis called.

"Right. Same time," she replied, without turning around.

Adjustment. When she got home next door to the preschool, which was really the church basement, she brushed her teeth and gargled though no liquor had touched her lips. She put a towel around her shoulders and sprayed her hair with sheen before picking it into a perfect circle with the comb. She smelled under her arms and was repelled by the odor of stained sweat on silk. She carefully tied a scarf around her head so as not to lose her hair's shape. She took off her dress and changed into a pressed pantsuit of white nylon, which made her look like a nurse. Satisfied with the mirror's image, she dashed out of the door to get her son.

"Here's Mama," Mrs. Johnson said, sitting at a children's table with Sam, who jumped from his seat and ran to squeeze his mother's legs. He was the last child to be picked up.

"Hi Baby," July said, squatting down to hold him tight.

"You haven't changed jobs, have you?" Mrs. Johnson said, carrying a wet painting of Sam's on her open palms.

"I'm still at the hotel, but I'm actually looking for new work, so if you hear of anything—"

"Oh, I thought you were working at the hospital. This would explain this beautiful painting." And she held it out, though her expression was one of warning.

Feeling defensive over her pantsuit and therefore put off, July stood up and looked at it. A large white building with a rainbow over it and an X over what looked like the door.

"I thought Sam must have seen a red cross at your work," Mrs. Johnson said suspiciously.

"That's not a red cross, it looks like an X, right Sam?"

"X!" Sam exclaimed.

"I had a book on Malcolm X and he became fascinated with his name. This looks like our place. Isn't that home, Sam?"

"My mom and I live right *here*," Sam pointed at the door with a fat, stubby finger and looked up at Mrs. Johnson.

"All you have to do is ask him if you have a question," July said, almost sternly. "He's happy to talk about his paintings, isn't that right, Sam?" July picked him up, put him on her hip, and took the gooey painting in her other hand.

When they got outside, the neighbor across the street was watering his yard, creating a high arc of spray with his hose. A rainbow sparkled through the early evening summer sun.

"Look at this, my baby, your rainbow! And it almost touches our door," she exclaimed, stretching the truth.

"I wanna get Miss Jun-sun," Sam said, trying to scoot out from her grasp. July held onto him.

"No, stay with me Baby. This rainbow is just for us, it won't last long, anyway, so let's watch it and enjoy."

The neighbor looked up at them and waved, changing the direction of the hose, and the rainbow was gone. July waved back at him.

Sam peered up at July with the face he used in the moment of deciding whether or not to cry. She squeezed his cheeks.

"Let's go inside now, and make more magic." She took his hand and led him across the street at the pace of his small-legged steps.

9

Dinner with the Neighbors

Aching, pining. Sam didn't think this cooler weather could get to him. He thought he'd welcome the moist change, but the smell clinging to the wet breeze of nearby redwood, thousands of years old, nearly does him in. In the town of Little River just below Mendocino, he looks out of his cabin window in the morning, beyond the garden's pink lilies that splatter all along the California roads this time of year. Anywhere in this beauty, he searches for a memory of his mother that would not hurt. It is as if her murderer ran again from the scene of the crime, now crouching in the woods, waiting to spring on him, force a mental picture on him of all that happened to her.

Barefoot, he takes his coffee outside on the porch, sits on the cushioned bench swing, rubbing his feet together to keep warm. He locks his ankles and rocks. If Haley were here, she would lay his head down in her lap, caress his temples, knead his hair, and talk about the constellations. Love is a trap he doesn't deserve. If he truly let himself go with Haley, then something might happen to her too.

The phone rings, butting into his serenity of aloneness. He picks himself up off the swing, not realizing he'd laid down in it to try and go back to sleep after an insomniac night.

"D'you find 'em?" he asks Joe first thing when he answers.

"What?"

"Mom's *papers*," he says exasperated.

"Sorry for worrying you son, I did."

"Why didn't you call me?"

"Don't know how I missed them before, but Zeke was here, and he told me to look again, and there they were."

"*Zeke*?"

"He's been hanging out a lot."

"Why?"

"The wheelchair got me a little interested in welding things other than what is useful. Zeke does sculpture next door. You know that?"

"Zeke? A sculptor? Can you call it that? Suddenly you're interested in *art*? What the hell was he doing in Mom's things?"

"He was not in your mother's things, son. He knew how frustrated I was thinking I had misplaced them, but he told me to look again and they were there. Simple. Sometimes those kind of things happen. Maybe I'm senile." Joe scratches near his tonsils with the back of his tongue, making a cough-choke sound.

"What a bunch of crap, Joe!"

"Be happy I found them and leave it at that."

"What are you telling people about my mother's business for, Joe?" his voice cracks, and he sniffles.

"You sound like hell, son, what's going on with you? You okay?"

"Yes, I'm okay," Sam sighs. "I'm just mad. Look who's talking, anyway. Just tired is all, I didn't get much sleep last night."

"Zeke's sister is up around there, somewhere."

"Zeke, Zeke, Zeke."

"You always liked her, didn't you? Why don't you give her and Andrew a call?"

"Don't have their number."

"Got it right here for you, son."

Sam pretends to write it down. He continues to stare out of the window, still angry with Joe for disturbing the singular depth of his pain.

"You listening to me?"

"Yeah."

When he hangs up with Joe, he lies inside on the corner built-in daybed with striped pink cushions. Sheba would like this room, he thinks, from the look of her house. He had neglected to buy a single souvenir for her in the last few towns. He contributes so much to her image, the imprint of that single night of feeling that hot for someone he wanted for such a long time. Haley and he seem like they could never recover the heat of their very first time. His day with Carmel Wendy was nothing remotely like the desire he once felt for Haley. But he shouldn't think too much about any of it. He is not a sex addict, he doesn't go looking for it, and there is nothing to say other than he tends to get lucky that way.

Two days later at a gas station in Fort Bragg, Sam eyes the stickers on an entering Ford Ranger pickup full of guys: TOMMY REDNECK with the Confederate flag, and SAVE A MOUSE, EAT A PUSSY. As he screws the cap on his tank, he gets a call from Zeke's sister Paige, inviting him for dinner at a restaurant twenty minutes past. Miffed for a moment that Joe wouldn't let it go—and reluctant to backtrack no matter how short the trip—he still accepts the invitation with relief. Would be nice to have the company, and get out of the hermit mode, so seductive to self-pity.

Worrying about what to wear, continuing to feel out of place in all of these whitest of white communities, he buys a red polo-style T and baggy, beige, polished cotton pants. He grabs the cheapest room at the edge of Fort Bragg, washes, combs his hair, patting it down in a tidier configuration of very independent kinks. Looking in the mirror from three-quarter angle to the other of his face, he wishes he'd bought spray to make his hair shine. He grabs the bottle of perfume from his bag, spritzes it on his wrist, and rubs it against his chest. As the scent rises, he continues to pat his chest as if he could salve his heart.

Sam walks into the restaurant, eyes first on the wide, bloodwood plank floor, then up to the high vaulted rough-sawn ceiling and exposed, galvanized air ducts mixing an industrial feeling to the castle's barn. The blond walls are washed in faint yellow, with butter-colored French windows, the cast iron chandeliers are on low light. Sitting at one of the formal white clothed tables for four is Paige with her common-law husband, Andrew. Her hair is dark, and fashioned overglamorously in a sixties movie star bouffant, slightly curled toward her chin. Andrew, who from afar looks like he could be a fortyish rock star himself, stands, shakes Sam's hand with an air of self-assuming generosity. Sam bends to gallantly kiss Paige's cheek; though American, she turns her head to receive another, European style.

"There's that wonderful scent. So sweet, I'd wear it myself. When are you going to tell me what it is?" Paige asks. Sam holds his hands open before he sits down.

"Well, don't deny a chap his mystery, darling," Andrew says, smug but with charm.

"I left you a note a month or so ago, Sam, did you get it?" Paige asks worried, her big brown eyes plaintive, her face as disagreeably sectioned as a Picasso painting.

Sam looks around the restaurant as if the note was hidden there, and shrugs.

Andrew laughs. "Well, who could understand *that* cacography, anyway," he says in his thick upper-middle-class Englishman's accent. His face is acne-scarred and pitted, yet considerably prettier than Paige's.

"I left it two weeks before Zeke was to arrive, I just wanted you to look out for my bromeliads up front, under the mailbox. It's the only place not covered by automatic sprinklers," Paige says, batting her painted eyelids.

"You should get more natives," Sam says, straightening his collar, and swallowing.

"Bromeliads *are* native, I thought," Paige says, screwing together her brows, creating two deep lines like parentheses. When Sam shrugs again, her expression softens to that of a flirtatious girl's.

"They're Australian, love. But don't hold that against them." Andrew wiggles his nose as if he might sneeze; it is pinched in two points at the top of the button. "So how long will you be on holiday, then?" he asks Sam, sitting back in his seat.

"I don't know. The month of August is a start."

"Well, we're a few days into it then, aren't we? Over before you know it." Andrew snaps, turns playfully alarmed toward Paige, then scoots his butt away from her in his chair. "Was that my wamble or yours, love?" Paige flips her hand. "Rather loud, wasn't it?"

"Did you fart?" Sam asks. "I didn't hear anything."

"His stomach *growled*," Paige says, shaking her head, flushing red.

"I could eat a rhinoceros, I'm famished." Andrew smiles devilishly, giving Sam the impression that he swung both ways. He fixates on the deep impression above Andrew's lip. He could choke Joe for telling them he was in the area.

"The woman starves me, really," Andrew goes on, patting Paige's thigh. "And when she does make an attempt, well, let's just say there's never a thing esculent on her table, I can assure you!" he cackles. Paige folds her arms, chuckles, shakes her head.

The waiter approaches, she is thin, with a large head framed by blown out camel-colored curls giving her the appearance of a lioness.

"Having a good time, I see, before I've even started you off on drinks," she says in a naughty tone, zeroing in on Andrew.

"They started before I got here," Sam says, pointing to them with his thumb. The waiter looks at him, as if put off by distraction.

"I'll have a whiskey and Coke," Paige says, looking jealous.

"Awful, isn't it?" Andrew asks, looking up at the waiter's eyes, shifting not so subtly to her breasts. "Coke. Deadens the taste buds, really. Spoils the appetite, as well, love." He snorts loudly as he laughs, the waiter joins in.

"I'll give you the wine list. You'll like a bottle. We have a few really good locals here, no doubt you've done some tasting during your stay?"

"We live less than a half hour away on our *own* winery," Andrew boasts.

"Surprised I haven't seen you before," the waiter says, still looking only at him.

"It's possible you didn't take notice that day," Sam says, giving her a fake half smile. The waiter looks at him now, irritated to recognize he's cute.

"I still want my whiskey and Coke."

"Why don't you surprise us with your favorite Coro," Andrew says, smiling. "That way I can rate *your* taste." He raises his index finger at her.

"I won't disappoint you," she says, closing up the list. "I'll be back with the wine, your whiskey, and the chef's specials." She turns slowly on her heels, making use of the nice fit of her tailored black pants.

"Full of persiflage, isn't she?" Andrew says, dismissing the thought of her with his hand.

"Full of mammary, I'd say is the one thing you really noticed," Paige says, squinting her eyes so that the reflection of candlelight flashes in them.

Sam inhales and exhales loudly.

"I'd say, Sam, you must have broken down and taken up yoga with the rest of them?"

"And what I have to do to get his attention!" Paige exclaims, spreading her mouth, lips tightly shut.

"Let's bore him with the connubial details, shall we?" Andrew says, now taking a serious tone. Paige flips her hand at him, pats the back of her hair in place.

The waiter returns with a competitive Pinot Noir, dismissing the Coro. After she chatters about the specials and pours each glass, Andrew tries not to tease or entertain her as he orders the appetizers. Sam stares her down, daring her to show she's attracted to him. Paige excuses herself for the bathroom.

"Zeke's been hanging out with Joe a lot these days," Sam says, putting his elbows on the table, then removes them, remembering manners.

"Ezekiel," Andrew says, shaking his head. "They don't have the same father, to be honest. Did you know that?"

"Yes."

"If Zeke had gone to university he might have made something of himself," Andrew says, wiping the corner of his mouth. "As it is, I'm afraid he's an empty hat."

Sam bites the bottom inside of his cheek, turns up his bottom lip. "So what do you think about nurses, empty caps?"

"Ach," Andrew waves his hand. "You studied, did you not? What's the difference? Nurse, podiatrist, pomologist. Put your head to something, that's what matters, I say."

"I hadn't heard that you did anything with your degrees," Sam says, stroking both sides of his chin as if he had a beard. "It's your parents' winery, isn't it?"

"I have my stake in it."

"Or so you say to Paige?"

"Rubbish." Andrew narrows his eyes at Sam. "Ah love," he

says, recovering his temperament, easily and quickly as he does, and pulls out Paige's chair. Ladylike, she tucks her black and white seersucker skirt under before sitting down. "Sam here was just beginning to worry me about Ezekiel."

"What?"

"Well, it seems our brother has been cavorting with Joe when he told us he was in hospital for an ulcer."

"Cavorting? I can't imagine Joe doing much of that."

"No, the old fellow is rather lucky to be up to titivating," Andrew says, turning to Sam. "Rather a mess, your house, isn't it?" Pointedly he turns to Paige, "Still, I don't see how Ezekiel could be hanging out at Joe's when he told us he was in hospital." Andrew feels his pockets for cigarettes, before excusing himself to smoke outside. "Will you order the game for me, love? I need a fag before I digest that I've just bought our brother another pair of bloody brogans, rather than paid the tab for his ulcer." He walks off like a dancer in his loafers, the dark gray cords tight at his butt, thighs, and knees, flaring at the legs.

Paige blows and vibrates air through a tight space between the roof of her mouth and tongue. The noise is chilling to Sam. "He acts like it's all about *his* money. What about mine?"

The busser brings their appetizers; Paige ignores him when he asks if they would like fresh pepper. In deference, Sam nods his head.

"My mother wasn't *stupid*, you know. She wasn't another vain stage mother. She put my money away for me. She took good care of us."

Sam clears his throat, uncomfortable to be between anyone but his two varied selves.

"Andrew's the one who gets taken in by Zeke." She forks a buffalo mozzarella and stuffs it in her mouth, continuing to talk as she chews. "I never pay him much attention. He used to be into counterfeiting, did he tell you?"

86

"Andrew?"

"Zeke."

"What?"

"He was quite good at it then the law caught up with him. He got off, but it scared him straight, thank God."

Sam swallows his salad, the lettuce a tickling lump down his throat.

"What does he live off now, exactly?"

"I told you, my mother invested well for us. She's shrewd, and he's a spoiled brat, basically. Mothers and sons, you know how it is." Paige wolfs down more, and then remembering Sam's story, covers her mouth with her hand, her eyes bashful and regretting. Andrew takes his chair, surveys the dug-into dishes.

"Edacious, isn't she?" Andrew says to Sam, shaking his head with affection for her.

"Have you decided?" the waiter returns to their table, hands clasped behind her.

"Yes, love, I'll have the rabbit, rare, and she will have the chicken," Andrew says, Paige glaring at him. "What will you have, Sam?"

"The bass," he says, clearing his throat, wanting to run out to call Joe about Zeke the counterfeiter.

"I've figured out who it is that you remind me of," the waiter says pointing at Paige, looking her directly in the eye.

"Elizabeth Taylor," Andrew says, bored.

"No—"

"Stockard Channing," he says, raising his brow and sticking out his bottom lip as if a comedian in a sketch. Paige's chest rises in both good and bad anticipation of being recognized, though this hasn't happened since she looked her teen star self.

"No, no, wait, I have it," she says, snapping. "San-dra Bern-hard."

"Sandra Bernhard? Darling, that's a first!" Andrew exclaims.

"Couldn't be farther from the truth, love," he says to Paige. With her eyes she ices the waiter, who walks away in a defensive manner to place their orders.

When Paige is done brooding, she invites Sam for a movie at their house after dinner, but he declines. The meal is rich and lousy—though the couple would beg to differ—the conversation worse, as he imagines all the ways that Zeke could have violated him, Joe, and July.

In his dream that night July appears in a white house, which seemed to be every home he shared with her; the turquoise dining room becomes an aquarium with glass walls, nothing swimming behind. July happily holds up different picture frames, trying their positions against the glass walls, and looks to her son for approval. When Zeke tries to enter the room, Sam blocks him at the door. July protests, happy to see Zeke (whom she's never met) and merrily pointing at Joe (whom Sam can't see). Then she picks up the frames again, motioning for Sam to help her as if it were a game.

10

Calling Abel

Just before sunset, Sam makes the unceremonious crossing over the California state line into Oregon. Numbing to beautiful landscape, he remains steady and uninspired on Highway 101. Fighting paranoia of skinheads and militia, he looks for opportunities to size up the locals in every FLAGGERS AHEAD sign that twice so far yields no construction workers. A local radio station informs him of the August heat inland driving the natives to the coast. After a third failure to luck upon any decent or fairly priced room on a Saturday night, he finally settles for a dive in the town of Brookings.

He knows he's in trouble when he asks where to buy a good cup of coffee and the motel clerk replies the Chevron station. Sam heads for the bar instead, redwood, gable roof, and the lopsided feeling of a log cabin. Keno is everywhere. He strolls in at attention, avoiding eye contact. The bartender is relaxed, pleasantly disinterested.

Eyeing Sam with overt suspicion is a rough neck woman who couldn't be much more than five feet. Sam sits, his vision adjusting to the low light. He tries to ignore her, and orders a beer. The door opens to dusk and a young thin man strolls in with long, dark brown hair, a curled mustache, and goatee. He is pale under the eyes like Abel, his delicate nose bridge resembling Sam's best friend as well. The guy orders as Sam is paying, then turns to look at him and smiles with a twinkle that Sam can't be sure what means.

"You're not a local, are you?" the guy says, near chuckling, but in catching Sam's discomfort tones it down.

"No."

The guy raises his chin before the bartender puts the beer in front of him. He reaches back for his wallet, looks at Sam after he puts the money down.

"Staying long?" the guy asks.

"No," Sam says and breathes in impatiently, contemplating whether the guy thinks he might make a drug sale. He turns to face the counter in dismissal but it comes off as shy the way he'd rather mean it.

"Well, later," the guy says, tapping the countertop once near Sam's hand.

"Later," Sam replies, looking into the guy's eyes long enough to wonder if he really couldn't be the one friend he'd have if he were forced to remain in this town. As the guy walks toward the back of the bar, Sam imagines doing coke with him in some beat-up room overlooking an elk crossing sign. In an alternative notion, the guy is some kind of artist Sam could claim the way Joe has suddenly latched onto a snake like Zeke.

"Have you seen a man who could be your father around here?" the short, rough woman startles him. She now straddles the seat on his left.

"What?"

"Have you seen a man who doesn't look a hell of a lot unlike you, only discolored at the jaw, around sixty years old?"

"No," Sam says, looking at her, terror budding. "Why?" he asks, making his mouth wide, elongating the syllable.

"I'm looking for him is all," she says.

"Why?"

"I'm looking for him is all," she repeats. She stares him down for one full second, Sam afraid of the clearness of her irises, as if nothing were behind them like fortune. He puts his hands on his own knees, to see if they don't actually exist. He looks up at her again as she raps the bar with her knuckle. The bartender nods and pours her a shot of vodka. He has a kind and pink pudgy face.

The woman lights a cigarette, her hands are at once veined and childlike, though the fingernails are stained, and the skin tough. The tiny crosshatch of wrinkles at her lips moves Sam to look at the lines in his own palms as if he might find a patch of the very same pattern. He orders a shot to go with his beer, and the bartender smiles as if to say, *See, you're getting it.*

"Are you visiting someone?" she asks in the same brusque voice.

"Are you kidding me?"

"No." She looks at him, meanly squinting those space age eyes, and he sees through them to something, changing his mind about her.

"I'm not visiting anyone. Why? Are you from around here?"

"Eureka, originally." She downs the rest of her vodka, puckering her wrinkled lips, her short hair and round nose are also puckish, and if Sam weren't sure she'd rather he was a girl, he'd want to kiss her tenderly for never considering being anyone's mother.

"You have kids?" he asks, doubting himself, and taking a long swig.

"No. I'm off duty. I'm not here for chitchat, but it's my luck you walked in. Your name Sam Brown?"

Sam chokes, beats his chest once with his fist. She slaps him on the back twice.

"That's what I thought. I have word that the parolee Shawn Lamb might have crossed the state line, presumably on your tracks. So, take this, my card. I'm a police officer. If you see him, give me a call, and I'll grab the motherfucker."

The sting in Sam's throat causes his eyes to burn and tear. Inside, it is as if someone puts a kidney belt on him and pulls hard on the straps. He swallows, a taste like iron in his tongue.

"So you've seen him," she says.

"A silver Toyota, dented, early nineties," he coughs out.

"That's not the vehicle description I have."

"I saw one in LA, one in Santa Barbara, but I haven't seen it since."

"Did you see *him*?"

"Just the car, parked in Santa Barbara and leaving the street I spent the night in LA."

"I'll let his parole officer know what you saw." She pushes her card into his front jean pocket, pulls a pen from the back of hers, dropping the ballpoint by butting its end on her chin.

"Why don't you just stay with me if you know he's after me?"

"It's not my job to guard you, and you just happened to walk in here. Lamb hasn't done anything yet. What's your number?" She asks dully, pen poised, not looking at Sam. He clears his throat and tells her the number, trying hard not to break down in sobs.

"Where are you headed?"

"Not sure."

"Listen to me," she says, looking at him now, her eyes taking on the shine of crystals. "Lamb's parole officer is a friend, and he asked me to nab him if I saw him. He thought Lamb was following the victim's family, because Lamb told him he needed to talk to you. This may be unusual, still more often than not if they wanna talk, they got conscience to clear, you're just the unlucky receiver."

"I'll kill him," Sam says, his nose running.

"I assure you, you won't, or it's you I'm taking in." She slaps him on the back again. "I'll find him before he gets to you. I used to be a bounty hunter—"

"But you haven't seen him!" Sam interrupts.

"Like I said," her eyes narrow, "if it happens that you do, call me. If you don't, I have him. And I'll let you know."

"Don't I get some kind of protection or something?"

"I'll give the local department Lamb's description, but he hasn't broken the law, that we know of, so I can't do more than that," she says, before she walks out.

Sam turns every light on in his motel room. He pushes the shoddy, scraped nightstand up against the door. Sweat spreads evenly, dense as mesh. He rechecks the locked bathroom window, too small to crawl through; he flops back on the bed, lies glassy-eyed. Snippets of ill-fated scenarios deviate in his head. He stares into the splotched wall in front of him, his will to focus twitters. Ghouls call with every headlight reflected through the droopy curtained view of the parking lot. What at first feels miniscule in his ears—phantom pustules of sound—now bulge and hiss grotesquely. He could easily fall through the vortex.

Now wholly servile to his fear, his heart is immune to any more fantasies of revenge. While Shawn Lamb was still behind bars, Sam's courage elaborated upon itself, and clung fast. His love for his mother was often wrapped opulently inside it, other times only beside it. Courage equaled allegiance and allegiance equaled courage. Circumstances now being otherwise transform the enraged screaming inside into a trill, self-preserving and limp.

When he should really call Joe to warn and ineffectively reassure him, he clutches the phone with the police officer's number already encoded in speed dial, then hits the button for Abel's instead.

"Yeah?" Abel says, peals of laughter behind him.

"Where are you, A?" Sam asks, voice wobbling.

"I'm at my brother's in LA, if you can believe that."

"I can't."

"Well, neither can I. They're having a dinner party, mostly his wife's friends. Not all of them stinking. I can't help feeling, nevertheless, that it's always about my negation."

Sam says nothing. His desire to hang up undiscovered makes arcs around his urge to tell Abel off for being too swiftly recovered and unrecognizing of Sam's suffering.

"My brother's pretending he's ready to just let it all be water under the bridge, you know? He's pretending to understand me, he's making a good case for himself that he cares. But he's also siccing his wife on me." Abel waits for a response, but Sam holds the phone with both hands, breathes in deep, pacing himself before cutting loose.

"She's really a nutcase, if I may say so myself," Abel says, near whispering, now buoyant, close to chuckling. Sam listens, so intent on all of the sounds in and around the motel that as Abel kicks a door shut, Sam jumps, feeling all the more vulnerable. "Before the party, you know, she comes into my room, and asks me how I like her 'midriff.' And the way she says the word *midriff*, you know? With all of this pomp, all of this offhand *arrogance*, like she's forthright and 'up front,' but really she has the genuineness of a slut.

"I'm sitting here," he continues, lighting up a cigarette, taking on an indignant timber, "and get this, my arm all stitched up, bandaged and *madly* itching, and my *brother* proceeds to tell me, last night in fact, that he wouldn't mind at all if I just went into her room and did her! Can you believe *that*?" He blows the smoke out. "Never an end to the sickness with him. He actually told me, listen to this, 'She's having fantasies about you, little brother, and I for one would welcome—"

"A, man," Sam at last interrupts verging hysteria, "he's after me, Abel, he's after me, he's after me," quivering on the last word until the sound of his own voice moves him to tears.

"He is *not* after you, Sam," Abel says firmly.

"A cop warned me in a bar tonight! He's crossed the state line, following *me*!"

"Where are you?" Abel asks, too calm.

"I'm in Oregon, some town called Bookings."

"*Brookings*."

"What do you know about it?" Sam asks sniffling.

"I'll fly into Medford, you come pick me up at the airport."

"I don't need you coming up here, man, getting mixed up in all this."

"I'm hanging up to make the arrangements."

"No! I've gotta face all this myself, I don't need you coming up here getting mixed up in it."

"I'll drive with you north. I need to get the hell away from here, anyway! Listen, he doesn't want to hurt you. He's tracking you down, to say he's sorry. I know he is. The cop'll have him before my plane leaves, before the night is over, I bet. I'm hanging up to get a flight for the morning. I'll call back with the flight number, Medford airport."

"I'm not picking you up. I don't want to leave the coast, A."

"You don't want to leave your room, you're saying."

"I don't want to leave the coast!"

"What the fuck does *that* mean?"

"I can't," he says, thinking of July and the dream pictures she sends of the ocean. "I'm not picking you up, you're not coming. I won't tell you where I am."

"Bullshit, man. Stay where you are then, and when I call back I'll get it out of you, and I'll make it to your hotel," Abel says and hangs up on him.

The morning brings Sam a newfound welcoming to peril. He could kiss the dirty asphalt of the parking lot as he stuffs his bag in the car. He could billow along in the cloud, his stomach a kite, all the way two hours north to his next stop, Gold

Beach. Even the passing sights of dramatic cliffs, tsunami wave warning signs, and driftwood packed on the sand like a bone-yard, do nothing but tantalize him all the more in this sudden appeal to death.

He doesn't answer Abel's call as he checks into the new motel. He won't hear Abel's message until he's taken in with pleasure the fustiness but odd warmth of his room with a difficult view of the beach, and a place for his bag, next to the kitchen, which gives the illusion of a hearth.

At the beach, Sam lies defiant in the sand, which blows into his hair, face, and eyes. This is what it feels like to remain very still and at peace, while the rest of the world whirls and makes a fuss out of living. The sound of the sea is violent, just as the wind proves itself as formidable opponent or partner. Sam can't decide in the moment, since in being is all the effort he's willing to put anything. He scrunches up his nose to the sand breaking and entering; the sun peers through and seems to burn a circle around him. Either aliens are coming to get him, or July watches over without making her aromatic presence known. He is suffused with readiness for the light, as long as he can stand it. The warmth slowly fuzzes off and falls with bite into cold, contorting what little faith he might have left.

Back in his room, hair freshly washed and dripping, ears soggy, he shakes his head out like a dog. His leg hairs glisten, his skin is soap smooth and a beautiful nut brown, set against the small white towel around his waist. He sits on the bed to call the cop in Brookings.

"Officer Wally," she answers.

"Have you found Shawn Lamb, yet? This is Sam Brown."

"No, where are you?"

"Gold Beach."

"I'll let the local department know."

"Has his parole officer heard from him?" Sam asks, his pronunciation sibilant, barely audible like a hoarse girl's.

"Can you speak up?"

Sam clears his throat. "Has his *parole* officer heard from him?"

"Not that I know of."

"You don't seem to be on it."

"I've got a few cases, Sam Brown, but I am *on* them all. Now that you're in Gold Beach, you're out of my jurisdiction, but I'll let the proper authorities know. Lamb was out of the San Diego County area when he last called his parole officer, but it cannot yet be confirmed that he ever crossed the state line into Oregon. At this point, no one knows of his whereabouts whatsoever."

"Well, how did *you* find me in that bar, anyway?"

"I told you, I wasn't looking for you, but Lamb. I was off duty, and you walked in."

"But how did you know about me?

"Your father let the parole officer know where you were."

"*Joe* knows about this?"

"I did not speak to any Joe directly, I was given your information by Lamb's parole officer."

"So, surely when he's found he'll be taken into custody? That he ever left the San Diego County area alone even is a technical violation of parole, isn't it? He'll be locked up again, won't he?" he pleads, voice lilting upwards again.

It is her time to clear her throat. "Take that up with your governor," she says with sharpness, before hanging up.

Just before Sam's vision narrows into gray, and takes him almost out into unconsciousness, he sees the filigree of lines around the officer's clear-as-water eyes, and the new nothingness behind them. How she must have been flung like scum with dishonor from space. He hits the button "END" on his phone, and it rings.

"WHERE ARE YOU, ASSHOLE?"

"Gold Beach."

"What's the hotel?"

"Ireland's Rustic Lodge."

"*Address*, Princess."

Sam searches for the notebook guide and tells him carefully, ready to spell out numbers if he has to. "But I'm coming to get you, A."

"Fuck you, I'm taking a bus." Abel hangs up.

At crucial times, Joe has a strange way of showing fatherly concern, and Sam in some uncertain terms tells him so. They are both frail as they speak, Sam's voice wandering through unnatural octaves as he asks why Joe didn't call him when he first learned about Lamb. The connection doesn't help as Joe plods about, making Sam feel as if being his son is the only reason in the world Joe bothers to get up in the morning. When Sam tries to diffuse the intensity, he actually sets the stakes higher, love making clumps in his chest until he wants to strike out against him. But Joe obviously understands this. So when Sam lays his head down to go to sleep at dusk, he hears the Neil Young song "Old Man" playing in his head, the way July used to play it on the guitar before he was old enough to cognitively file away that she did.

11

Joe's July

"Look like Angela Davis, anybody ever tell you that?" Joe asked July, sitting alone on lunch break, her back toward him where he stood paying for his food at the counter. She turned with animated surprise, still holding a bitten hot pastrami sandwich that looked raw and alive, escaping messily from her hands.

"If this weren't 1987 and I still had my 'fro you might have gotten away with that," she said, wiping her long fingers and their clean, unpolished nails. She smiled, thumbed the corner of her mouth for a spot of mustard. Joe then stood in front of her, and though they were inside the deli, she kept looking back down sheepishly as if his stare were the glare of the sun in her heavy-lidded eyes.

"Lips proud and childlike. Pout or challenge?"

"Do you know her?"

Joe grinned, his fat cheeks puckering like beggars for a kiss.

"Do you? Because I was still there, you know, at UCLA in the philosophy department just a year before she arrived."

Joe laughed lustily.

"What? Dating myself?"

"To answer your first question: Don't know her, but I'd like to know *you*. As for your second, I would have said you were in your twenties." He pulled a chair out, his chin down, brows up, as if asking for permission but not waiting for the answer.

July looked at him bewildered, not able to tell if he was making fun of her or not.

"Black don't crack," he said, putting one side of his kind, daisylike face in his hand to study her.

"That's right. I'm forty-one, I look nothing like Angela Davis, and I was just leaving. I'm late getting back to work," July said, folding the paper plate as a cradle for the sandwich, and covering it with napkins. She scooted out her chair too quickly, nearly toppling back. Now standing, she realigned the shoulder pads in her red, gray, and white plaid dress.

"Forty-one, who would believe it?" He shook his head slowly, looking at her from head to toe.

"Come on," she said, doggedly now, gathering the trash on the table.

"No come-ons. Sure I'm not the first person to take you for a young girl."

"No, you're not."

"Are you a professor?"

"I'm a clerk."

"What's a woman with a philosophy degree doing as a clerk?"

"I can think as I type. A professor needs more than a BA, which alone never gets people very far anyway, and certainly not in philosophy."

"Hey, don't need excuses." He held up his hands, which to her looked as strong and exaggerated in definition as a Charles Wilbur White charcoal.

"You've got enough info from me. I must be crazy," she said, putting the strap of her chocolate leather handbag on her shoulder, and holding it just over the small rip in the seam near the strap ring.

"As it happens, I'm down here to renew my business license, so may I accompany you across the street?"

July put her feet together so the square toes of her red shoes touched, and she checked it all out as if to make sure she were really there. She then leaned toward him, wondering if she might shake his hand, but decided against it as he looked at her with great mischief, like he could get her to run through the streets with him stark raving mad and naked.

Later that evening in bed, she was tempted to show him a photograph of herself pregnant with Sam, her hair newly styled in a 'fro, in solidarity with Angela Davis, whom she was heart-broken to have never met. Lying there so alert, ready, yet utterly relaxed and satisfied, July thought she might finally be in touch with her own very essence. It didn't matter anymore that she hadn't, like Angela, spent her junior year in France, that she hadn't graduated with honors, nor was she feeling inferior to anyone for not having furthered her studies in ethics in some place like Germany, gotten her Ph.D. right there in San Diego, then become a hated and radical thinker. (She dropped that part in her head about being incarcerated for two years and tried for murder).

Neither did July allow her old pining for a life in music to do any pinching or howling from the inside. She was a mother, a provider, and now a lover to only the fourth man she had let into her life. Wayland, Ernest, Ed, and then Joe. She wouldn't count that one time with Otis Hamilton when she saw him a few years after their encounter in a bar in San Diego, where she was able to accuse him face-to-face of sending that photograph of Ernest and his family. After she'd thought about it, she didn't buy that it had been Ernest's wife. So she accused him again, and that time Otis didn't deny it. He argued morality with her in a way that was far more convincing and sophisticated than she would have ever expected. Though she wasn't drinking—as she rarely did—she let him take her home. Hypocrisy itself was seductive, and she'd been alone a long time. Sam was conveniently spending the night with a friend, just as she sent her son to do this very first night she spent with Joe.

Joe didn't make much effort to win over Sam, who was still missing Ed, his partner in sweets. July admired Joe's reticence to ideologically insert himself anywhere in their lives, other than the occasional comments on physical health. He kept his faith in Allah for the most part private, and she respected his plans to build his business, however unglamorous a trade in plumbing parts might have been.

Something about Joe again inspired the fervent collector in her. She wasn't sure if it was the importance of all of those parts—the clutter in his warehouse—and her desire to have her own, or whether she was struggling to cling to the feminist, by playing down the need for him. When her mother would whip her out of school to move them somewhere tailing some man, July would pack first her latest collection: marbles, baseball cards, matinee idol magazines. So things became just as important as Joe was. Suddenly, sports figures were interesting and political heroes more affirming in a time when America was enamored with the very same cowboy who had brought down her Angela Davis. Indentured servant and slave contracts felt all the more appropriate, iconic.

July, looking for some control over mystery, lust, pushed aside all academic distaste and picked up an Aleister Crowley book to understand more about Kabbalah and tarot. When she found she had a knack for readings, even magic—her intuition for a friend's troubles came up in perfect unison with the cards—she started believing in her individuality again in a way that challenged the egos of the household. It was obvious to her that Sam didn't think his mother put him at the center of the universe anymore, when she seemed to be more pleased by a new purchase, or the look on a friend's face as he or she left the house after a reading.

This was all only the resistance of her sexual awakening, when she should have just lounged in it, July was later to harshly find. Up to her very last breath, she regretted not having trusted just taking it easier with a man, who had never set out to control her whatsoever.

12

The Tree Surgeon

The pounding on the hotel door stirs Sam's bowels nearly to the point of embarrassing emergency. In frenzied haze of having taken too late a nap, Sam grabs a chair for both blockade and weapon. He looks through the peephole and sees Abel's welcoming eyes, one lazy with the lid still a touch abnormally fat.

Sam opens the door and embraces him longer than Abel returns it. He's holding two bags of sandwiches, fries, and beers, his arm bandaged, and his royal blue duffel sits between his legs on the carpeted stairwell entry.

"I'd forgotten how sweet you smell," Abel says with disgust. "You pouring on the charm for me?"

So overcome with relief for the company, Sam stands there stupidly in Abel's way, still unable to return the teasing.

"Let me in then, will you, Princess?"

"How's it healing?" Sam asks, taking his bag as Abel hops over it gangling but graceful.

"Don't remind me, it itches like hell." Abel hands him the food too. "I'm hungry. Set us up then." With his fingers now on his fly, Abel runs into the bathroom, leaves the door open, and speaks over the exceedingly long, glugging stream. "So explain all this to me!"

Clearing the table, Sam throws the hotel information notebook like a Frisbee across the room. He litters the floor with yesterday's T-shirt, afro comb, and wallet.

"Tell me the story now. How did all this happen?" Abel asks, zipping up his pants in front of Sam, now setting the table. Sam pauses, steadying himself, hands spread at either side of the faux veneer surface, as if to set the stage for renewed panic, his role as the hanged man.

"He called his parole officer once, said he would have to leave San Diego for a couple days. The parole officer then didn't hear from him after that, but was anonymously tipped that he was following me. The parole officer called Joe, who knew of course where I was and told him, so he then informed the local police. She, the slag, has now washed her hands of it."

"What *slag*?"

"Officer *Bee* Wally of the Bookings Police Department," Sam says, his expression scrimping.

"*Brookings*. Why wouldn't he have caught up to you all this time, if he really was following you? I think he just skipped, and whoever tipped the parole officer guessed wrong."

Sam looks up at Abel with both pleading and dread that he is dead on.

Abel pulls out a chair, bites his chapped bottom lip, and rips open the hot foil on the steak sandwich. With his right foot, he pulls on the strap of his duffel bag until it's close enough for him to dig into. He rifles through for two vials of pills.

"Thought you wouldn't do that again," Sam says eyeing him.

"I don't want to talk about it, Sam."

"What do they have you on, this time?" Sam takes the bottles from him. "Wellbutrin and Lexapro cocktails? How are you feeling?"

"Fucked up. But enough about me, how about you?"

"I'm just glad you're here, A."

"Aw, shucks," Abel says. Sam tears open the ketchup and

covers his fries in artful ropes. Abel puts the pill on his tongue and chugs a beer.

"You *know* you shouldn't be doing that. What the hell's the matter with you?"

"No lectures, okay? *You* take a bus from the airport then hitchhike with a smelly farmer next time." Sam's bottle sits on the table and Abel clinks it with his.

"Hitchhike? Who does that anymore? Are you crazy?"

"Lot of people still hitchhiking up here. And yes, I might be crazy, and then again, so might be you."

"I don't know what's wrong with me. Before I talked to you, I was ready to die, you know?"

"Don't have to explain that to me. Don't think I haven't been there myself a thousand times." Abel swallows and looks him in the eye. "You know, it's true you petitioned in every possible way to keep the psychopath in prison, and he knows that. But I do believe in rehabilitation. I mean it is possible to be redeemed through prison theater, through *Hamlet*."

Simmering, Sam squints at Abel.

"I believe him. I believe he's rehabilitated. I believe he was going to tell you all of this face-to-face, free and as equals in his eyes, and then go on about his business. But then he changed his mind about emptying out on you, and he's gone off to figure out some other kind of penance since he's not *really* ready to be free."

"I'm sick of theorizing, A. You know I've thought of every possible possibility."

"In every paralleling parallel universe?" Abel raises his chin, teasing.

"Not funny."

"Not really kidding."

"You too?"

"Who too?"

"Haley. Ask her about multiverses and she'll let it rip."

"Conspiracy theorists unite!" Abel says, rubbing his hands together in mock glee.

"Quantum theorists make it plain," Sam commands with sarcasm. He takes a big chunk out of his sandwich.

"Where is Haley these days?" Abel says, opening another beer, but not yet touching his food.

"She's home, doing her thing. I haven't returned her last call. I met someone."

"When? When are you getting in the time for any romance during all this? Though from the smell of your cologne how could I doubt you."

"I met her last year on duty at the hospital."

"Traveling nurse?"

"A weather girl."

"A *weather* girl?"

"A patient. A TV personality."

"You're always going for those TV *personalities*, aren't you?"

"Huh?"

"Your neighbor, what's her name?"

"She's no TV personality."

"She was some kind of celebrity, wasn't she?"

"That was decades ago. The weather girl," Sam redirects edgily, his mouth full. He swallows, clears his throat with purpose. "Her name is Sheba Moses."

"Sheba Moses," Abel repeats, sticks out his split but rosy bottom lip.

"What's that s'posed to mean?"

"She's black?"

"Yes, what of it?"

Abel sticks out his bottom lip again. "So you've been two-timing Haley all this time?"

"No I haven't. And that's not what the lip is for," Sam says pointing to it. Abel sticks it out again, this time looking like he might be getting a little drunk. "Say it."

"Say what?" Abel asks, with a boyish giggle.

Sam takes the beer bottle from his hand. "What's your comment about her being black?"

"I didn't comment, I simply said, Hmn." He puts his index finger alongside his nose and mouth, feigning deep thought. Then places his hand on the table, crosses his legs, as if portraying an easily offended lady. "It's not like I've known you to go with the sisters. Kayla even made a comment about that."

"She the one who put that in your head?"

"I can think for myself."

"Man, you were pussywhipped from the get-go, admit it." Sam sticks a handful of fries into his mouth.

"Let's not talk about her. She messed up and I don't want to think about it," Abel gets serious again.

"While we're on the subject, I thought it a bit strange that once you and I became friends you later hooked up with a black girl."

Abel looks at him with an expression of deep offense. "Wow man, I don't know what you're getting at. I happened to meet you, and then a year after I happened to meet her, and nothing other than circumstance, coincidence, can be drawn from that."

"Create your own reality, A, isn't that what it's all about?"

"Then I guess you're doing the same, and you wanted your payback sooner than later."

"What's that supposed to mean?"

" 'Coming to your emotional rescue.' "

"Do I have to worry about you, A? Should I watch my back in the shower?"

" 'Some girls,' " Abel raises his brow, and laughs, now clearly drunk.

"Oh, leave the Stones out of it. You know it's times like this I remember your age."

"Come on, old man, tell a poor kid of twenty-eight what's what."

"Okay. Act your age, not your dick size."

The next morning after breakfast in the café where Sam buys a tall bottle of cranberry ketchup for Sheba Moses, he lets Abel drive the convertible shoebox so that he can crane his neck, peer into every car gaining on them. He had only allowed himself enough time to relax on the beach of charcoal sand and driftwood, to collect white stones also for Sheba. Maybe this was only to bug Abel, he couldn't be sure, because he was also thinking of Haley. A few hours into their journey together, Abel becomes more and more intrigued with the passing dunes. Ignoring Sam's protests, Abel pulls into the second ATV rental park they come upon.

"If I wanted to do this I'd go home, A."

"Have you done it before?"

"No, have *you?*"

"No, which is precisely why we should," he says, getting out of the car and slamming the creaky door shut. Sam remains inside, arms folded tight like a protesting boy's.

"Get out of the car!" Abel commands, opening up the passenger door and pulling Sam out.

"You're overdoing it with that arm, you know, A. We've got no business out here."

"It's not like we're going to get wet, Princess," Abel says, walking ahead, pulling a sweatshirt over his head so the long sleeves cover his arm dressing.

They stand in a long line, where Sam gazes out toward a highway he can hear but not see. When they reach the booth, Abel pulls down every large helmet, tries to get it onto Sam's head with no success. Finally he spots the one and only extra large. Sam holds his breath, hoping he would never find the right fit, and fights off Abel's fussing over him, since people are staring at them anyway.

Sam hears nothing of the recorded safety rules as they sit waiting for their slated quads to roll in. He stares at the double line of twelve, thinking they make you wait just for the torture. When the equipment guy takes them over, he tells them he's giving them the newest ones, and Sam is more thankful with his eyes than he has been with anyone. Abel jumps on, a stoked look on his face, and a thumbs up to the guy. A scrawny, cocky kid intercedes, too quickly points out the accelerator and the brake, then gets on the quad in front of them, instructing them to follow. With the kid way ahead, Sam blunders between stop and go. Abel hangs back to hen over him until Sam gets comfortable with the kick and takes off. Abel flies ahead with the kid, who leads them up an avalanche of sand and endless space meeting the big sky, a heaven as playground. *A white boy's playground*, Sam thinks, considering it a cure for any "urban" child.

"What are you tripping on, Princess? Let's gooooooo!" Abel calls, speeding down a slope. Sam struggles to follow. He mounts the next slipface, which is even steeper, and he doesn't realize to what extent he must accelerate in order to make it up the blowout without sinking his back tires into the convex nose of sand. At the top of the hairpin hill, Abel turns, recognizing Sam's stuck, and airborne, jumps the machine back down the parabolic mound to help.

"Get up," Abel says, standing in the sand, wiggling the fingers of his perfect hand.

"You think I'm going to let you lift this with your arm, A? Are you crazy? Back off!" Sam pushes Abel away, stands behind his back wheels, steadying his knees and hamstrings to lift what feels as heavy as a bank vault.

When Sam gets back on and this happens a second time where the hill goes concave and his rear tires sink in the quick, Abel makes him trade quads. Together they lift Sam's, and Sam takes off on Abel's. He realizes that when he leads, rather than follows, he can judge the hill, taking it as if made of the same shapes and essence. Abel lurks a few yards behind, a smile like putty molded to his face. Sam knows then he has his own joy-sick grin, which he can't take off.

They sit in a house café in Florence, Sam still ticked after finding out that Abel really had gone dune riding many times before, but lied to get him to try it. They sit staring out the window at a tree that looks like a Dr. Seuss character, a succulent creature that could be pineapple, artichoke. Abel breaks the silence by asking the waitress what it is, and she tells him it's a Monkey Puzzle tree. As she pours coffee at the neighboring table, Sam eavesdrops on their conversation—the waitress explaining that she is the owner along with her sister, and they had recently lost their mother in a car accident. They painted the walls behind the cash register a jolting, poisonous pink in honor of their mother's lipstick. Sam stares at the color, which had struck him as horrid before he realized that it was similar to the shades of minis that Haley wears. So long now used to his compulsion of mourning, he can't decide if he is sad for the café owners, miserable for himself, or regretful that he just can't connect with Haley. He really does love her, he says to himself. He looks up at Abel, the bluish, haggard transparency under his eyes, and feels the same depth of gratitude for him as well.

"Where did that sullen look go, Princess?" Abel asks, spreading his mouth and bearing his teeth like a clown. The circles under his eyes now look perversely festive.

"Were you listening to them?"

"I was," Abel nods, taking off his sweatshirt, looking down at his arm, then noisily sucking in air at either side of his tongue.

"Shit, A, you're oozing. *Goddammit,*" Sam says, putting his hand on Abel's forehead. "You're hot." Sam calls for the check and leads Abel down a hallway that suggests the nearness of a spoiled little girl's room. The bathroom is equally feminine, with flowered burlap covering on the walls and wastebasket. Sam undoes Abel's dressing.

"It looks a bit mad, doesn't it?" Abel asks, biting his tongue. The wound is hot, red, swollen, and drooling a yellowish-green fluid.

"When were you supposed to get the stitches out?"

Abel shrugs.

"*What*?"

"A couple days ago, I think. But it didn't look ready to me in the shower."

"Why didn't you *say* something?" Sam asks, getting angry.

"It's been all about you, hasn't it?"

Sam's exhale cooks the air. "We're going to the hospital now."

Sam is so very confident in his element upon arriving with his patient at the brick building on Ninth Street. They enter the demoted pink and green lobby, which has the synthetically strong suggestion of comfort. He is able to override a steering to the emergency room—a far more costly choice, Sam knows, since he discovered in the parking lot that Abel resigned his position and no longer has health insurance. This very efficient exchange with the triage nurse leads them upstairs to a waiting room for a resident she knows who can take a look at the infection and prescribe the antibiotics Sam anticipates. He would blow on his nails and buff them if he had the nerve. That the hospital is religiously based enormously helps his case with the injured chaplain.

After thirty minutes of waiting, Sam returns to worry. The lines on his forehead resemble a treasure hunt map pointing to his third eye. Abel chats like an exuberant eight-year-old after the fair, and Sam tries to laugh, while haunted by coastal Oregon's insistent grayness—elongated, gelid, and far more powerful than the flippant California sun. He's so deep in thought that he doesn't see the young woman sitting in a worker's uniform, her expression splintered. She trudges over to the water fountain, annoyed that her shoulder-length, bronze-tinged dark hair gets in the way of her zealous drink. Sam feels the immediate urge to give her a trim. He imagines her sitting in a barber's chair, her head back, neck cupped in the deep sensuous curve of the sink, her mouth open in surrender as he digs his fingers into her pliant scalp.

She glances at him now as if she has done so at least ten times before, and Sam is embarrassed not to have noticed her before she noticed him. She is very tall, but disproportionately short waisted. The encyclopedia dull green pants and shirt say something in turquoise near her significant breasts. With much impatient annoyance, she puts her thin, dark flyaway hair up in a ponytail on top of her head, and it stares at him too in comic book exaggeration. It points at him, Sam imagines, like he is indeed the one.

"We *live* in the hospital, man," Abel drawls.

"Tell me about it," Sam snaps. He looks at her. She flicks whatever is under her fingernail at the pristine floor under her substantially sized feet in scuffed golden work boots. She peers up at him, and it is as if the observer inside cranks the notch on zoom lens and there are her eyes—reddish brown and ready to narcotize.

"Miss Bends?" the volunteer calls.

"Yes." She pops up to approach the desk, sticks her hands in her back pockets as if offering her open chest to the woman.

"I'm beginning to think we should go back to emergency, or maybe the clinic across the street," Abel says, looking at his Camel cigarettes watch on his good arm.

"Hmn?"

Abel shows him his watch. "Where did you get that?" Sam's upper lip curls disagreeably.

"It's nearly four o'clock, Sam."

"You're right," he says, getting up, and Miss Bends, noting their rise, seems to slow her approach of the elevator. She hits the button, turns to look at them with a smile so big that the top lip is stuck on her pink gums.

"Where are you guys from?"

"LA," Abel says flirtatiously, his lids so heavy he looks high.

"I'm sorry."

"You're the fourth person to say that," Sam says, as they all step onto the elevator. "It's annoying, really, and we're not from LA, he's just claiming that for effect."

"Then you deserve the answer," she says, still smiling with challenge as the doors close. She presses her back against the elevator wall, Sam ogles her breasts and the inviting pocket that reads in embroidered turquoise lettering: SPARKY'S TREE SURGEONS.

"And so, what's your trouble?" she asks Abel, shifting her eyes, which aren't reddish-brown in this light, but rather macadamia nut.

"Infection. Stitches," Abel says, now squinting at her with resentment that she prefers Sam.

"Why aren't you in the emergency room?" The elevator doors open, and Miss Bends holds her arm out to keep them open. "After you," she says, smiling with the air of a private joke.

Abel walks off. "Tell me about it."

Sam looks behind him once wanting to throw her upside the elevator wall again, close the door, and lock it. She smiles at him, clearly returning the sentiment.

Some fifteen minutes later, they don't allow Sam in the examination room with Abel, and as excited as he is to see Miss Bends walk into the emergency waiting area, granola bar half eaten in her hand, he is not in the mood for games.

"What are you doing down here?" Sam asks. She sits down beside him, offering him a bite of the granola bar in gesture. Sam shakes his head, and she bites it down until there is nothing left. "Are you Sparky?"

"Sparky's upstairs, but I call him Tom."

"So you're a tree surgeon?"

"Tom needed me to take over his business while he's here—he's an arborist just outside of Eugene. We went to school together for a bit. I'm trained as a forest pathologist, but lately I'm . . . wavering," she says, smiling at her lap, then looks up at him. "I'm living up in Newport these days. What are you doing here?"

"What's a forest pathologist?"

"Tree disease expert, basically. What are you doing up here? Where are you really from?"

"Southern California desert. We're driving up to Canada." He decides in the moment.

"Beautiful trip," she says nodding. "What do you do?"

"I'm a nurse."

"Ah, a people person, then."

"Okay."

"Well, yes," she says, firmly, sitting up in her seat. "Genuine care for your fellow man."

"I treat others as I want to be treated," Sam says. "And as, I suppose, you want your trees to be treated as well."

"Correct," she says with her index finger.

"But I really can't claim to be that pure. Nurses are so scarce I could get a job anywhere, anytime."

"I don't believe that's what it's all about."

"Okay," he says, stretching his face imitating a doofus.

She throws her head back and laughs in cascades.

"It's not that funny," he says, and laughs with her.

Her ponytail falls, and she grabs her hair, winding it back around as if it mustn't dare do that to her again. Her laugh subsides and Sam watches her mystified.

"What's your name?" Sam asks.

"Greta."

"Greta," he says, a chuckle escapes.

"It's not that funny," she says, imitating him.

"Just, of course, *Greta*. You don't match your name, and that's a good thing. Greta is a beautiful name, and you're a beautiful woman, but you don't go together, and that's a good thing," he says, not knowing what he means as she looks into his eyes like he's crazy.

"And your name is Sam," she says, folding her arms over her chest.

"How did you know?"

"I heard your friend. So," she pauses, looking at him, taking him all in. "I have to get back up there and see if Tom's ready. I'm taking him to his grandmother's and dropping him there."

"He's okay?"

"He split open his leg, it's pretty much healed now. Stupid story, embarrasses us arborists. When I was a teen I worked on a Christmas tree farm, now *there's* where I saw some scary self-hacking. This was a stupid accident for Tom, taking care of his grandmother's yard." She gets up and goes to the desk. He watches her go, wishing she had just a little more rump, then again if she did she could lord her perfection over him. She comes back, that smile sitting up high on the gums. The teeth are straight but small, too small for the rest of her.

"This is my mobile. If your friend's up for it when he gets out of here, come on up to Newport. I can recommend a good place to stay," she says, writing, looking at the piece of paper as if it were a mirror she didn't recognize. Then she smiles again as she hands

116

it to him, returning the ballpoint with a click against her thigh. "Okay, Sam."

She reaches for a handshake and grips him hard as if to mock being the amazon she is. Sam looks up at her, breathes in as if smelling fresh fragrant jasmine. Her grin turns into one that seems to remember she was once a heartbreaker. He trusts her anyway, because she keeps turning around to look at him as she walks off.

13

Girlfriend's July

Teaching Ava the cards on Saturday afternoons became July's second best of intimate times. After roving garage and estate sales in the mornings, Ava would come over and join July in the deep turquoise dining room, which had the appearance of an aquarium with floating framed photographs of people like Gandhi, Che Guevara, Wilt Chamberlain, Martin Luther King, and Babe Ruth. Together they adventured in teas, tonics, and smoothies, discussed the latest in books, movies, and their respective bedrooms. Ava had two fresh, cynical preteen daughters and retained bitterness from her second marriage. She held a miffed expression that couldn't be taken seriously since she resembled a pretty version of a troll doll due to her exaggerated features. Inspired by Ava's face, July bought a troll and kept it on a shelf in the laundry room, coming to love its caramel skin, fuchsia hair, eyes, and rhinestone star belly button. Often before leaving with a load of folded clothes, she'd turn the doll around and giggle at the delightful perk of its butt.

July felt keenly aware of this new silliness in her life. Joe's nudist habits, Sam's peripheral vision for fun, along with her latest affection for a girlfriend, all took her mind off everything she'd previously considered grave, including her mother. Ava loved to tease Sam on his way in and out of the house during this rock-collecting phase, and July looked on, feeling proud of herself as a parent. Ava was also very enthusiastic with Joe—almost to a fault—but July considered herself long past jealousy. She even found herself welcoming challenge to the security she felt in her life.

She liked watching the growing expert counterclockwise movement of Ava's hands when she did a reading. It was like the pleasure of a nongambler dabbling at the tables and admiring the dealer. Everything Ava knew about tarot, July had taught her. On that particular afternoon, after scoring a box of photos of a black family taken in the fifties and sixties, instead of coveting their nuclear unit, July detected happiness in her grasp. It was the first time she removed herself from the psychological and sociological aspects of the cards—the subjective interpretations of human behavior, the mythological symbols. That studied interest she took in the cards' relationships, their potential cause and effect, had finally moved into the mystical arena. She just wasn't aware that belief had its hold on her.

The first center card was Five of Cups: Disappointment. Ava glanced up at her. July was puzzled since this was the only period in her life that she could ever remember not burning with question. This seemed to be the only instance when not only was the nature of any problem far from concern but that she no longer reached for notions of having been let down. Flanking Five of Cups was Seven of Swords, suggesting Futility at the heart of the situation, and the Ten of Wands, which described July's personality—in this instance—as one of Oppression. Ava read the cards as ill dignified. July crossed her arms, swallowed. She watched Ava's hands and listened to her voice as an instrument of the cards.

In the upper right corner of the fifteen-card spread, Three of Swords was read as Sorrow and Separation. The Ten of Swords suggested Disruption, Ruin, and Death. Even July couldn't help but agree with Ava's gasp, when turning up the twelfth card, the

Tower, which in this layout confirmed Destruction, more specifically danger or sudden death. The thirteenth card was the Hanged Man, which also symbolized her Growth Card year, and suggested the chance for her to break any patterns. Next to the Hanged Man were the Two of Disks, lying in the position of Possibility and Hope, yet Eight of Swords sat as a symbol of Interference and Unforeseen Challenges.

The lower left corner of the spread eluded Ava in the complications of its psychological interpretations, but was clear to July. The Seven of Cups represented her hiding from self, her unfulfilled promise, her guilt, delusion, attraction to the wrong men—even dangerous men, excluding Joe—and though debauchery fell under the card's meanings, July resisted any implications that this quality could refer to her. Ace of Swords was clearly Punishment, July knew she did this time and again with Mother, and her insistence upon Good and Evil, and the fundamentals of the coming wrath here on earth. Five of Swords emphasized weakness, loss, and defeat. It was cruel yet cowardly, which led July—through her medium Ava—to the lower right corner of her Destiny. She could fully believe in Fate, rather than will, in this instance, as it alleviated her of the responsibility to change. Nine of Swords lay in its cruelty; Seven of Disks played off the beastliness of the Nine, and reinforced the failure and disappointment that had already come up in the cards. Finally, the Magus was the Thief, the magician, looking yellow and innocent among the many images of swords, daggers, blues, violent orange fires, and bleeding pinks, and all of it lay there as real to her as anyone or anything in her life.

Why put stock in it? July asked herself. *What could be stronger than will?* she asked then, contradicting her need to be lazy, a victim. She could tool with logic, will none of this to be true, and yet superstition, acceptance had superseded reason. She had settled into belief.

Ava kept quiet for a long time after the reading. She was utterly spooked, convinced. Then she offered up the obvious, clearing her throat to do so: "But July, you can think of Death as transition."

"Well, I'm not going to wait to be struck down, Ava!"

"As you shouldn't. I meant it emotionally, symbolically. You're well warned here, girl. As a mother, it would be criminal to ignore it."

"They're only cards, Ava."

Ava held up her hands in surrender, and from beneath plucked-to-a-threat brows, looked up with purpose at July.

Two weeks after the menacing reading, hanging on Joe's arm as she entered a party, July zoned in on a guy whose ears and jawline exemplified a bad case of vitiligo. The spots of depigmentation gave him the look of a large puppy or scrawny cow. Unusual as he was, she couldn't figure out why he seemed familiar, and worked to place him in her history throughout the evening. She asked Joe who he might be, and he didn't know, nor did Ava. She inquired about him of her hosts, and with annoyance they pointed out who brought him. July didn't recognize his companion—who didn't seem to be his companion, as they barely spoke that night—and so finally July mingled her way toward him. She was determined to change what was freaky, jarring, and grotesque to her. Simply because his appearance disgusted her, she had to turn that around, much in the manner a merely tolerant person steps aside to let the disabled person get through the door first, and then pats him- or herself on the back for the common courtesy.

"Who would think that deviled eggs could taste this good?" she said, holding one up, exposing her throat, and slowly placing it into her mouth. She smiled hoping the yolk did not powder her adobe-clay colored lipstick.

He looked at her with interest that was neither remarkable nor unkind. July's energy flocked across the room, searching for Joe's position, but couldn't find him.

"So, how long have you known Sue and Charles?" she asked, knowing the answer.

"I don't," he said, putting his hand in his gray gabardine pocket, which betrayed the casual of his black Members Only jacket. "Carolyn, over there, brought me," he said pointing, his look adrift, his demeanor decidedly damaged.

July smiled and inhaled through her nose at the same time so that she looked as if she had smelled something foul but needed to make nice about it. "Is Carolyn your wife?"

"No," he said, appraising her now as if she were coming onto him within the pattern of the stuck-up and arrogant. "And I gather that's not your husband," he said, looking down at her ringless finger, long and graceful as a pianist's.

July bit the corner of her lip and narrowed her eyes. "We've met before," she said, shifting her weight to center. She grew impatient with the long pauses between her questions and his responses, though she hadn't realized that she'd actually made a majority of statements. "Tell me where it was," she said, liking the sound of her voice in control.

"That bar over there on—"

"You're Otis Hamilton's friend," she interrupted, nodding.

"Otis Hamilton?" he asked, with the sudden, detectable accent she couldn't place. Boston? A black Boston accent?

"Yes, Otis Hamilton. Otis Hamilton from LA."

"Don't know if I'd call him a friend. Is that where you're from?" He smiled for the first time.

"No," she lied. "Where are you from?"

"Western Mass. Springfield," he said, picking up a couple nuts from the dish and jiggling them in his hand with an assuredness that peeved her. "I haven't been here but a few months and don't know too many people around here."

"And you're sure you don't know Otis," she said, narrowing her eyes again, looking at him so carefully that it was clear he attracted her. She was beginning to see that the sexual confidence she found with Joe gave her an urge to conquer whoever stood out.

"I remember you from that bar," he said. "I didn't say I don't know him, but Otis isn't no friend."

July spotted Joe from the corner of her eye, and tried to catch his attention. He was busy charming the hostess, following behind her with a heavy box in his arms. July felt intent on leaving without ever having introduced herself by name. She could feel his interest grow as she was losing hers.

"I wouldn't mind meeting you again at that bar, though. Hell, I'd meet you in church if you wanted," he said, chewing the rest of the nuts, and clapping the dust from his hands.

July walked away as if she'd never spoke to him before and wouldn't think of it again. Ava stopped her midstride, grabbing her by the elbow, that miffed expression on her face, which was meant more for the wandering July than some guy, her prey, a poor victim of maculation.

14

Water Is the Tune

"You're just a ball rolling out into the traffic, aren't you?" Abel asks, dropping a few fresh Oregon blueberries onto the passenger's seat. It's too cold to have the top down. Abel scoots up, head smashed against the canvas ceiling. Looking straitjacketed, he turns to grab the stray berries from falling into the crack. He pinches one too hard, squeezing the juice, and cusses to himself under his breath. "Aren't you just a ball?" he repeats, returning himself into comfortable position, looking at Sam with a *gotcha* face.

"Put on your seatbelt, will you?"

Abel complies. The sound of metal scooping into plastic is a relief to Sam.

"First it's Sheba, then it's Greta," Abel says in nursery rhyme. He eats each berry one at a time, his tongue and bottom lip purple with it.

"Sheba's not far from my mind," Sam says, zipping up his jacket at the stoplight in Yachats on the 101. "Here's another town that cute built," Sam says, looking past the quaint stores to a sign that says POPULATION 635.

"Perhaps it should be *Haley* not far from your mind."

"You never met Sheba, A. She's incredible."

"Memory is mythology, Princess," Abel says, holding up a berry to Sam's mouth. Sam glares at him as if to say, *I'm not gay.*

"When was the last time I spoke to Haley, anyway?"

"I don't know, you tell me," Abel says, still playful.

"She's back in the club, and I'm sick of it."

"So we're on our merry way to Miss Greta's in Newport," Abel says, squashing the now empty carton of berries, and rubbing his stomach.

Sam looks in the rearview mirror as he frequently does in increasing surreptitious terror of Shawn Lamb. "What's the harm in looking her up?" he asks, hoping Abel doesn't notice his paranoia.

"No harm for you, friend, the question is, How long will I be holed up in Newport waiting for you and our trip to Canada like Godot?" Abel looks past Sam's face to the sea in the distance. He sighs.

Sam turns to look at him. "I never said I was going to Canada, A."

"You said north. North up the coast, so let's go all the way!" Abel calls to the sea.

Sam's forehead aligns in grooves with worry—Abel's antibiotics, Wellbutrin SR and Lexapro mix.

"What are all the tsunami wave warning signs about?" Sam asks, trying to keep his attention. Abel says nothing, now looking the opposite direction from the jagged shoreline of pines growing in hummocky windblown shapes. "Huh?" Sam asks.

"Earthquakes," Abel mutters. He turns around again to dig in his duffel bag for a pack of cigarettes. All with his left hand, he rolls down the passenger window, lights up, blows away from Sam, but the smoke hits him anyway, and Sam flips it.

"When do you ever hear of Oregon earthquakes, man?"

Abel reaches over his own chest to flick the ash out of the window. "Earthquakes aren't of much concern, I'd say the volcano watch has taken center natural disaster stage in the moment."

"Funny to me how scared people are of earthquakes in California, when it's Florida wiped out by a hurricane every other month on the news. *They're* the ones who are crazy."

"Why are you talking about the South in all of this Pacific Northwest beauty? Just look," Abel says, taking a long drag.

"Burl to the left, burl to the right."

"Hey, Myrtlewoods are people too."

"What's with the white-peaked rocks in the middle of the ocean? Is it birdshit?"

"It really is beautiful up here, I could live here you know," Abel says in a different voice, as if speaking to someone else in the car.

"I thought you did at one point."

"I told you I spent a summer in Portland and traveled around a bit. You ever hear anything anyone says?" Abel asks.

"What's up with you, A?"

"I refuse to stay holed up while you're fucking this Greta, you hear me?"

"Who said I was? And if you want to talk like that, I can drive you back to the airport. I appreciate you coming out here for me, but I'm not going to take your moral authority. Not right now, A. I'm as messed up as I could be at the moment."

"And I'm just fine and dandy," Abel says, his lashes dewy with weather. He throws the cigarette out of the window.

"Don't throw anything out of my car, man. You know I hate that."

Abel sighs like an old lady.

"I'm sorry for all of this crap, okay? I'm sorry about your infection, but it's not my fault. You're a big boy now and can remember your own doctor's appointments." He looks at Abel. "What's with your brother, man? Wasn't he paying any attention?"

"Ugh," he groans.

Sam raises his hands in surrender, his knees still at the steering wheel.

As they approach the Yaquina Bay Bridge into Newport, Sam calls Greta for directions to her house. Abel is quiet the entire way. Sam voices surprise at the modest bustle of the town and the bank's temperature sign announcing a warm seventy degrees. Abel sits under his canopy of gloom, pointedly ignoring the excitement in Sam's eyes and posture as he makes the turn for Greta's neighborhood.

As they pass the Eureka Cemetery and Mausoleum, Sam's gung ho shrinks slightly. He can almost hear Abel's resignation not to further tamper with the mood. He takes Yaquina Heights Drive to a dead-end street speckled with hydrangeas. There are blue spruces near the Newport School, giving it the permanent feel of Christmas. He circles past the water tower painted with a tree façade. Pinot Noir vine leaves grow wild along the hill and down the short incline to her very private home.

Greta's house is a timber frame set back deep into what appears to be her own forest. The squeak of the car doors opening seems to produce her with velocity from the side entrance. Sam is punched smitten at the sight of her.

"Hey guys!" she exclaims, galloping down the dirt path of the drive for Abel's duffel. She wears a thin, washed-out orange sweater, sleeves pushed up, revealing light fur at the forearms.

"I got it," Abel snaps. "I'm not *that* feeble," he says softening in tone.

"What can I take?" she asks, standing taller than Sam, facing him with elation filled to the brim. Her hair is caught high in a ponytail at the back of her head making her look like a giant cheerleader.

"Sheba, Sheba, Sheba—" Abel whispers from behind him.

"You can take these cherries," Sam says over Abel's voice. He bends into the car and hands her the small, crumpled grocery bag. He pulls his own bag from the trunk and glares at Abel.

Sam follows her up the walk, watching the no-ness of her backside in high-waisted jeans. He trips over the threshold and catches himself with awe at her log cabin style of mismatched wood. There are high-beamed ceilings, exposed and intricately laid copper piping, a granite and stone fireplace. At the center of the living area, a fountain pours in polyphonic percussion. She sets the bleeding bag of cherries down on the metal dining table, and when Abel asks for directions, she leads him partway to the bathroom.

"This is incredible," Sam says, looking around him.

"It's all recycled wood," Greta says. "Besides what I was given through work, I went to demolition sales for the rest. The entire house is insulated in sheep's wool."

"My house is insulated with cans of salt," Sam declares with pride. "Solar paneled as well."

"You see these cisterns here? They collect rainwater, and I filter it for drinking. I recycle all the wastewater—dishwasher, washer machine—for the toilet. There are next to no off-gases anywhere, and I used low VOC paint for the little color there is."

Hands on hips, Greta looks up at the ceiling and across the length of the house. Her top lip appears stuck on her pink gums as she flashes a grin at Sam. It is as if she can't believe he stands there in front of her. Sam scats in his heart like Ella Fitzgerald.

Abel opens the door just as he flushes. Though he slouches, he plasters a new attitude across his face. "It's like a shrine in there," he says brightly, his dark hair aglow under the skylights.

"That's because of the milk glass windows," she says. Sam looks at her long chin.

"This really is a beautiful place, so incredible, it's like you're living in the middle of a forest. You're very fortunate, you know," Abel says.

"Thank you, and I do know," she answers, very pleased with herself. "You guys hungry?"

"I'm not," Abel says, walking toward the stereo.

"I'm starving," Sam says, scanning the coffee table, noting *Mother Jones* and *Nation* subscriptions. He picks up the latter, flipping through it without stopping on a page, and puts it back down. Many Noam Chomsky books stand out on the shelves, as well as Spearhead, Rage Against the Machine, and Audioslave CDs in stacks. Abel examines inside the jewel case of Yes. Sam joins him as he puts it on.

"One night," Abel whispers to him. "I'm staying here for only *one* night."

"So how's Sparky?" Sam calls to her in the kitchen.

"Much better, thanks," she says distracted. She is in front of the open fridge studying it, holding her bottom lip together in a fold between thumb and forefinger.

"Can I have some water?" Abel asks, joining her in the kitchen.

"Of course." She pulls out a tall brown ceramic mug that would be better for coffee; Abel wears an expression of distaste.

She turns to Sam. "Sparky has two people working for him, and they can handle the load. I was just helping out for a couple of days." She scratches just beneath her ponytail, bending down looking into her vegetable drawer. "How does a cucumber, avocado, tomato, and nut cheese sandwich sound?"

"*Blaagh*," Abel says, with his tongue hanging out.

"Sounds good to me," Sam says, climbing into the hammock on the far corner of the house. As soon as his body feels snug, his head swivels down the labyrinthine fear. He becomes mortified that he threatens Greta's safety, puts all of their lives at risk.

"So what do you do, Abel?" Greta asks, pulling out bread and hummus.

"I was a chaplain, I consoled the dying at the same hospital Sam worked."

"Hah," she says. "A chaplain is the last thing in the world I'd imagine for you."

"It's weird hearing him say that he *was* a chaplain." Sam shakes his head, folds his arms, swinging himself in pretense that he hasn't a care in the world.

"Let's face it," Abel says, walking over to Sam. "I'm having an identity crisis."

Greta laughs robustly, a knife of hummus dripping on the counter. She thumbs it up, licks her fingers. "Then, I'm having one too!" she declares merrily, looking behind her for the sharp knife to cut the tomatoes and cucumbers.

Abel, appearing tentative and all the more rudderless, walks back into the kitchen to face her. Sam realizes Abel's pacing is making both of them nervous. "My girlfriend says I'm going through my Saturn Return."

"What is that, exactly? I'm not much into astrology," Greta says, slicing and dicing, Abel's eyes fixed on the escaping pulp.

"You'll have to ask her, I don't know much about it either."

"Someone's getting their pasts and presents mixed up, I think," Sam interjects.

"And someone talks like there's a toddler in the house," Abel says, turning to glare at him.

"What sign are you?" Greta asks, with a wink at Sam.

"Pisces," he says, trying to shrug off the nagging paranoia, and even more so wanting to lift her up and push her down on the countertop.

"I'm a Leo," she says, "but again, I know nothing about what that means." She chuckles.

"That's not nut cheese, you know," Abel says.

"Come here," Greta says, putting the knives down, and opening her arms. "You look like you need a hug."

She takes him in, careful of his wound. The embrace is long and quiets them both, jealousy excavating its way through Sam's marrow.

"Thank you," Abel says. "I needed that." He blushes, backing away from her. "I'm a Gemini," he adds. "You didn't ask, but I thought I'd tell you."

"Speaking of twins, I'm feeling right now like I'd love to have *seven* clones of myself, and send them all off to lead entirely different lives, you know what I mean?" she asks, looking back at Sam, who returns the once-over with suspicion that she's flighty. "One could be a classical musician, one a traveler, one an astrophysicist, one a philosopher, one a farmer, one a painter, one an activist."

"A philosopher, huh?" Sam says, clearing his throat. He resents her for putting him off balance.

"Then I'd be free to concentrate on what I love: trees." She pulls tin plates down making Sam feel like he's in the army. And yet he feels cozy under the roof of still another woman with her own home.

They sit together at the metal table. She opens a bottle of Oregon hard cider, as Abel sparkles from ear to ear.

It's past ten at night when Sam and Greta leave Abel asleep on the hammock. They run tiptoe to her old Suburban, which she says she's embarrassed to drive but can't give up for her work. It's the cadence of Greta's speech that strikes him, Sam realizes in the truck as they drive through the dark to the water. Now that she is speaking lower, as if voice should be proportionate to light, he hears the understory, lush with slope and falling husk.

Greta pulls into her favorite spot on the Yaquina River, and before she can tell him any more details of Central Oregon Coast history he doesn't listen to, he leans in as she turns off the motor, the only other sound he tunes into besides the beating in his chest is a barred owl stammering "*Who cooks for-you!*" in the distance. He meets the short snub of her nose, and the clench of her gaze from this close moves him to mash her lips. He mauls her mouth until she shuts her lids. Her eyeteeth feel long and sharp as fangs, and she is just as vehement, snatching the clothes from him as he bobs for any part of her. The scuttle to the backseats, their knock and drop into awkward bed, the plush of her breasts, the nipples thudding against his tongue, the confluence of the sweet, spicy stink of her, pull the girdles tighter around his balls.

The car becomes a capsule after six hours. The dawn's cold, the window's breath, their mixed potion of smear and grist on skin and upholstery, bring Sam to a compulsive confession of love. The art of escape. Greta's expression slides from frayed, pliable, to supplicant and all of the nuances in between. He wants to take it back as she gets dressed, her eyes like gauze. He wants to shout it out over the roaring hum of frogs, but she climbs into the front, and there's nothing left but to pull on his pants, as she turns on the engine leaving him no time to buckle up.

"I think I love you too," she says, almost glumly but in that low deciduous voice of hers, as they make their way back up the hill to her house.

She cuts off the ignition at the top of her driveway, lets the truck roll down the graveled drive into place. In silence, he follows her to the side entrance, where he hadn't noticed before the view to the back of an attached terrarium with glass ceiling, her bed in the center of it.

This girl is a dream, he says to himself, *I created her in my mind so in need of a break*. He takes her hand, the sound of the coffee machine grinding on the other side of the wall.

"Abel," he says aloud to her, "has anxiety disorder, so we can't stay, you know, we can't imposition you any further, as I really do have to take care of him."

"Lie down," she says, smiling the way he feels he knows with the gums showing. "Let's go to sleep and see about it all in a couple hours."

132

15

Shadow Puppets

When Sam opens his eyes slowly to the attack of spotted light from all sides of glass, he doesn't know where he is, but wonders why his mother chooses now to visit. His head hot from the halo of her concentration, he rolls over to his side, thumb and index digging into pressure points beneath his brows above the inner corner of his eyes. Pressing there interrupts the blood vessel spasms he feels across his forehead, and as he pushes to the level of pain, he stops the nausea from coming on, wishing he could also stop all he imagines that happened to her.

The door creeps open. Vision temporarily blurred, he is convinced he's dreaming when Haley walks in with dark airy hair. The closer she comes, the odder she appears, her mouth in an unrecognizable, prim O.

"You have a headache?" Greta asks, carefully approaching the bed as if he might be in need of exorcism. Reality modulates. He knows Haley isn't here at all, but that he's in the bedroom of his new lover, his best friend waiting for him somewhere outside of it.

"Yeah," he says in slow motion, pushing himself up. "What time is it?"

"It's a little after four, Abel's gone for a walk. I'll get you some aspirin," Greta says, formally.

While she's gone, Sam looks around him. Trees close in on the glass, the sun sparkles in the room like thousands of trinkets. In the mirror, he finds his image abhorrent, as the last thing he can stand to see is someone idle and in pain. Greta returns. Walking with measure and a full glass, her other large hand is open. He takes a last glimpse at his own expression, now mawkish. He mourns their mutual afterglow, the one they didn't get to experience.

"Thank you," he says, taking the pills from her pale palm. She sits down on the bed next to him, upsetting his balance. She hands him the glass of water, her shoulder touching his.

"This is the sunniest I've seen it up here," he says.

"You brought the sun," she says, smiling in her gaudy way. Her eyebrows are thin and unruly but this sets off the alive and nutty brown gleam to her irises. He takes in her smell and remembers how completely he could give himself. He pushes stray hairs back from her cheek and kisses it. She closes her eyes and opens them with a flutter.

"You had a nightmare this morning, you know," she says.

"What did I say?"

"I don't know, I tried to wake you up, but it was as if I pushed you deeper into sleep, and you quieted down. Still it was frightening."

"My mother was killed."

"In your dream?"

"No. My mother was actually *murdered*."

"Oh my God," Greta says, her jaw hanging down like a drawbridge.

Sam's eyes roll up in his head, before he looks at Greta, making a sound like someone choked him.

"Oh my God," she repeats, reaching around him to put her hand on his chest.

He lurches forward and catches himself back to the bed. It's only then that he realizes he means to rock himself like a baby. Greta rocks with him, her arm making a comfortable fit.

"This happened a long time ago," he says. He looks at her with his nostrils growing wider. "I was only fif-teen." His face breaks into a grimace. "But it still hurts, it still feels like it happened this morning." He cries more easily since he has been crying so much these past days on the road.

"I'm being such a baby," he says, biting his knuckle before throwing his arms around her and sobbing into her neck. When his tears and snot become a gush, he grabs his T-shirt from the floor and lovingly wipes it off of her. Her long neck is soft with golden down at the throat. He stares at it, pets the hollow with his finger, and kisses her there. His tongue finds its warm, hot way in her mouth, tickling her palate, getting to know the bumps and lines.

"Hello!" Abel yells testily from outside the door, "I'm back! Can I talk to you, Sam?"

Sam wipes his face with the heels of both hands, sniffles, looks into Greta's eyes, and smiles. Her hand is on his cock, and he's hard, and her upper lip rides the top of her gum, as she looks like she might break into laughter.

"I'm coming!" Sam calls, straightening himself in his pants. Greta has nothing to fix, none of her is in disarray.

Abel wears the same clothes from yesterday, a frumpy royal blue jersey and baggy black pants. He holds his wounded arm to his heart, looks at Sam with large, droopy eyes, his lips pursed like a teacher ready to scold. Greta makes her way past them sideways through the door, Abel waits until she's out of earshot.

"I'm staying," Sam says, beating him to it.

"What did I say?"

"What did you say? You're acting like a jerk, you want to take my car? Go ahead."

"Are you crazy?" Abel asks, putting his good hand on the doorframe and leaning into Sam's face.

"Well, what do you want? I can drive you to the airport."

"Does Miss Greta *know* you're staying? Because she and I had quite an interesting conversation earlier today."

Sam stares at him like *Spit it out.*

"One, *Sparky* is her boyfriend, and two, she's looking for a job. Three, her father, who paid for this little castle in the forest, wouldn't you know, is due to arrive at the end of the week."

Sam widens his stance so as not to give Abel the satisfaction of seeing him wince from the punch.

"That's right, Princess, sulk it up. But haven't I always told you, look before you leap! Have you thought about the fact that you're putting her in danger by staying here?"

Greta returns noisily, but with much sensitivity. "Are you guys hungry?" she asks, peering from the corridor.

"I could use a beer," Sam says, looking at her with accusation. She walks in between them, and looks at one and the other.

"What's going on here?"

"Nothing," Sam says, appraising her as if she were a wall of feminine hieroglyphs, meant to confuse men.

"Something's going on and I'd appreciate it if you said it to my face," she snaps.

"Abel informed me of a few things, and so I see I'm in your way."

"You're not in my way," she says. She munches her lips up, mad like a monkey. She turns to Abel. "You're both welcome as long as you're respectful of me."

Abel walks past them both out into the living room.

She stands there near the threshold with her arms folded. Sam looks at her determined to keep a shield over his heart. "Sparky's your boyfriend?"

"Tom *was* my boyfriend, as if that's any of your business."

"Well—"

"Well, *what?*" she interrupts. "I'm thirty-eight years old, I'm a big girl, I know what I'm doing."

Sam clears his throat. "Look, I don't mean to be in your way. Abel and I can leave this evening."

"I don't want you to leave."

Sam clears his throat again. "Isn't your father on his way?"

"My Dad called while Abel and I were having coffee. I told him after I got off the phone that Dad said he'd like to visit. We have no plans. Wow. What's up with Abel? Is he in love with you or something?"

"*No*," Sam says, looking at her indignantly. "We're both just going through a lot right now, and I guess, we've been in misery-loves-company for some years now. It's a hard habit to break."

"Okay then," Greta says, clicking her heels. She puts her hands on her hips, cocks her head like the heartbreaker he caught in her for a moment at the hospital. "Let's get those beers. And something for your stomach, all right?"

Two hours later and thankful that Greta found an old joint where Sparky used to hide them in the cupboard, they all lie high in various positions on the gray Tibetan prayer mats, spread out on the colorful rug. Sam's cell phone rings from on top of his bag—still in the middle of the floor from yesterday—but he doesn't get up to answer it. He knows it's Joe, who has checked in with him every evening since Brookings. Sam continues to lie there, the only one also half drunk, but just as easy and pleasant as his companions. Abel skillfully makes shadow puppets against the kitchen counter wall. Greta crawls over to Sam, plunks her head down in his lap. She claps for Abel, as Sam fondles her braless, plump, and fleshy orbs.

Abel flies his shadow bird just in front of the latticework, giving a jungle feel to his showcase. Greta is giddy now with her comments, as Sam mutters to himself now that the phone rings a third time.

When Sam answers, Joe's voice comes across devoid of toss or puff as he asks how he is. The all too brief relaxation recedes. Sam gets that old familiar tingle of fear, asks Joe to hurry up and get to the point. Joe tells him Shawn Lamb was found dead by the Winchuck River. Sam repeats what he says to take in the facts. He could implode over Joe's choice to deliver such a dry and technical statement. Without fatherly wisdom or advice, Joe rewords his news that Shawn Lamb was found by the river at the California/Oregon border, dead of suicide.

Sam stands in the kitchen. Abel's shadow puppets take the height of Sam's head. The shadow skims his face, as Joe adds that the eye doctor told him today that he's at the very beginning stage of glaucoma. Sam remains quiet. The devil took his life. As Abel's and Greta's laughter grows louder in his head, Sam stands there, housed in rage, not knowing what to do. It's not until he feels his friends' fear creep from the crevices of the room that he realizes he flails out at a God who would fool him into thinking he could ever come close to any kind of peace or resolution.

16

Oregon's July

There was no good reason to lie about going to see her mother, yet that was what July did. She told herself it was because Mother was sick, and she didn't want to worry Sam over a delinquent grandmother he'd never met. July also suspected the menacing tarot card reading might have something to do instead with her mother's pending death.

Mother had moved to Portland, Oregon, a few years after July left Los Angeles. The man she'd followed to Chicago didn't work out. There she met a retired pilot who brought her to Portland, set her up in a rinky-dink apartment in the tiny black section of town, while he lived by himself in the small fishing village of Garibaldi. It was Mother's first and only white man, and for as much venom as she'd previously held for his entire race, he seemed an unusual choice to July.

Upon her arrival in Portland, July rented a car and planned to take her mother to the coast for fresh sea air. As she climbed the mottled concrete steps to the building, she wrinkled her nose at the withering, unkempt landscape. Mother had left the door unlocked, no doubt for a more theatrical witnessing of her decline. The bedroom was open, and there she laid so thin her hands looked like claws against the nubby orange blanket. She wore a white pullover with a rhinestone star, casting hundreds of dotted rainbows about the room. It was as if a petri dish of culture were reflected on the overhead.

"Come in, girl," she said to July with a general's command. The rhinestone effect remained a fantastical sight as Mother breathed, and all of the refracted light made July dizzy.

"Have you been eating anything at all?" July asked, looking at the shape of Mother's cranium, her bed hair pressed flat.

"You don't look so good yourself," Mother said, appraising her face as if she had poison oak.

"You're so skinny, Mother, what is this? It's sweets and booze you can't have, not food."

"Great diet, isn't it? Just forget about all of it." She pushed the covers aside.

"You're happy not eating?"

"Are we here to be happy?" Mother asked, looking meanly at her.

"Well, run or be dragged," July said, folding her arms.

"I don't need to do either when I have the Lord," Mother said, swinging her legs out of bed. "So how's your plumber?" she asked with disgust.

"He's not a plumber, Mother—"

"He deals in pipes, doesn't he?" She stopped in front of July, looking up at her defiantly. "Then he's a *plumber*. What other woman on this earth trades in a white collar for a blue?"

"One that's sick of doing laundry."

"Everybody's drawers gets dirty and a plumber's even dirtier!" She shook her finger at her, then snatched the curtains closed.

"Thank you," July said. "I was losing my sense of gravity in your rhinestone intergalactic. Let's get out of here and get some fresh air. Did you pack a weekend bag, like I asked you?"

Mother kept walking into the bathroom and shut the door hard as if they were having a fight rather than talking to one another the way they always had.

*   *   *

During the drive to the coast, July became convinced that Mother was far from dying. She felt small in a world where a woman like that could fall swiftly into neediness. She'd never shown July vulnerability before. She had always thought that all her mother had to give was spunk, and the rest of it she had to find for herself. She looked over at her in the passenger seat, astonished that Mother managed to maintain a hag's soul in a glamorous woman's body. All done up now in her Tina Turner natural hair wig and makeup, it was as if the illness—the diabetes she'd claimed was destroying her—had packed up too and left for the opposite direction.

"I haven't seen one of us this entire drive." July sighed, taking the first of three turns to the retired pilot's house without hesitation.

"There aren't any of us up here!"

"What are you doing here then?"

"What do I need to see colored people for? I've seen them all my life!"

"This is a strange twist to your plot, isn't it, Mother? You couldn't have given me any more loathsome an impression of white people when I was young."

"Wasn't much at the time I didn't loathe them for."

"LA wasn't bad, don't know why you left."

"Are you kidding me, girl? I'd been there long enough. I was born there, you know that! And you knew about the color bar, we couldn't go *nowhere* they didn't want us to. It was written into the deeds. They made sure we couldn't get our hands on shit."

"I know. CC&Rs."

"CC and whose?"

"Covenants, Conditions, and Restrictions."

"That too. So what are you talking about? Stupid girl, living down there in San Diego, which can't be much different from

141

here. Who'd know you had any learning up in that head." She pointed out the next turn, and looked at her with a confidential expression, approaching a whisper. "I'm so glad you got rid of those naps, by the way. Only picture of my grandson, and there you are holding him with a head full of them!"

"It's called a natural, Mother."

"You'd long ago missed Black Power, anyway. You were always too late. Born late, probably gonna die late too. And that's no blessing, as I'm proof that getting old is no holiday."

"Sorry to have kept you waiting."

"I'm not waiting on you, Gwendolyn."

"So what's the self-pity for? You're only fifty-nine, act so much older, but look nowhere near it."

"That's 'cause my youth was stolen from me, and the Lord is intent on my reward."

"Guess I'll have more to say when I'm dead too."

"You read all the wrong books when there's only one that matters," Mother said. She pointed with her thumb at the last turn, and nodded at the house as July came upon it.

When they knocked on the retired pilot's door, there was no answer. Mother shrugged, sauntered back down the three steps, and admitted she'd never called him to have lunch, as she'd rather have surprised him. As they scoured the small town full of banners and signs she'd paid no attention to, July half believed the clerks who all said there wasn't a room in town for the celebration of Garibaldi Days. After the fifth motel, she got them back on the road, and drove south.

They stopped in Newport, thinking they could find a hotel after a lunch Mother barely touched. Overlooking the water, July noted that the sun hadn't followed them from Garibaldi, and she watched the grayness suck compliance out of her mother, which made her uncomfortable.

"Your father was putty of a man, he was," Mother said, chin in hand. July looked at the sheath of age spots, which rather than betraying her years, posed as freckles and beauty marks. "But I had to run with him, I'd gotten tired of my father mistaking me for a wife."

"You don't have to tell me this," July said, imagining her mother's mouth a nozzle that she could turn off.

"You should look him up, Gwendolyn." Mother looked into July's eyes for the first time. "You should. He'd be proud of you."

July stared back at her, not sure if her mother really knew or not that she'd impaled her, then spliced her down to size. Mother opened her purse, and took out a small cardboard phonebook held together by a rubber band. She found the letter *E*, then took out a pen, scrawled a name and number on the napkin with the same abrupt scurry July always found so odd. She offered it to her.

"You're thinking this will save your soul, Mother?" July asked as she snatched the napkin then dangled it in front of her.

"My soul's already saved, I accepted Jesus as my savior. You are an adulterer, a single mother, a Communist, and an atheist with a Muslim in your bed. You got a lot to pray for. Look up your father, he might surprise you with some direction."

"I doubt I've ever been all of those things at once, Mother, and yet, somehow I imagine you've accomplished even more than all that."

"Take me back home," Mother hissed, pointing at July's face.

"I see we're well past counseling, so I'll do exactly that."

"Counseling!"

"*You're a vat of hell, woman, you know that?*" July spit. "And I'm so glad you're up here, because California isn't big enough."

Mother, ordinarily pecan hued, paled to the silt and gravel-stoned Oregon sand. She put on her blazer, embossed with fake designer letters. She stood up, the booth cushion like a suction loudly releasing air.

July watched her go to the pay phone outside, as if she were making other arrangements to get home. She turned from that old, familiar view, the tower of mother, and looked out at the water, thinking how few dramatic scenes she'd ever had, and how the accumulation of all of those soft-focused memories were really the essence of life. She gazed so long out at the water that it became as still as a painting. She realized how much she liked the control she could have, like standing ready for a ball being thrown, and knowing that if she slowed it down, she was sure to hit it. Time was like that, amenable as long as she respected its resistance to beginnings and ends.

Mother was standing there long after July had paid the check. She looked out at the street, as if she'd called a cab, her legs looking skimpy in dark hose and patent leather, square-toed pumps. July didn't need to say a word. She walked right past her to the rental car, and after some paces, listened to the rhythmic echoing click of her mother's heels on the pavement behind her.

17

Nanodiamonds Are Forever

"It's not easy being free," Abel says to Sam at the Portland airport curbside drop-off.

"Why sympathize with him, man? I wanted the *death penalty*, not an early parole with luxury and choice to end it for himself."

"I'm talking about you," Abel says, taking Sam's hand from where it rests on the driver's windowsill. "Forget about forgiveness—"

"*Forgiveness?*" Sam interrupts.

"I'm saying there seems to be no way you'll ever do that, so try with *his death* to just let it go. It can be over. It's up to you."

Abel, who was as sullen as Sam the whole ride from Newport to here, now gives him a smile brimming with luck. His bandage off now, infection gone, stitches out by Greta's doctor, his healing wound shines in the city heat-wave sun. As he turns to walk off, Sam misses him with a tattletale whine and ache in the gut, momentarily wishing he'd chosen a road trip with the one who understands him best over the unknown with a stranger who can only offer the comfort of hot sex.

Greta is on her period this day, their fifth together alone. She mixes chocolate paste in a pot of near-boiling whole milk and sugar. One hand is on the back of her hip, as she stirs with the other. In this pose she appears pregnant, as Sam fantasizes that he could feel happy about it. The smell of the simmering chocolate, the sound of the water playing in the fountain hypnotizes him into domestic complacency.

She lifts a teaspoonful to her lips and blows, as he leaves her to sit on the other side of the island. She tells him she's running out of money since she's been without work for nearly six months. She tastes the hot cocoa, making a steamy slurping sound.

What am I playing house for? Sam asks himself, hoping he hasn't said this aloud. But he does hear himself ask her how she's been making it, as she explains how she has been helping out Sparky "here and there" and that she got a loan from her dad. He can't cover the gash in his tone when he asks if she's still sleeping with her old boyfriend.

"I told you I wasn't." Her voice pulls and breathes like an accordion.

"Okay, then."

She pours the hot chocolate into the first of two large, spotted purple mugs, and spills some on the floor. She jumps back. "Dammit," she says between closed teeth.

"I got it," Sam says.

"The floor is filthy," she whines, ripping a paper towel from the roll, accidentally tearing it in half.

"Where's your mop? Huh? Go sit down, I'll bring your cup to you."

Greta goes outside for the mop, as Sam, with a kitchen towel, wipes the concrete floor that's ground with bits of straw and twigs. She comes back with the broom as well, and gasps.

"Don't use that towel on the floor, that's gross," she grunts, scrunching her top lip to her nose. Sam takes the mop from her, and she looks at him as if he better keep his temper in check. She takes her cup to her favorite spot on the living room floor, and unfolds her prayer mat on the area rug of soft, plush, and splash-dyed woven hemp.

"Seems a waste of my degree," she says aloud to herself, as she looks out the window.

"What?"

"I don't know. I'm thinking I want to start a business doing something else all together. It's not that I don't still care about trees, I'm just feeling a pull but I don't know where that is."

"What's your degree in?" Sam asks, mopping the length of the floor.

"Forest pathology, I told you."

"I still don't understand what you do. What kind of diseases do trees get, anyway?"

"Swiss needle cast, a fungus that affects Douglas-fir forest here near the coast, is one, and that's mostly due to water stress. Sudden Oak Death is a big one, destroying the Northern California coast all the way up to Oregon's. And there are all kinds of root diseases, fungi, pests, dwarf mistletoes—"

"How do you know when a tree is sick? It's not like they can tell you where it hurts."

"With something like Swiss needle cast, the needles turn yellow and fall from the tree. There are many things that can go wrong with a tree, and you can tell from the position of a trunk, moving from vertical to leaning, you can look at gaps, fissures in the soil, weak limbs, branches, cracks, hollow cavities, mushrooms. With Sudden Oak Death the bark can even bleed."

"Bleed?"

"A thick sap that actually looks like blood, and underneath there's a canker with dark patches of infected tissue—"

"Okay, stop, that's enough," he interrupts again. "So who did you work for?"

"The Oregon Department of Forestry. Long time ago I worked for the Department of Agriculture, doing inspections, giving phytosanitary certificates, but I hated that. It was so much more about the marketplace."

She lies flat on the ground now, hands on her abdomen, touching. Sam mops up to the area rug where she lies, leans it against the wall, and lies down next to her. He pinches her big toe, and notices for the first time that she has bunions. She turns to him, gives him her gummy view, her eyes mischievously lit.

"Why are you a nurse?" she asks.

"I enjoy being around women all day," he says, slyly.

"Oh yeah?"

"Yeah."

"There are a few male nurses out there, right?" she says, looking at his lips.

"Sure, but unlike me, they tend to go for ER and ICU, you know, the excitement of codes."

"Codes?"

"No breathing, no pulse."

"Ah, flatlining."

"Yes, but no such thing, really. The monitor usually shows some kind of activity. That's the movies making it simple, making it stupid."

She leans over and kisses him, being meticulous with her tongue, as if to take the last residue of chocolate from his taste buds. He slides her navy sweats down, and she gets up to fetch a bath towel, when she comes back she has to work to get him hard, which is easy when she foregoes the condom. The slippery, warm, gush of her blood swallows him up to a time when he could breathe water.

Later upon her immediate request, he soaks the stain from the prayer mat with an oxygen scrub. She sits next to him with her head hanging down, her hair wild, limp and thin as uncut ryegrass. The towel drapes around her waist, her long legs together, feet pointing and flexing.

"What was your mother's name?" she asks.

"July."

"July."

"It was her birth month, and she started referring to herself as that when she was in her teens, it caught on."

"She spoke of herself in third person?"

Sam, annoyed, has to think about it. "Yes, I guess so. No, I don't know. She introduced herself as July, okay?"

"So what was her real name?"

"Julia."

"So she called herself that for short."

"Julia Brown is what's on her birth certificate, and she started calling herself July in her teens," he says with much impatience.

"Where was she born?"

"Memphis. Can we talk about something else?"

"Yes," she says. She flips her hair back out of her face, then as if the feel of it revolted her, she lassoes it between her fingers, winds it into a tight knot at the top of her head.

"My mother, Tess," she hesitates before continuing. "She ran over my father so much that he's physically weak before his time. He does weird things like burying his old TV in the backyard, just to avoid carrying it up the hill to the front where someone can come take it away."

Sam stops scrubbing, resigning himself to banter.

"He was her slave until she left him." She clasps her hands together, looks at the rug. "My mother was a great beauty, still is really, and it affected both my half sister Rabina and me a lot growing up. It had so much to do with our development, our sense of self, you know, made us defensive. Rabina's a smoke-jumper. She parachutes in to fight fires—"

"Yes, I know I what a smokejumper is," he interrupts.

"Anyway, you can understand how both of my parents feel safe they'll never lose me, in comparison to her." She looks at him measuring his interest. Sam can feel the small chunk of resentment grow for his lack of enthusiastic attention.

"What did your mother's murderer do to get out?" she asks like a slap.

"He was up for parole."

"Yes, but why did they grant it?"

"He participated in some kind of Shakespeare theater therapy—he acted in the play—and became a Buddhist on *excellent* behavior."

"Maybe he was repentant, you know? Maybe that's why he killed himself."

"I'm just sick of talking about it really. People are so obsessed with murder, and they give me all the pity in the world, then try to drag the details out of me." ˙

"People are fascinated with it because they almost envy the victim, you know, it's like that final agonizing mystery ends, she got it over with, no more terror, she's dead!"

She lies there statuesque, her upper lids shiny as if she had applied Vaseline, a smudge of blood on her thigh like the Rorschach test mirror of his. The pendulum of anger swings against his sternum so hard he thinks he hears it clank. He drops the rag and goes outside into the slosh of mud, walks out farther into the spongy footing of the forest floor. The thick mist kisses his face and shimmers on the ends of his matted hair like gossamer. The density of green all around puts him in a trance of homage to his mother, the star, her image before him defying belief that she was ever dead at all.

With Greta out of the house on vague errands, Sam takes Haley's phone call into the bedroom, and closes the door. He sits on the chest at the foot of the bed, facing the one solid wall with the painting called *White Heart Rot*. It is a small abstract by some friend inspired by Greta's explanation of a city tree disease compared to tuberculosis in humans. The title reminds him instead of people who give Greta and him second and third looks when they take walks together through the neighborhood.

Haley is yacking about when they first met and the ring he gave her because she always wanted it—peridot, her birthstone. He's not sure how this leads her to describe the incredible wingspan of some bird she just saw, or how this segues to the reminder of the older guy she used to see, the one who worked for NASA calculating trajectories to the moon. She mentions meteor showers that will be happening next week in hope that he could somehow join her. He won't go into everything that has happened up until now, other than the fact that Abel was with him for a week, and that Shawn Lamb was found dead. He hears the probe in her tone, and he clamps down on it. Not long after he's sure he's built a sturdy barricade does she come barging through. She's able to get most of it out of him, including the depth of his pain and fear when he thought he was being followed. She's surprisingly valiant upon the news of Greta, and sits silent with it for a while before purging her own guilt for a one-night stand. He goes queasy with her excessive details, and finally stops her in the name of abuse. Her silence again comes through like tentacles, arranging him into a rumpled, heartsick heap. She knows it and coos at first cuddly, then frothy, and as he twitches, useless in trying to resist, she slithers into a low, nasty voice, lubricated with heat. She tells him all she misses him doing to her, and all she misses doing to him. He lies back on the bed, frees himself from his button-down pants, and begs her to see it, begs her to touch it, pleads with her to swallow it down.

After he comes, his promises of nanodiamonds are unnecessary. She reminds him that they aren't necessarily presolar or forever, and he protests her literal mindedness. She tells him she has to break up with him now, because otherwise he'll always make excuses for taking her for granted, or worse yet blame her for never finding himself.

18

Science of Mind's July

Before July was close to Ava, Joe often confused her with Yvonne. This was a small irritation to July because she thought if Joe were truly interested in everything about her, he would get her friends straight, just as she did his. Yvonne was distinguished in many things, and one was that she was married to Brian Cook, who had long ago offered July a job in management at his medical billing firm. July turned it down, but she was heartened by their belief in her. She remained impressed with Yvonne, who had a bachelor's in psychology, a master's in theology, and a doctorate in thanatology. That Yvonne was so versed in the medical, psychological, and sociological aspects of death attracted July tremendously. Yvonne believed alienation to be at the core of everyone's problems; July would argue that anyone could be taught to use this unavoidable state to their advantage. Fixating on the self-centered was limiting, so it wasn't the estrangement, the feeling of being isolated or withdrawn that interested July, but rather the notion that one's world was unreal. It was that quality of reality—or unreality—that one had created for oneself that she found most interesting. She thought Yvonne should stress these points in her counseling of the grieving and the dying, often telling her so.

There was a strong competitive side to Yvonne; the more July talked about the cards and Ava, the more Yvonne took July upon herself like a cause. She was soon able to do what neither Mother nor Joe could, which was to bring July inside a house of worship for worship's sake. Because it was the Science of Mind church, informal, less religious than spiritual, more of a center or gathering than a denomination, July felt less turned off. Since Saturday afternoons with Ava and Sundays with Yvonne took up most of her weekends, July thought she depended on Joe for very little emotional tuning, and this left her less needy for her man's attention. But it wasn't like he would have denied her.

After the Oregon visit with Mother (which she'd told Joe and Sam was a Las Vegas trip with Ava), July grew increasingly focused on finding racist city planning, CC&Rs, and color bar documents. She had already amassed a small gallery collection of slave bills of sale, tax assessments, and inventory lists including "bucks and wenches," along with her latest, an 1851 warning poster to the colored people of Boston to avoid contact with kidnappers and slave catchers.

This 1851 original poster she got from Shawn Lamb, who said he acquired it from his adoptive parents still living in Springfield, Massachusetts. She ran into him in church, just where he said he'd follow her. Entirely erased was that initial stultification she'd felt at their first meeting. She'd actually used the word "fatuous" to describe him to Ava that night at the party, and yet when she ran into him in church all she noticed was his sinuous chest under a clingy navy blue shirt, the intelligent crinkle at the corner of his eyes, his evanescent attentiveness, this time suggesting an active mind.

When July introduced him to very light-hued Yvonne—who wore her permed and crimped hair in a bun—she looked at him as if he were rabble. July questioned the kind of counselor Yvonne could be with that attitude, and chafed at her own naïveté and choice of friends. July then focused on the aberration of his patchwork skin, and imagined Mother's outraged witness to this new rattle of her loins.

153

The walk to Yvonne's car brought out discussion of July's passion in collecting, and Shawn Lamb was quick to mention this original Boston warning poster, which he said he could get for her. He said he'd call her with a price, and she corrected him that it was she who would call him. And as she took his card, Yvonne had already revved the engine.

More than a month passed before July picked up the phone. Meanwhile, Yvonne had pulled her into some volunteering at the counseling center, stirring up a personal interest in psychology and entertainment of going back to school for another degree.

July tried not to worry that since Sam was starting tenth grade, and a year younger than most of his class, he had gone from a high sense of fun to a mangled low of sexual confusion. She knew it was a phase and unavoidable. Sam's best friend, Wayne, was short, chubby, and hobbled on a broken leg from a car accident. He was as smart as Sam, but ahead of him in the field of smut, as evidenced from the hardcore stash that July found in Sam's room. Sam said it belonged to Wayne, and she believed him. She didn't want to embarrass her boy. She then allocated the matter to Joe—as this is where Sam needed a father in his life—and as she saw later that the exchange went well, she began reading up on course offerings and financial aid at UCSD and San Diego State University.

It was fall of 1987, she considered applying for entry, the deadline December. Yvonne encouraged her; Ava discouraged her. One night Joe surprised her with a diaphanous red panty and bra trimmed in gold. With an inappropriate kind of sportsmanship, she shimmied in her new undies, their baptism far from mind. She then lunged into bed, colliding with Joe's wrong move to catch her, and launched into details of her plans. Joe said this was all "fine and dandy," but that lately he'd found himself craving a baby. July recalled her age for him of forty-two, to which he replied that his own mother hadn't stopped there. She reminded him of the impermanence of cravings then got up to fix him a stack of buttermilk pancakes.

Shawn Lamb asked if he could meet her at the center, now that he had the document, and she shivered at the fact that she'd never mentioned volunteering there. Sensing her discomfort, he quickly suggested the bar, at which she also scoffed. He told her about a seahorse he found in Point Loma near the new lighthouse, and how there was a nice place they could meet to make the exchange by the old one at the Cabrillo monument. She agreed.

It was good to be by the water in a different section of town from the county office building, but as she climbed the hill of the park, she was overwhelmed by loyalty and sacrifice, surrounded by the veterans' cemetery on both sides. When she passed the anechoic pool of the Space and Naval Warfare Systems Center, she had a strange feeling of déjà vu, but assumed this was because the moon was visible in the bright light of day, rare.

Shawn Lamb waited for her in the parking lot and asked if she would like to take a walk along the Bayside Trail, which winds along the old military defense road. She told him she didn't have much time on her lunch hour for a two-mile hike. She tried to remain pleasant, but was impatient for the poster. He went to his car, which she was too distracted to recognize even for color, and upon his return with the large envelope, she appraised the document as an original with her keen eye and paid him without hesitation.

The attraction she'd felt in church was totally gone in the bright of day. She wondered if she'd confused eros with agape. He had a small tuft of hair under his bottom lip, and his eyes seemed to poke out at her. This time his shirt was a cheery periwinkle, and his pressed corduroy slacks seemed casual and fashionable to her. She considered having a snack with him at the gift shop, but then she noticed the waking goop in the inner corner of his eyes, and coupled with his skin, she lost her appetite.

As she hurried to her car with her latest prided document—having insisted that she wanted to walk alone—she pictured herself in an antiseptic room where she could cast out all evidence of having been infected.

19

Comet Dust and Satellite Ghosts

At the Samaritan Pacific Communities Hospital, Sam pores over the seventeen available positions in Nursing/Patient Care. Two of them he might consider, though he is overqualified. What's more, he would need to get Oregon RN licensure, even limited status, which scares him. But when July came to him in a dream, she gave him the distinct feeling that he should stay there.

He takes a walk through town, bristling at the turn his life seems to be taking. There's Greta, brandishing her politics, cursing Evangelicals, and making him numb. With her ennui rubbing off on him and her newspaper-want-ads pushing, he still feels shocked to have left the hot and dry for the cold and wet. He misses Haley, he misses Abel, and he misses Joe.

Sam huddles in his jacket, imagining mildew growing between its layers. The sound of his own shoes on the pavement gives him frenzy. He dials Joe, who puts him on hold for what seems like a full five minutes, before coming back to him with tenuous jitters.

"Should I be calling you at all, or are you always going to have bad news for me?" Sam asks, trying to be light but failing.

"That's why I didn't call you today, son."

"What *now*?"

"Maybe you're just following your mother, son," Joe says, his tone apologetic.

"*What?*"

"Got word today from this guy, Cowells—he knew your grandmother—well he called to say that she passed yesterday, and he's burying her up there, right there in Portland on Friday."

"I'm not in Portland," Sam protests, "I'm in *Newport*."

"Did you hear what I said, boy? Your grandmother died, and she's right up there next to you in Portland," Joe says, getting angry and flabbergasted. When Sam doesn't say anything, Joe continues, trying to believe it. "He tracked me down through your mother's letters, he couldn't find us in San Diego, of course, but he got us on the Net. She'd even kept the court adoption papers," Joe says trailing off. "I just can't imagine why she never answered," he whispers with a wheeze.

"Did you not really want me, Joe?"

"Of course I *did*," Joe says with a spit in it that Sam can hear. "I'm trying to figure out what kind of woman stays out of her daughter's life, is all. Didn't she want to *understand* what happened?"

"Who's going to understand it?"

Joe sighs. "Not me." He's quiet for a while, then his voice goes hoarse. "You want the address or not? I agree either way."

"Not."

"Okay then."

"I might take a job here."

"Seems like some kind of sign, you know, you're up there in Oregon of all places and your grandmother dies, right up there next to you?"

"I thought you said you agree either way."

"I do, son. It's just unearthly, is what it is. I'd put her aside in my mind. And if your mother didn't want you knowing her, then it wasn't up to me to fill you in."

"No, it wasn't," Sam says, his voice hard.

"So, you're taking a job up there?"

"She doesn't deserve my presence."

"Don't think so either, son," Joe says, with a period on it. "So you're taking a job?"

"I might."

"Must be some lady."

"Well."

"Well, what?"

"I think I'll call you tonight, Joe. I just gotta think a bit, then I'll call you tonight. Maybe I should go."

"Okay, son. Love you." Joe hangs up, and Sam stands as if encased between the lines on the sidewalk. He squats right there, not caring who's looking, burying his face in his hand, never having heard Joe say that before.

At three a.m. Sam stays up with Greta to see the meteor showers, Perseids, named for the constellation Perseus, Haley had told him. They stand outside in a clearing, Sam with a blanket over his shoulders, giggling every time he catches a burning burst, spattering its trail, the radiant as if directly overhead. Like a child he yanks Greta's arm, pulling on it, so that her airy hair flounces this way and that. He tries capturing her with his thick, plaid woolen blanket, but she gets away, dashing inside to turn on opera, pointing the speakers so the voices echo in their forest with the glimmering drama of the sky. This makes him laugh with the kind of glee and abandon he can't remember ever feeling.

When the streaks grow fewer, connecting less and less dots between the stars and him, Sam enters the bedroom. Greta follows humming with the last of the music, her nose red and wet.

"This is fantastic," Sam says. He plops himself out, spread eagle on the bed. He looks around him in the three-sides of glass room, under a skylight of quieted stars. Greta brushes her tangled hair and stares at Sam as if trying to recognize him. "Isn't this fantastic?" he asks, arms folded under his head, looking into her eyes.

"Most incredible, it is." She holds up an index finger. "With the exception of seeing iceblink when I went to Greenland."

"Iceblink?"

"Sunlight reflecting off of ice can make a bright band on the underside of low clouds. When I saw it, it had this overwhelming and deep yellowish glow."

"In Greenland, huh?"

"I went dog sledding there, to a place called Disko Bay. The entire trip was spectacular."

"Alaska's closer than Greenland."

"The guy I was seeing had already been sledding there, and Greenland was next on his list of adventures," she says. She puts her hand on his face, contouring it with her fingers. "My sister was just in Alaska though, for all the fires."

"Who was the guy?"

"The one who painted *White Heart Rot*."

"Thought you said he was a friend."

"He is a friend, now." She peels off her clothes and gets under the covers, and since he is on top of them, she pulls so he might roll off. When he sits up, she helps him with his layers.

"Have you ever repeated a word to the point that it stops making sense, becomes totally unrecognizable?" Greta asks, tossing his sweater on the floor.

"Of course," Sam replies, cagey and irritated with her spoiling his past meteor moment.

"Well, it's the same thing as staring into the mirror, you know. Staring and staring until you are wholly unrecognizable to yourself, finally apart from yourself, just an observer of an observer."

"Yeah," he says, a bit bored, impatient, as if she were taking him for stupid.

"I think about that a lot here when I'm alone. The aloneness is not the point, it's about how I fit into this universe, however small, however connected or unconnected I might feel at any given time."

"Yeah, I know what you mean."

She wraps her naked body around his as he joins her under the covers.

"Stay with me," she says, closing her eyes and holding onto him, nuzzling him with her thighs.

I thought I was doing just that, he says to himself. But the sound of her command—tempting as it is to obey—doesn't accommodate.

At the service in Portland for Mavis Maud Purvis, Sam sits in the very back row of the small Episcopalian church. He is one of seven there. The only other white man present besides the minister, Sam concludes, is Travis Cowells, who protrudes with discomfort in the front row. There are five women, four of them black, one of them Latina, all dressed in church lady finery. Sam brushes off his dustless, brand new, starched black khakis from Newport, straightens the thin striped tie over his white button-down shirt, and tugs the lapels of his ill-fitting, houndstooth check, thrift shop blazer he just picked up down the street. The minister has already welcomed everyone of the small gathering, and no one cries, sniffles, or makes a sound. Sam fights the urge to get up and testify to what a cold and unloving woman she was, and how wrongly they celebrate her memory. He tries disconnecting from the pain of the only other funeral he'd ever been to, his mother's, services postponed two months due to mistakes in presophisticated 1980s forensics and DNA technology.

The minister speaks of the limited time assigned human beings on earth, and the consequences of not using it wisely. Sadistically hoping for the deceased's roast, Sam tunes in with a keen ear but is disappointed to find the sermon remains general in advice toward the path to freedom. It makes him think of Abel, and the unnecessary muck he'd stirred in their last phone conversation. Just because Sam wasn't clear on his own next few steps, he turned the tables on his friend, pushing him on depression, joblessness, familial estrangement, and worse, impotence. Sam looks at the one-page leaflet in his hand, a stranger lacking trace of his mother's features, a name wholly irrelevant, a biographical paragraph with an insignificant link to Los Angeles, and no mention of Memphis, where his mother was born. *What makes Joe so sure this is my grandmother at all?* he asks himself in a raspy whisper.

At the end of the service, he leers inside of the open casket, malicious thoughts clotting his chest. Her skin is thick and stretched like a wetsuit, her face gussied up with lipstick, rouge, and powder in all the wrong hues. Her hands are thin and veined in rivulets. Her white lace collar swallows her neck, and her dress is a navy so dark it suggests an abyss.

He doesn't realize how long he stands there until a headache comes on, the corpse's image more and more murky in his melting vision. They must have turned up the heat in the church, Sam thinks, as he lays his hand on his forehead, clamminess forming between. Someone handles his shoulder, the feel displeasing since his jacket's pads are lopsidedly stitched. He hears his name in the form of a question, which only makes him angry, and he walks away from the casket, not turning around to face the voice's owner.

Disapproving hens cluck at either side, he thinks, as he walks up what seems to be ever the steepest aisle. Then he hears the name "Cowells" behind him very plainly, the church door opening to enticing fresh air, with the slight grimy scent of city.

"Getting a hold of yourself?" Cowells's voice carries, blatant with resentment.

"Leave me alone then, if it's such a *bother*," Sam says, now squeezing together his eyes, cheeks, and mouth muscles.

"Come with me then, and we'll escape Mavis's bridge club, do us both some good."

Sam follows his reluctant host for two blocks to a diner, and as the haze of heat lifts from his brain, he's surprised to feel as comfortable and on edge as he did in the heart of Hollywood streets when he was in school. Cowells is quick to find a booth, and he orders for them both without opening menus. Sam sits stupid and sick with grief for everything ever denied him. As he focuses on this old man, neither feeble in form nor posture, he envies him the privilege of intimacy with his beloved mother's mother.

"Ach, it's more hellish than I thought," Cowells says, chewing down on gum like cud.

"That it is," Sam agrees, looking into his eyes, and the skin of his face, which appears rinsed at once in a translucent blue and yellowing cigarette smoke. The comb is apparent in the separation of gelled gray hair.

"I'm taking her ashes up with me to drop over Lake Tahoe," he says, not leaning back for the coffee put down in front of him. Sam looks up in thanks for his at the waitress, who doesn't return the acknowledgment. "A lot of it will blow back on me, of course, but so be it."

"She loved Lake Tahoe?"

"*I* love Lake Tahoe."

"So what's it got to do with her?"

"Everything that had to do with me did with her. She preferred things that way."

Sam flares his nostrils. "You were the sun, rising and setting."

"Don't go getting all riled up," Cowells says, a touch of mirth in his bloodshot eyes. "This was an old-fashioned woman."

"She was only seventy-four, she must have lived long enough to know better than to blindly follow some man."

"Seventy-four isn't young either." Cowells sits back in his seat, feeling for a handkerchief or cigarettes that aren't there.

"I can see you're a positive thinker," Sam nearly spits.

"Positive thinker? Now he's nothing but a little mustard spread on the meat of almighty negative," he says, taking a sip of his coffee, with an obvious distaste for it. He looks at Sam, warming up in proportion to Sam's irritation.

Sam studies Cowells's nose, which would act as a treacherous overhang for the person, size of a pea, surely to fall into his cup.

"So what do you do?" Cowells asks, putting one elbow on the banquette, in a pointed, casual manner.

"I'm a nurse."

"A *nurse*?"

Sam gives him a weary look.

"Remind me not to take ill on your watch."

"What's that mean?"

"That you can't even take care of yourself," he says, picking up the butter knife from the table, and turning it over a few times, his other arm still resting on the booth.

"And wasn't it a male nurse who killed all those people? Mavis was always anxiously talking about it in the hospital."

Sam folds his arms, sinks down in his seat.

"Tranquility comes, you know, when you stop giving a damn what they say."

"*Tranquility*," Sam says, shaking his head. "Man." He chuckles to himself.

"Do you fly at all?"

"What do you think?"

"Mavis loved to fly with me."

Sam nods, trying not to get too interested in her.

"You fish at all?"

"Nah, man."

"It's there too, you know, in the stillness of the water," Cowells says, going quiet and into himself.

They sit there in silence until the waitress brings their plates.

Cowells immediately cuts into his sirloin, while Sam mashes his mashed potatoes. He stares at Cowells again, wondering what it would have been like to be a passenger on his plane. It's at this moment that he can't believe he's never flown before, never before this had reason or impetus to leave his state. He puts the potatoes in his mouth, chewing more with his tongue like a baby, feeling like one too for being so inexperienced.

After Cowells has been through three quarters of his steak, he looks up at Sam, as if just remembering he was there.

"So, you have a girlfriend?" Cowells asks, wiping the corners of his mouth with the napkin as if the gesture disturbed him.

"Yes," Sam answers.

"Is she here?"

"No."

"What's her name?"

"Haley." Sam cuts into his meat, flummoxed by his own decisions at every turn, he realizes.

"Dirty snowball," Cowell says.

"That's 'holly' she's like 'hail.'"

"As you have it. Treat her like a queen?"

"I should."

"She a looker?"

"Yes."

"Then don't. That spoils them, you know."

"Not into spoiling my grandmother, I take it? Was she some kind of servant to you or something?" Sam snaps.

"Watch your temper, and what you're implying," Cowells says, talking to him and pointing with a cut of steak on his fork.

Sam sits steaming, not knowing why he doesn't hit him.

"This state, you know, after the Civil War, was colonized by white flight from the South. Exclusion laws in place, there were more Klan here by the twenties than any state in the Union. I was born here, then. So if you want to talk about racism, we can, but you wouldn't begin to have an idea of the attitudes I've known, nor what a woman like your grandmother—whom I respected very deeply—went through in her time." He still talks with his meat end fork. He then swallows as if it hurts. "There's *nothing* you can't have now, and if you don't take it, then you've got no one else but yourself to blame." He puts the forkful in his mouth, and chews, looking at Sam carefully now, as if searching for Mavis.

Sam pushes his half-eaten plate of food to the center of the table, gets up, and buys a pack of cigarettes from the cashier. He brings it back and lights up at the table, blowing the smoke not directly at Cowells, who looks at him with pity.

"Your father seems like such a sensible man," Cowells says, pushing his plate toward the edge.

"This is a nonsmoking section, kindly put that out," the waitress says coldly. Sam raises his lids like heavy garage doors, looks her up and down once, then snuffs it out on his plate. He coughs, his cheeks flush.

"I think it would be rude to miss Mavis's gals gathering," Cowells says, gesturing for the check. "You're welcome to come with me."

"I don't think so."

"Played canasta with them once, they're very adept, though bridge is their game."

"Are they from her church?"

"She never told me what church she went to," Cowells says, reaching for his wallet as the waitress places the bill on the table. Sam looks at him, his mouth agape.

"How can you not know something as basic as that?"

"Mystery is what keeps love alive, friend, so don't go spilling it all to your girlfriend. They pretend like that's all they want, but when you give it to them, they hang you with it, then blame you for supplying them the noose." Cowells scoots out of the booth, looking his age only for that moment of getting up.

Greta soaks his feet in a large, eggshell pink, ceramic bowl of peppermint oil, mineral crystals, and Epsom salts. He looks down at the top of her head, her thoughtful brow, and wonders where she'll be when she takes her last breath. How old she is, whom she's with.

"What?" she asks, looking up at him with a flirtatious giggle.

"Let's have meat tonight," he says, smiling at her with gratitude.

"I only eat game—hunted, freshly killed. Don't want to slow myself down with old meat. It's not worth it. Besides, didn't you have steak this afternoon?"

"It was awful, the old man ate his, though."

"Did you tell him about your mother?"

"No," he says, wincing. Though she massages his right foot, the crystals and salts sloughing his sole, and it feels so good.

"Wasn't there food at the church ladies'? You told me that when I called, you *said* you were eating." Greta cradles his feet, but her tone takes a turn.

"I didn't eat much, there were casseroles, pastas, I don't know what else, kinda nasty."

"I would have cooked then, but there's nothing in the house, I had a sandwich, since you'd eaten, so that's it."

"Calm down, woman. I'm not starving," he says, playfully.

She washes off the salts, and starts on the other foot. She works in silence for so long that Sam falls into a meditation. In his trance, soothed by the sound of the water on his feet and the water in the fountain, her voice some twenty minutes into it comes as a harsh disturbance.

"Even if there's no such thing as reincarnation," she says, breathing in as if midconversation and had gone too fast, "there might be something to recognizing just a small percentage of someone's energy, you know?"

"Yes," he says, lazily, encouraging her to put her all into quiet and his foot.

"Because I recognize you," she says looking up at him, kneading between his toes, and he moans. "Maybe you were three percent of a tree, and I remember being four percent of the grass surrounding it." He smiles, closes his eyes, and nods, *yes*.

"We could have been bits of anything that met, or even bits that went together."

"Uhn-hmn," he says, as she grabs a towel, and rather roughly dries each foot.

When she's done, he teases, lifts the front flap of robe, and rubs his foot between her legs. As she makes more room for him, he inserts his big toe as far up as it will go.

20

Otis's July

Playing confidante was never her thrill, but July enjoyed coaching people on how to look at a problem. She thought this was perhaps how Shawn Lamb became attached, hanging on her words of why he lost his only kid to the mother. If he weren't so wretched with pain over it, July would never have allowed him to appear at the most inappropriate moments—though, not once in front of Joe—the worst being on her arrival home with Sam from a conference with his English teacher. He had written a worrisome essay with a lewd reference, signs of anger and depression. The teacher also felt that some of it had been plagiarized, and so cautioned them both that Jesus was the only philosopher one need quote. Bringing her religion into the classroom enraged July, and she told her so.

On the short ride home under California blue sky and dulling warmth in early December, July mused aloud how ready she felt to pluck Sam from the public school. Silently she agonized over where she might get money for private. As they pulled up to their front walk, she saw Shawn Lamb waiting in the car across the street, and this was nothing beside her horror that Otis Hamilton sat there next to him in the passenger seat. Sam's head still being at the conference, he wouldn't recall seeing either man, though it could have made a difference.

"Go on in, Sam, I'm running next door to Mrs. Bell's for some eggs."

Leaving her purse in the car, July patted her loose bun, and straightened her striped gingham dress as Sam walked into the house, not sure of what he could be getting away with.

"What are you doing here, Otis?" July asked, hurrying over with a scared lisp she hadn't heard in herself in years.

"I wondered if you might join us for a drink," Otis replied with his usual calm, pugnacious tone.

She put her fists on her lips. "You know I got a man, and I'm committed to him."

"That never stopped you before," Otis said, leaning in toward Shawn Lamb, so he could look up into her eyes.

"He could use your spine to pick his teeth." Her throat parched, her chest thumped with as much fear as remembrance of her own desire during their one time in bed.

"Come on. Everything is copacetic. No need for insult, now."

July put the kiss-curl tendrils behind her ears, eyes locked with Otis.

"Ah, come on out with us, Gwen," he said, sweetening his voice. "I'm not in town long. I miss you."

"Why didn't you admit that you were friends?" July asked Lamb, looking at him now as if released from ambush. He should be on her side, she said with her eyes, showing the full circles of her sparkling deep brown irises.

"Shawn tells me about your collection," Otis said. "I could add to it you know. There's a peculiar WANTED notice for a slave, fifty dollars for her reward. She was very unusual—a fighter—and I know you'd like her. Maybe I'll make it a Christmas gift."

"I'm not interested," July said, scraping the soles of her new shoes on the asphalt as she pivoted to dash away. A car turned the corner and broke sharply not to hit her.

"Take care of yourself, Gwen," Otis called to her as she skipped the porch stairs into the house, her bladder about to burst.

She'd broken a sweat, and had the piss chills on the toilet, as she thought she'd never empty out. In her bedroom, she closed the door and got on her knees, facing the direction she'd seen Joe do a thousand times, and she prayed with an ache in her heart that they could afford to move. And for that good while, her own guilt and fear acted as a magnifier over Sam's dilemma with his English teacher.

Early Christmas Eve July opened the front door to Yvonne and Brian Cook, his bald spot perfect as a coaster at the top of his head. July hadn't realized she was remiss in accompanying them to an interfaith service, as she'd already planned for Ava to stop by for an exchange of presents. The Cooks stayed long enough to share thick eggnog and rum, which Joe passed on, though he sat at the dining table trying to be a part of the festivities. He caught dissatisfied glances as he rolled and twiddled his thumbs, July sure that he was contributing to her increasing nervousness. When Ava finally arrived along with her girls, who went straight to Sam's room, the Cooks excused themselves to run to church. Ava hadn't laid down her coat on the couch before July sprung up feeling wholly in the spirit of the holiday. She called everyone she knew to stop by for a drink. Joe by this time was only half there, she could see—as he had expressed feeling waxy with resentment over her distance and filled calendar. Whenever she took the time to really be with him, head-to-head and heart-to-heart, he was completely there and open. She knew that she was the one afraid of intimacy.

July pulled out her unwrapped gift for Ava, an antique modern lamp with a shade of stars. Ava seemed touched but hesitant for July to open hers, which was a framed deed for one square inch of Yukon Gold Rush country, originally distributed in Quaker Oats Puffed Wheat boxes in the fifties. July responded with how cute it was, and tried to chuckle jollylike as Santa. She listened halfhearted to the movie Ava had just seen, the girls' trickles of laughter from Sam's room, and Joe's attempt to fill in actor names that Ava was forgetting.

July couldn't get her mind off the WANTED FOR REWARD document that Shawn called to describe to her two days after she saw them. She knew it had become her aeon; he said Otis left it there with him for her. A slave named Rebecca, six feet tall, slim, with a long face, "long teeth, black gums, white eyes, and plaited hair." The subscriber stated—Shawn read—that Rebecca was the "biggest devil that ever lived" having poisoned a stud horse and set a stable on fire. She had escaped four times before, badly mauling and abusing the slave who caught her. Shawn wouldn't read to July the details of Rebecca's crimes, using it as intrigue to get her to meet him. Which she did.

21

Smoke Gets in Your Eyes

"Your cologne is on the sweet side. Like gardenias," Greta says with a tone of agenda. She twists her bottom lip between her fingers.

"And?"

"And it seems like you've been wearing it even more since you've been working."

"Why haven't you said anything before, if you didn't like it?"

"I don't know, guess I didn't want to hurt your feelings."

Sam shrugs. A headache comes on, though he confuses it with anger.

"I mean, is it for my benefit? Or is there someone you like at the hospital?"

Sam walks away from her and to the bathroom cabinet for some aspirin. She follows him, stands in the hallway. He takes two tablets, turns on the faucet, cups his hands together, and bends to gulp in the water. He splashes his face, opens his mouth wide, and looks in the mirror, mesmerized by the drips creeping down his neck to his white T-shirt collar.

"So what is it?" she asks. He looks up at Greta, her arms folded, her skin flushed. Hair high in a flyaway ponytail, her pink button-down shirt is crumpled and opens low. She's sexy when she's mad, and he wishes she would jump him right there so they could hurt one another.

"You're not going to answer?"

"Your question doesn't dignify," Sam says, moving to the doorway to face her.

"You piss me off, Sam, you know that?" She turns to walk away, heading for the kitchen, and he follows her.

She pulls out a box of cornmeal from the cabinet, slamming the fridge closed after she gets the carton of eggs.

"I took a job today," she says, not looking at him, as she pours the meal into a measuring cup.

"That's good."

"Don't you want to know what it is?"

"Yes, tell me," he says curtly. He rubs his temples, beginning to sear.

"With your crazy hours, we'll never see one another."

"What's the job, Greta?"

"With the Oregon Parks and Recreations Department. I'm overqualified for it, but I'll be working on state park projects up and down the coast, assisting the Natural Resource Specialist."

"Sounds just fine for now, doesn't it?"

"And my sister will be here tomorrow—*God, it's the worst timing*—and we'll have even less time together."

"It's just a couple of weeks."

"Why do you have to work so many evenings? I couldn't understand why you took that job, when you were better—"

"It's surgery, patient care, Greta," he interrupts. "And part time is good for me right now, the full time was Emergency Room, you know I can't stand that."

"There were *other* choices, Sam."

"Are we going to continue to fight about it? If so, you talk to the range here, and fire away. I'm going for a walk."

The pain pierces like a knitting needle thrust between his eyes through the back of his neck. He doesn't want to talk to her about Joe's news that once they found it wasn't suicide with Shawn

Lamb, they had reopened his mother's case. The whole universe opens up again to swallow him whole. Trust sifts for Joe, as he had to know about all of this a lot sooner than he let on. He resents him for taking the lead in all things concerning his mom.

"Sam! Are you okay? Come on inside, already," Greta says, outside with him now, pulling him up from his knees. "Come in and lie down," she says, lulling him now with her voice. "Lean on me, baby. *I just don't understand this.* You gotta take better care of yourself. Isn't there something we can do for these migraines?"

Holding onto her, he quickens his pace, leading to the bathroom, but throws up on the threshold.

"Have you had this checked out yet, Sam? *Jesus.* You have to take better care of yourself," she repeats, rushing off for paper towels, washcloth, and ice. Sam steps over the mess, kicks off his shoes, strips off his shirt, pants, and gets into the shower, letting the water run over him. His head tilts back, eyes closed, mouth open.

"You're at the hospital now almost every night, do I have to take you by the hand to the doctor, myself?" He didn't know she'd come back so quickly, her voice carries over the shower door, startling him.

Sam doesn't know how long he lets the shower run over him but the pounding, nausea, and Greta are all gone by the time he steps out.

Having forgotten about her imminent arrival, Sam is frightened by the vision of a woman standing in the foyer, and she in turn is just as shaken.

"Who are you?" she spouts.

"Sam. Who are you?"

"Sam," she says, coming toward him, extending her sturdy hand. "I'm Rabina. She didn't tell me you were black."

"She didn't tell me you were rude."

"I'm sorry," she says. She takes back her hand without apparent concern for his assessment of the sincerity of her apology.

Golden with swimmer's shoulders, Rabina is dressed for summer in early October. Her lightweight clothes accentuate a thick waist and muscular legs. Her blond hair is cut short, and her pert nose looks as though it should be on a petite girl. She has an underbite, giving her thin but shapely lips a naughty insolence. She looks more like a Greta than Greta does, Sam realizes, and Greta looks more like a Rabina. With next to zero filial resemblance, the only similarity Sam notes as he watches her critically observing the space around her is that extraverted confidence.

"So where is she?"

"At the store."

"Okay, then." She smiles, picking up her bag and throwing it with force to the couch near the stereo. She paces near the fountain, touching anything in reach, Sam imagines nothing could calm her down.

"Aren't you s'posed to be at the hospital or something?"

"I work evenings, mostly. Neither of us were expecting you in the morning."

"I'm early."

"I could call her, let her know you're here."

"I could call her too. It's okay, I'll wait." She plops down on the couch next to the bag, her knees spread wide apart. She looks at Sam, where he stands in the kitchen, getting himself a glass of water.

"So you're the older one?" Sam asks.

"Younger." She nods, stretching her jaw like she knows he's trying to get to her.

"You gotta be an adrenaline junkie to do what you do," Sam says, taking a sponge and wiping the counter where he splashed.

She smiles. He's not sure if she has gum or if the strange jaw movement, every so often, is a nervous habit.

"It's the danger you like, then," he says.

"Maybe. But it's a lot more than that. Great sights, the unpredictability of the job. Never know where I'll be. And there's the traveling when fire season's over."

"There can't be many women doing what you do."

"Not a whole lot, but we're out there." She leans back into the couch, lays her arms out along the top of each side. "What you don't see are a lot of African Americans."

"The first black military smokejumpers were the Triple Nickels," Sam says, taken aback by his own enthusiasm. "Think it was called the 555th Parachute Infantry. And it was in Oregon, as a matter of fact, where they trained, it was um—"

"Pendleton."

"You know the story?"

"No. How do you know it?"

"I worked in a naval hospital years ago, a friend there told me a lot of stories about his father, his uncles, his grandfather, it was everybody in his family in the military."

"Yeah."

"Anyway, the Triple Nickels fought forest fires all up along here caused by Japanese balloon bombs."

"Okay," she says, smiling, clearly humoring him. She pops her jaw again.

"I'm surprised I remembered that."

She yawns, stretches her arms up in the air.

"Tired?"

"Got up at five this morning to make the drive."

"Why?"

"It's almost four hours from Redmond to here."

"Trying to get here at nine?"

"I was trying to catch Greta before she left for work."

"She doesn't start until tomorrow."

Rabina gets up and shrugs. "Guess I got it wrong, then."

She walks over to the fountain, puts her finger through the miniature falls, running it back and forth slowly, sensuously through the water. She seems mesmerized for a spell, and then wakes up out of it, turning to Sam.

"Can I get you anything before I go?" Sam asks.

"I'm fine," she says. She flicks the water from her index finger at him, it doesn't reach but the sudden playfulness sets him off balance.

Late after his shift at the hospital, Sam sits in the dark of the parking lot with Abel on the phone. He strokes his thumbnail as he tells Abel about the migraine medication he snagged—his first theft ever—instead of seeing a doctor here for a prescription. He worries aloud about not recognizing Joe, who has thrown himself into Ramadan after years of halfhearted acknowledgment. Sam pulls the lever on the driver seat, and lays it back. He clutches his unzipped jacket together at his chest, and looks up at the canvas ceiling. Finally, he tells Abel about the reopened case, but his friend is uncharacteristically silent.

"I wish I was a drug addict," Sam says, one hand up the sleeve of his jacket, pinching on the soft, wrinkled skin of his elbow.

"No you don't."

"Yes, I do. Then I wouldn't have to think about any of it."

Abel is quiet, and Sam wants to ask about what's going on with him, but at the same time doesn't want to lose focus on himself.

"This call must be costing you," Abel says dryly.

"I upgraded the calling plan."

"Okay."

"Okay, what?"

"Good for you, then, Princess."

"What's up with you, man?"

"Do you remember our last conversation?"

"Yeah."

"So what do you expect?"

"I'm sorry, A."

"The sorries run thin."

"What do you want me to do, then? I didn't mean any of it. I'm just *upset*, okay?"

"It's always all about you."

"I said I'm sorry, okay?"

"Joe told you about the glaucoma, right? He's not doing so hot, really. Not exactly good for business."

Sam sits up in his seat, puts his hands on the steering wheel.

"And, of course, how could you ever feel for Shawn Lamb, but his daughter, you might mention her at some point, you could pay your respects, say a prayer at least," Abel adds with a touch of venom.

"What are you talking about?"

"What do you mean *what am I talking about?*"

"Just what I said, A! Stop fucking around."

"Joe didn't tell you?"

"Tell me *what?*"

"Lamb's daughter was found dead in Santa Barbara. She was a grad student at UCSB. Everything done to your mother was done to her."

"*What?*" Sam says, making a screeching sound with tongue vibrating against the roof of his mouth, his eyes welling up. "Then *he* did it. That monster did it to his own daughter and he killed himself!"

"No, he did not do it, Sam. That's why the case was reopened. It took them a couple months to tie the two together, but that's when they figured out that it wasn't suicide either. He must have been telling the truth about someone else. His daughter must have been the thing the real murderer hung over his head."

"He was there, A, you *know*, he was. You know what they found in my mother."

"He raped her, yes, or they had rough sex, I don't know, Sam, but there was someone else too. There's no more denying it. How can we?"

"*Why wouldn't he name him then*!" Sam screams.

"I don't know, Sam. He's not a squealer. Who knows why he wouldn't name him? He was threatened. Probably afraid to lose his daughter. I mean, who knows."

"Why didn't Joe tell me?" Sam whispers, barely audible.

"Maybe you should just come on home, man. This is all a lot to deal with. I thought you knew. I must have misunderstood Joe."

"Or he left the dirty work up to you?"

"Don't blame him, man. Just quit the damn job in Oregon, Sam. What are you doing there anyway? It's over now with that girl, isn't it? You barely mention her as it is."

Sam breaks down into sobs, Abel makes a shushing sound for a minute, then falls silent again to the point that Sam can't be sure if he's still there. He lets it all out until there's no more left, and when he whispers Abel's name, his friend repeats that he should just come on back home.

"You know what I think?" Greta says to him, as Sam lies in the crook of her arm in bed that night, his tears fully spent from car time with Abel. "I think that in death our energy just splits off and recombines, so you don't have to think of your mother as really gone, you know, that's why you feel her, she's real somewhere around you. Maybe you came to find her here."

"I should go home is what I should do. You know, Joe needs me right now."

Greta is quiet, then she breathes deeply. "You probably should then."

"I hear what you're saying about spirit, though." Sam turns to his stomach, props up to look into her face.

"Yeah." She smiles wide, her gums catching part of her top lip.

He realizes it's this part that makes him crazy for her. "Spirit's like air, don't you think?"

"I don't know."

"And it's never the same air—you know, like you can't step into the same river twice—and so you're breathing it out, gulping it back in again, and it's different. You're changing, you're kinda part of everything else, all the time. Your mother is there somewhere."

As salve for the pain in his stomach every time she said the word "mother" he now bites her top lip, sucks on it so that it will engorge to twice its size, into something he could eat. He pins her shoulders down, hungry now as she meets him. She buckles upward with her pelvis, as in a rodeo, until he enters. He bangs into her as hard as he can, so that she might call out loud enough to disturb Rabina.

The two sisters stand together in front of the stove: Greta, dressed in new khakis and hiking boots, and Rabina, shiny with sweat in her red running shorts and nylon tank. Her short gold hair forms in spikes, lit by the morning sun. Sam pours himself a tall glass of coffee, thinking to himself he doesn't know whom he wants more, and this is proof enough that it's time to go home.

" 'We gotta harvest the trees before they burn down!' " Greta says in a mock Texan voice.

"That's not what he said." Rabina shakes her head.

" 'What happens in these forests . . . they're not harvested, not taken care of, they're like tinderboxes.' " Greta nods cockily, her Texan voice dead-on.

"Well, they can be, Greta. Come on. Some thinning is necessary, and you know I don't mean old growth—"

"You missed it last night, Sam," Greta interrupts.

"You told me when I got home, remember?" He sips his coffee, focuses on Greta, trying to squeeze Rabina out of his vision.

"Sam's totally disinterested in the debates."

"Can you blame him, living with you?" Rabina smiles, winks. "I'll be glad when this is all over."

"It's not about '*healthy forests*' it's about the timber industry," Greta says, getting worked up now.

"Are you forgetting Dad?"

"Dad's retired."

Rabina throws up her hands.

"That man's got no understanding of the disease triangle."

"He's not a *pathologist*, Greta."

"No, but he's pathological."

"I knew you were going to say that." Rabina points her finger at her. "Get out of here, will ya? Aren't you late yet for work?"

"Greta, late?" Sam asks, holding his coffee glass, looking at Rabina in the eyes for the first time this morning. Rabina laughs.

"What's so funny?" Greta asks.

"Greta is *always* late," Rabina says, pointing again, her jaw pops out once.

"That's strange, not once has she been late with me."

"She hasn't been *working*, Sam. Give her a few days, and you'll see what I mean."

Greta flips Rabina off, tucks in her shirt, and kisses Sam fully on the mouth. She looks at him, proudly, possessively, her goofy smile ablaze. He doesn't realize he's sweating too until she gently blows his forehead and into his hair. He watches her walk out the door. Her car isn't out of the drive before Rabina warms up.

"You wanna see a movie?"

"In the morning?"

"This afternoon," Rabina says, not looking at him as he crosses the kitchen to pour a cup of coffee.

"Long as it's over by four, I can go," Sam says, not looking at her either.

22

July's July

July couldn't remember when she became afraid of the dark again. She was as intimidated by and dread-filled of it as she had been as a little girl. She told herself the culprit was the warmth of the bed, the incredible heat emanating from Joe's body in the plush of the sheets and down comforter that forced the idea of getting up to pee—no matter how bursting her bladder—into a most difficult feat imaginable. But she knew that what really kept her from leaving the small universe with Joe was the terror of what seemed to lie on the path of the corridor between the bed and the toilet, the terror of the unknown.

When she tried concentrating on what she knew to be there, the dark bombarded her with phantasms both clear and distorted, but all hideous, all hellish, all evil. She felt inappropriate lying there with surely faulty perceptions and irrelevant value judgments. All that lurked there was entirely of her creation. Exactly how she could give in to this creation would depend upon the strength of her unfounded beliefs, superstitions, and thoughts of victimization. In one word, it was fear, and inside it was empty, erroneous.

And still, she lay in bed, holding her urine.

It was a new year, 1988, and July longed to keep a resolution. On the way to work, she pulled over to a phone booth and called her mother. She kept the door open, leaning out partly into the sun.

She lifted her leg and made a short sucking sound with her tongue when she saw the small run in her stocking, which was two shades too light.

"Best wishes, Mother," July said as soon as her mother picked up the phone.

"Gwendolyn?"

"You have any other children?"

"Not that I know of." Mother laughed, causing July to take the phone from her ear and look at it. July's smile was bright.

"Did you have a nice holiday?"

"Can't complain."

"Wouldn't you like to know how Sam is?" Between her long fingers, July wound the stiff wire connecting the receiver.

"If you would give me your telephone number, you know I'd call him myself to find out."

"No, you wouldn't."

"Try me."

July looked out at the early morning downtown traffic, the wind whisking up her nostrils, and though softened by the sea, the carbon suffocated. She slammed the phone booth door shut. It was quiet, frightening, and intimate inside.

"Gwen." July heard her mother's voice clearly.

"Yes, Mother."

"I said, *try me*."

"I don't want you preaching to him, it's that simple."

"Has the poor boy ever seen the inside of a church?"

"No. And that's because in your mean-spirited ideology, even the Dalai Lama isn't saved."

"No, he isn't, and neither is your Muslim."

"What sense does that make?"

"You're so selfish, Gwendolyn."

"What do you mean?" July asked, getting excited. The recording came on asking for more coins, and Mother spoke over it.

"You think you can just dodge pain while on your foolish earthly hopscotch to happiness. You won't find heaven here."

"Dodge *pain?*"

"That's right."

"Dodge pain with you?" July shoved more coins so hard into the slot she tore the delicate skin and cuticle of her index.

"Dodge pain with anybody."

"While you were so twisted, so contorted by faith, you let that man *beat* me, Mother."

"Is this what you called me for?"

"Didn't you?"

"Girl, you were nine years old and didn't have the sense to tell me."

"*Tell you*, Mother?"

"Well, I didn't STAY WITH HIM, DID I?" Mother roared out, angrier than July had ever heard her.

"God damn you," July said with articulation.

"You're the one who's damned, and you *know* it. Taking the Lord's name—"

July lightly but with purpose put the phone in its cradle.

At her desk, July repeatedly misstepped on the keyboard, her ring fingers lazy and envious of the thumbs. The wait to hear about grad school was becoming fiercely unpleasant. She looked at Joe's picture on her desk and felt love and the grip of guilt.

"That's a nice pin," one of her fellow clerks said to her, coming closer with her pincers extended. "It's a turtle! How lovely!" she said, bending to touch it. The pin sat so close to July's throat that this felt as intrusive as a white stranger reaching out to touch her hair—as if she welcomed strangers' dirty fingers when she wore it natural.

"Thank you," July said with an uneasy, false smile.

"Where'd you get it?"

"It was a Christmas gift from my son," July proudly lied, as Sam hadn't given her anything but an unsigned card.

The clerk gasped. "You're so lucky! My kids didn't even think to wish me Merry!"

"Your kids are all in elementary school, Mariam. What do you expect? My kid'll be fifteen next month."

"Already? My gosh. Meanwhile, you look like his sister."

"I do not."

"Oh, yes you do. Really, I should be so lucky," the clerk said sweetly, flipping her hand and walking off.

The sight of this woman's small pale hand fluttering as if without a care in the world, bothered July. Because they were stuck there, they were both stuck there, and this woman acted as if this weren't the case. She couldn't remember feeling like that since her brief marriage—ready to move on—but she was, and it was too early to feel this way, as her out would still be a while yet.

July's desire for Otis's wanted document that Shawn Lamb said he had but didn't when she last met with him, intensified in itch as she remembered the grandmother she never met was named Rebecca. It was a trivial coincidence that this slave had the same name, but worth infusing with meaning so she may justify the fact that she had to have it in her collection. She hadn't rebuked him for not bringing the document since she felt empathy for him as he went on and on about the daughter he wasn't allowed to see. His pain brought out hers in keeping Sam away from his natural father.

She called Shawn Lamb again and asked him to tell Otis that she would take him up on his offer that the document be a late Christmas present. He said it would take him a few weeks or so to get it.

En route to the lighthouse on a cool Saturday afternoon in late February, July got dizzy up a slow incline in Point Loma. She couldn't understand why she felt such a headache coming on. She turned back around and parked closer to town, where she could call Joe to come get her. The pain seared. Joe told her to buy some aspirin and sit down by the marina. He was due to join a prayer group he'd been putting off for months. July wanted to whine, but then thought she didn't deserve to. She hung up holding her head, asking herself if she really should go ahead and meet Lamb.

Choices seemed no longer debatable since he soon drove up with Otis in the car. She gave into her desire, into her fear, right then and there. Why prolong it anymore with pretense that she didn't want in the car? she asked herself, rubbing her temples, as the throb was deadening. She smelled Otis's breath, mouthwash fresh and medicinal, as he leaned over from the front passenger seat to kiss her where she sat in back. He reminded her of Ernest, when she was younger and confused, and she missed that time before she bore the responsibility of motherhood. She liked the idea of slumming.

"Let's see it," July said, as Lamb looked over his shoulder to pull into what little traffic there was.

"It's at the house just a little ways over here," Otis said, putting his arm around his bucket seat to look at her, his safety belt off, and the warning light on.

"I thought you said you were a longshoreman, Shawn, how can you afford to live over here?" July asked, relaxing now, her headache on the way to forgotten.

"He unloads cargo on the docks, yes," Otis said, and laughed with the sound of phlegm in his throat. "But he's house-sitting."

"Why don't I believe that?"

"Why don't you?" Lamb asked, looking into the rearview mirror at her. Since all July could see were his eyes and nose, he seemed handsome and discoloration free.

Lamb made a left onto one of the partially paved neighbor-hood streets. Devoid of sidewalks, it had the loose, down-home feel of the country, though the seventies ranch-style houses were decidedly upscale. Near the end of the block, he pulled into a long private driveway of small pebbles, enclosed by mature pines. July followed them out of the car into the large garden sprinkled with teak benches, which she stopped to admire. Lamb led her through the back door, where they passed the Italian mosaic service porch and sprawling mauve marble kitchen. She asked for a tour of what she thought was a one-story house, but after languorous pleasure as a voyeur examining the white, middle-aged, childless couple's family photos and placing their personalities in the three starkly contrasting bedrooms and baths, she found that Lamb had saved the best for last, a grandly laid out, dark stained oak paneling game room and bar in the basement. Red leather chairs and books, it had the look of a smoking room though the pool table and dartboard moments recalled an English pub. July felt as though she were traveling without having to leave the city.

Otis mixed Lamb a Manhattan ice tea and poured July a glass of cranberry juice by request. Lamb complimented Otis on the drink.

"I used to bartend, you know," Otis said, his eyes on July as if she were rapturous looking.

"Where was that?"

"All over," he laughed, drinking gin straight. "There isn't a state I haven't been."

"Really?" July asked, then glanced at Lamb, who was quiet and looking uncomfortably at the floor.

"I used to train-hop as a kid," Otis said. He sat down in the chair across from July. "If I liked it, I'd stay and find work as a mechanic, or bartender, or whatever. I can play me some pool."

"A hobo and a hustler," Lamb said. He rubbed his hands as if he were cold, then clasped them and looked up at July.

"What's Ernest up to?" July asked Otis, looking into his eyes, turned on that they'd spent a night together, and have a history in one man.

"Ernest is still married, if that's what you mean."

July smiled, glad to be over it.

"And he's still got a thing on the side," Otis added. July's smile dropped. "You haven't changed either, Gwen."

"I'll never get used to this 'Gwen,'" Lamb said, shaking his head at her.

"So where's Rebecca?" July asked, crossing her legs ladylike.

"Miss *wanted* Rebecca," Otis said, mouth exaggeratedly parted, and smiling. "'The biggest *devil.*'" He laughed. "Bet she made it all the way to the Gullah is-*lands*," he said, going for the requisite accent.

"She burned down a barn, a stud horse, as well as some other general's stable and stockyard," Lamb added with genuine awe.

"Now why do you suppose a slave could do all that, escape five times, and still be wanted *alive* for fifty dollars?" Otis asked in the manner of a game show host, the deep dimple in his chin still vile to her after all these years.

"Where's the document, Otis, you've teased me enough," July asked sharply.

"Well now, humor me, Gwen, and answer the question."

July folded her arms and realized her three-quarter-length sleeves were too tight.

"Well?"

"I'm beginning to think you don't even have it," July said, lips pursed to frowning.

"Oh, I have it all right, but how grateful will you be for it?" Otis asked, his eyes lit, as he leaned toward her. Lamb swallowed, stood, and walked over to the bar to pour himself some water.

"I won't be grateful at all," July said. "Because you can either have some money for it, or keep the damn thing. How desperate could I be?"

"Now, now. Don't get your girdle twisted, Gwen. But you sure are *fine* when you're angry."

"Shawn?"

"Yes?"

"You want to take me back to my car now?"

"I do, as a matter of fact."

"And what makes you think I'm wearing a girdle!" July stood up indignantly. She patted her hips, and straightened her dress that was Saturday afternoon casual but fitted, with a print of the world map. Amply filling her décolletage, she unnecessarily wore a padded bra.

Otis stood too, getting between her and Lamb. "I was just kidding, beauty."

He cupped the side of her face, looked into her mink brown eyes. His thumb caressed her bottom lip, pressing as if trying to make an imprint of her teeth, and she sighed as he kissed it. He brushed his thumb so lightly against her nipple that her clitoris engorged until it hurt. The fizzing sound of his hand on the pantyhose between her thighs was as erotic as the touch. She heard Lamb walk away, ascend the basement steps, and was shocked by her own disappointment. Otis easily lifted her and laid her down on the pool table, pushed her dress up waist high, though she'd have rather he cut it off. He took her finger and made her smell then taste herself, before he entered.

Lamb came running back down when she yelled out, but she wasn't in pain, she was coming. This false alarm must have made him angry, she thought, because Otis was ramming too hard, and Lamb instead of helping her, grabbed her head. She understood then it was Otis who spurred him on, as Lamb stuck himself inside of her mouth. He pushed until she choked and gagged with thick, warm, gooey spit. Though it was Lamb she bit, Otis was the one who slapped her.

"I told you," Lamb said, holding himself, and looking wide-eyed at Otis. July propped herself up with difficulty, and yet she couldn't understand why she wasn't afraid. She wiped her face with the back of her hand, and she smoothed her hair. She glared at both of them with arrogance and hate. She didn't have time to think before rage propelled her off the table, and she yanked down a pool stick. She extended it in front of her with both hands, like a martial artist's staff. Otis was still hard, as he hadn't yet ejaculated.

"Go get the document for this bitch, she *deserves* it," Otis said, grabbing his erection. "And fire it up too!" he called after him. July glanced briefly at Lamb as he lit up the stairs again, and she wondered why he followed Otis's orders like a well-trained dog.

"Now, Gwen, you're gonna have to apologize to the gentleman who just got you off so good," he said, spacing his words so he might appear to maintain his temper. July quickly pulled her bra back up around her breasts. Her dress only wrinkled and hanging crooked, she still felt strong despite the hose and panties on the floor.

"You hear me, Gwen?" Otis said, creeping closer and taking an even calmer tone. Then a foot away, July pointed the cue between his eyes.

"You think you're scaring me?" Otis's eyes blazed. "Lamb!" he called again, getting furious. He stood his ground.

July didn't know her mouth was open, until she felt a trickle of drool run down. This disturbed her since her tongue felt scraped and dry.

"Lamb!" Otis ferociously called again. Lamb came running back down with a rolled poster and some rope. "Open it up for her," Otis commanded, standing there smiling. Lamb unrolled it, July glanced quickly at what was only a bad quality Xerox pasted on laminated poster. "Read it to her."

Lamb slowly read the details of Rebecca's features, her clothes when she disappeared, her crimes against animals and property. When he got to the part about Rebecca having branded and scalped the slave who captured her upon the fourth time she'd escaped, Otis asked him to repeat it. July lost her balance for a moment, and Otis easily grabbed the pool stick from her, turned her body around into him, her neck in a chokehold.

It seemed to her she struggled with everything in her and yet with cruel speed her arms were tied above her head, which she banged twice against the hardwood floor. Her clothes were stripped off her, and she heard Otis sing in a horrid disco voice, " '*Are you ready, are you ready for this? Do you like it, do you like it like this?*' " He sang this as he tore into her, and in a lower bass warriorlike chant, repeated the chorus, " '*Push, push in the bush.*' "

July turned out the lights in her head when the bruising hit her uterus and she concentrated on leaving her body. She was so successful in this that she passed out from the smell of the iron searing into her flesh five times down her back and buttocks to spell the letters SL, "for slut," Otis spit into her ear as her mind entered slow wave sleep. But she couldn't maintain the depth of her sleep when she felt as if the top of her head were missing, and didn't know if it was she or Lamb or Otis who was screaming. Then she felt a bubble of air in her neck and hot liquid pouring down the front of her body.

"It's not me who's dying," she tried to say loud enough for her son to hear, but the words were smothered in her throat. "I am the water, I am the fire, I am the dust, I am the air."

"He can't kill me," she said, without effort through her mouth, as she no longer struggled with her breath.

23

Blood Relative

In the moment of dark just before the trailers in the movie theater, Rabina puts her feet up on the seat in front of her. She makes two comments about race. One references the widely discussed political documentary for which the only part she holds respect is when the African American representatives stood up with no senatorial backing. The second comment inadvertently dismisses Sam, as she squeakily pulls and pushes her straw through the cup cap hole, making little stomping sounds on the ice, then jiggling it in her hand. He hears this noise over her talk of being unfamiliar with the "serious" black actor they are about to see. Rabina adds that she has never been much interested in hip hop, comics, or basketball stars, who seem to be the only African Americans ever on the screen.

Upon deciding she can think of little else in his regard, Sam remains quiet. He reaches for his cup in the ring between them, without looking Rabina lifts the popcorn from her lap to make it easier. He glares at her as if she is offering stale toast, but she doesn't take notice. He grabs a handful of popcorn, and as he puts one kernel at a time in his mouth, she pulls out the Raisinets, looks at him mischievously, rips open the box, and then pours its entire contents into the buttery bucket.

The disharmony continues over lunch at a sweet café in town where they both have salmon sandwiches, Sam a bit paranoid after remembering Greta's mercury warnings. Sitting on a barstool, staring out the window, he can't wait to get to the hospital. He hadn't realized until this moment how attached he's become to a jeweler who just had thirty percent of his liver removed, but with complications. In his late sixties, the jeweler also plays a ragtime trumpet, and has gotten into a game of name-that-tune with Sam, whenever he enters his door.

"Did I tell you I'm going to Costa Rica?" Rabina asks, interrupting his thoughts in an unusually gentle manner. "Next week."

"No," Sam says. He takes a sip of his blueberry lemonade. "How do you keep something like that under your hat?"

"I don't know," Rabina says. She leans back on her stool, running her hand through the spikes in her hair that Sam realizes is gelled. He smiles at this touch of vanity so opposite from her sister. "I don't like bragging. Besides, I've been to a lot of great places, thanks to my job's lengthy time off."

Though Sam smiles, he can still feel the worry on his forehead. He doesn't believe that his mother is always at the source of it, and so wonders if anxiety might be his natural state, his emotion of choice, his psychological addiction.

"My sister seems a bit stuck to me," Rabina offers, again with a soft tone Sam realizes is making him uncomfortable. "The faces and the places might change, but it's still Greta spinning her wheels."

"To what do I owe this so *wanted* analysis?"

"I was going to say that you seem just a bit stuck yourself."

"You're a bitch, you know that?" Sam says, turning the upper half of his body toward her, his upper lip trembling. Rabina grins, and Sam sits there incredulous. "How can I just sit here? How could I sit through you talking about the '*good black*'—"

"I thought you weren't listening to a word I was saying!" Rabina raises her finger, mouth open, but pleased. "I was telling you about being a rookie on a hotshot crew, and thinking it was my fault in getting everyone close to serious trouble. But then it was me who found the *good black*—that is the area that's already burned and safe. It was my first failure and my first success all wrapped into one. Two years of it and I decided to go for jumping then."

Sam looks at her like he won't let her get away with it.

"You don't *believe* me?" She looks at him with the expression, *What's up with you?*

"Nevermind, man." Sam raises his hands only as high as the table in front of them. He leans away from her to get his wallet out of his back pocket, but it is in the wrong direction. With irritation, he leans back toward her to retrieve the wallet from his right pocket.

She smiles at him, but when he looks too meanly at her, she pops her jaw.

"No, I got this," she says, whipping out her money just in time to place it on the bill tray their waiter holds with a neighborly smile that is neither hopeful nor greedy. Vulnerably, she looks at Sam. Her dark blue eyes are bloodshot and watery, but her face is as fresh and young as a soap commercial.

"I gotta get to work," Sam says.

She nods, rolls her tongue over her top row of teeth. He stands up unsure of whether she is flirting, but glad he escapes the moment to find out.

"It takes intelligence and individuality not to be anyone's pawn," Greta says to Sam, who doesn't know why he ever expects anything light to come of her pillow talk.

"Ai, yi, yi," Sam responds while still spooning her, but then rolls over to his side, naked back to hers. With his thighs, he can feel the goosebumps and fine hair on the back of hers.

"I now work for a yes-man, is all, and it's profoundly disappointing."

"All of life is profoundly disappointing, Greta." Sam cradles his own head in the crook of his arm. With aggression, he removes his feet from footsy position with hers.

"Wow," she says. She turns over to look at him, he feels her eyes on his skull. "You really see it that way, don't you?"

"Duh."

"Don't you see how wrong that is?"

"We just had a nice—no—a *really* good time of it, and you launch into the shortcomings of your boss right afterward. Can't you see how disappointing that is? And how things like this happen over and over again?"

"Wow." She then makes a humph sound that rings false. "It's all my fault then?"

"Are you kidding me? Can you be that self-centered?" He turns to face her.

"And can you expand your consciousness for one damn moment?" she asks, propping herself up angrily, her breath hot and milky, just short of foul.

He wants to push her away in every sense of it.

"Can you accept your present? Can you live in the *now*?" Her eyes gleam demonically to him.

"I am living in the *now*, Greta, a now in which I want you to shut the fuck up."

He gets up out of bed, runs to the linen closet, and makes himself a flannel blanket bed in the hallway near the bathroom.

Before work, Greta steps over him. He sneaks a peek at the still stunned and angry expression lining her face. He grabs her ankle before she can pass.

"I'm sorry." He looks up at her from the floor, his hair sticking out on top and matted on the sides like a variant Mohawk.

Greta stares down at him, then pulls her leg from him and continues haughtily down the corridor.

"Never again," he says to himself and slowly shakes his head. Anyone who can't accept an apology, he thinks, doesn't deserve one.

After a shower, he finds the sisters: Rabina, in her running clothes, sitting on the couch bed in the middle of conversation, and next to her, Greta, bending to put on her shoes. Rabina's bare heels dig into the cushion, arms around her knees, her coffee cup held between her legs, and the stereo turned on low.

"You understand that if a lot of thinning were done it could create a lot of stumps that are entrance courts for forest root diseases, as well as uneven aged stands encouraging parasitic plants to spread in the forest," Greta says with gravity.

"Thinning cuts down on fire hazard, and you know that's a fact, Greta. There are millions of acres of clogged forest lands—"

"We're talking about *ecosystems*, Rab, a lot of plant and animal life depending on one another as we depend on them—"

"Since the cutback on the timber industry, we're destroying forests in other countries where little or no management happens. They cut just for our appetite. Now admit it, trees are a renewable resource—"

"Tell that to the dying out tanoaks, Rab, and while you're at it, why don't you give me your argument for the betterment of all animals who are close to extinction."

"Not everything is so bleak. Look at the African woman, the ecologist who just won the Nobel."

"Which is wonderful, we'll take any credit we can get, but still a hell of a lot more people need to pay serious attention."

"Morning, Sam," Rabina says, looking up at him with new ease and familiarity.

"Good morning to you, though I can see that Greta's chopping your head off too."

Greta bears her teeth like a wolf. She puts her hand on her

sister's knee to get up, and rolls her eyes at him as she heads for her car keys on the counter. Sam follows her past the water fountain into the kitchen and grabs himself a tall glass for coffee, bites on the half-eaten muffin he knows is Greta's. He looks at her, hoping for a look of intimacy, but she glances back at her sister, then glares at him, and walks out of the door without a word.

"What did you do?" Rabina asks grinning. She stretches her jaw rather than popping it out once.

"Tried to sleep, as far as I can tell."

"What's that smell?"

"What?"

"That sickeningly sweet smell like . . . magnolia . . . no sandal-wood?" Rabina looks up at him, her eyes bright this morning and full of appreciation.

"Your mother sure invested a lot in charm school on the two of you."

Rabina laughs recklessly, and Sam is surprised to love the sound of it—out of breath, desperate with abandonment. "Your cologne, then," she says, still laughing, she reaches for his hand, and he gives it. He sits down next to her, while she tries to catch her breath.

"My real father actually is charming," Rabina coughs out, trying to make herself stop laughing. "He didn't raise me though, Mom and Dad did, Greta's blood father. He was generous enough to forgive our mother her affair. 'Affairs,' I should say."

"You're lucky then."

"What do you mean?" she asks, smiling in the afterglow of her burst of merriment.

"I never met my father. I've got a picture of him, and that's it."

"Can I see it?"

He looks at her surprised, wondering why no one has ever asked him before. In fairness he remembers Haley. But knowing where it was she had tried to take it from his wallet, and she hadn't asked.

Sam is quick about running to his bag in the bedroom, and pulling it out of the pocket he'd moved it to after feeling spooked by Shawn Lamb's death. He thought he might have been causing all of the bad luck by keeping the father he never met so close to him. Like it was spitting in Joe's face, as karma licked back at him for it.

He hands her the photo with a shaky thumb and forefinger. She takes it from him, and he notices her nails are jagged and bitten.

"That's something," Rabina says, raising her beautifully arched and natural brows.

"Hmn?"

"Your eyes are much bigger than his, but there's the same intensity. That 'I am' intensity."

" 'I am'?"

"I am. I exist. It's not unlike my mother. Greta show you her picture?"

"No."

"There must be one around here somewhere," she says, looking around and passing his father's photo back to him. She gets up, the sweaty nylon shorts sticking to her. He wonders why he can't smell her.

She looks around the few shelves, wanders through the hall, and he follows her into the bedroom. She looks on the top of the spare and austere industrial-style vanity, then opens a few of its drawers.

"You can't do that," Sam says, offended.

She opens the rest of them, digs around.

"Invading her privacy like that," he continues. She puts her hands on hips and looks around the room for any clues she might have missed. "How do you have the right?"

She dismissively flicks her hand at him, looks up at the glass ceiling, and the trees above their heads.

"Every second I have the opportunity to like you a little, you snatch it back from me."

"*Pobrecito.*"

"Where'd *you* learn Spanish?"

She grins at him. "This is an incredible bedroom, isn't it?"

"It is," Sam says, and looks at her.

She grabs his cheeks and chin like an overzealous auntie, causing him to pucker. She laughs at the look of it. Then she kisses him on the mouth, moves her grasp down to his throat. If she grasped any tighter he'd choke, but her temerity makes him hard. He can smell her now, even underneath the overpowering sweetness of his cologne. And he can feel that, like the married Tallulah Larkin, his first real lover, she is into punishment as she pushes him sharply onto the bed. He rolls from his back to his side, afraid. His lips hum with her.

"What's the matter with you?" Rabina whispers softly into the back of his neck before biting in. She grabs onto his cock, and he pushes her away. He sits up, equilibrium beyond reach.

"Can I have a little privacy?"

Rabina gets off the bed, her elegant brows knit, her pert nose flared. Without a trace of self-consciousness, she tugs the nylon shorts out of the crack of her rump, and walks out. She reminds him of a superhero. As he watches her figure until it disappears around the bend of the hallway, it's as if his mother takes shape in her absence, and hurries toward him with heat. Her image seems to have collided with him so fast that he can't see or feel where she went. He looks above him at the trees. The late morning light stipples the leaves so brilliantly they appear to be ablaze. He calls out to July, and he can't be sure if the burning trees are a vision or a sign.

*   *   *

Sam cannot know how he got on the floor, his head precariously close to the wooden chest at the foot of the bed, his tongue sore, like he'd clamped down hard on it. He licks his bottom lip and it stings as if split. His heart thumps with panic, wondering if someone had broken in and knocked him out. Grounding his palms, he pushes his way up to a seated position, then dizzy, takes his time in standing up. Everything in the room looks as it did before, and through the glass, the forest sits serious and undisturbed, not even by mild breeze. The incident with Rabina returns. He calls for her but hears no response. When he looks at the clock radio it's past noon, but he can't remember the time he'd noted when they first walked into the bedroom. His phone sits next to the clock, so he picks it up and dials Haley, who isn't there. The hesitation to leave a message is so long that it makes the decision for him, and so he hangs up without saying anything.

When Sam returns home from his hospital shift at midnight, lights out, he sees no sign of Rabina. Greta is already in bed, pretending to be asleep, as far as he can tell. She is on her back, wears a thin, gray knit T, the long sleeves pulled up over half her hands though her arms are up stretched. The full moon glows hallowed yellow through black and blue branches that are eerily alive. Greta appears like a sickly goddess under a spell awaiting the kiss of a powerful and evil prince, who can reverse the curse, and unleash it upon the world.

Sam strips down to his briefs, slips under the covers next to her; the warmth escapes its trap and wraps him in gratitude. She doesn't stir. From his easy view on the pillow, he gazes at the slopes and curves of her face until she is magnified, giant. He frightens himself with the thought that she is dead. Even as her chest rises and she slowly turns her face away from him, he can't control the expectation that he will rob her of something, maim her with his stare. He wants to touch the gentle litheness of her neck that seems tense as a bow when she's awake. He wants to trace the fragile intricacy of her veins.

He goes behind his own eyes for the pixilated color and trails of blood. He is relieved to be a dreamer, watching himself, and not his mother, acting upon lusts. It isn't this house, and it isn't the one he grew up in, but rather a version of his and Joe's that he shows Rabina the way through. The only traces of his mother are her documents, haphazardly nailed up here and there. When they get to Sam's room, it is outside somehow, and Rabina playfully stands on her head, brags of being a gymnast. He is quick to enter her, just like that as she stands on her head. Though she enjoys herself, he can also see her face compounding in red until it is about to burst. She could crack her neck. He lays her down. She laughs, and it's easy, because they are lying in the grass of his room, and he's happy. Even when she pulls out a knife and asks him to play that he's raping her. He needs a little convincing, which she does amorously enough, and while he's inside of her with his hand over her mouth, the other hand holds the knife to her throat. He's flooded with the warmth of his own come, and doesn't realize it is Rabina's blood until he opens his eyes.

"I have violent dreams," Sam confesses to Joe on the phone, as he sits on the ground outside in the cold.

"It's natural, son."

"I mean, dreams where I am the perpetrator."

"Still say it's natural. What is not is to pay them no mind."

"What do you mean?"

"Over and over getting the same sign in your dreams? Read it."

"Read what?"

"Read the damn sign in front of your face!"

"Why are you getting so mad?"

"I'm not getting mad."

"You are."

"I'm *not*."

"*Now*, you are."

"Times like this you remind me of your mother."

"She had violent dreams?"

"She insisted on her own assumptions, pressed until they came true."

"Did she have violent dreams?"

"Don't know. Would suppose so, like everybody else. But she never woke me up in a sweat."

"So you never had to tell her to read the 'damn sign' in front of her face?"

"Boy, don't you *ever* imply that I didn't look out for that woman, because I did. You know that." Joe spits.

"Well, I'm calling you, Joe, like she did. I'm feeling sick and dizzy like she said she was. You gonna come pick me up quickly this time?"

Joe hangs up on Sam, the chill filling his throat, as he wishes he could take back what he just said.

24

To the Lighthouse

Citing family emergency in the morning after his mother came clearly to him, Sam leaves notice for his boss at the hospital. He says good-bye to his favorite patient, the jeweler, who is still unconscious under anesthesia, after a third surgery. For Greta, who has already left for work, he doubles back to the house with an envelope holding two weeks' pay and a torn piece of map from his car, a section of Oregon with the town Florence at its center.

"Where are you going?" Rabina asks, startling Sam, who jumps in the kitchen with the envelope still in hand.

"Where'd you come from?"

"I'm staying in a motel in town."

"But where's your car?"

"I ran."

"But Greta's not here."

"I know that."

Not knowing where to leave it, he bends the envelope in half, puts it in his back pocket, and folds his arms. Not wanting to betray Greta the private romance of the torn map, he looks at Rabina hoping she won't ask what he has.

"So where are you going?" she asks again, grins.

"San Diego."

"What's in San Diego?" With the back of her hand she wipes the sweat from the side of her neck.

"Guess we all can't go to Costa Rica."

"Why the hell not. What's stopping you?"

"Are you kidding?"

She looks at him like she couldn't care less. "Are you in a hurry this morning?"

Sam studies her curiously.

"Well, are you?" she repeats.

"Why?"

"I really feel like going to the lighthouse. I was wondering if you might want to come with me."

Sam's face inflames with shock and anger. "What do you know about it, Rabina? Are you trying to play with my head?"

"The working lighthouse. Yaquina Head, not Yaquina Bay. The one with the twelve-foot-high Fresnel lens. What do you mean *play with you*? Why are you getting so mad?" She stretches her jaw, pops it to the right, then the left.

He stands there speechless.

"What's the matter with you!" she asks loudly now, using her lips as if he were hard of hearing.

"That's where I'm going," he answers so quietly, he's not sure if he really responded. It is as if Rabina actually was there when his mother came to him, standing in front of the lighthouse.

"You're going to the lighthouse?" Her face quizzical now, melting as if they were truly simpatico, and she'd known it all along.

"In San Diego," he says, his face breaking into a smile. His eyes well up.

"Oh. Come on then." She puts her hands on her hips, standing her ground.

"There are two of them there, too," he says, trying not to cry.

"I'll go with you," she says.

"How do you know I'll have you?"

"You'll have me."

"What about Costa Rica?"

"I'm still going."

"But how can you just drop everything and go?"

"Drop what? I told you I'm off, and doing whatever the hell I want when I'm off is the whole point of it."

"Okay—" He clears his throat, looks shyly at her. Wondering why she knows she is supposed to be there with him. "Okay, okay, then."

After the rigmarole of driving to her motel, waiting for her to pack, then returning in separate cars to Greta's so that Rabina can leave hers in the drive, Sam forgets about leaving Greta the envelope. And this even while Rabina takes the time to write her sister of her whereabouts. Rabina takes Sam's wheel. He lies back in the passenger seat, content to watch her nodding and humming to the classic rock stations of every town they pass through on the 101.

After a late lunch in Bandon, Oregon, overlooking the marina, and dinner in a twenty-four-hour Eureka diner, Rabina drives straight through the night, Sam waking up to the car parked in the lot of a lemon yellow country style inn at sunrise. Not sure of where he is in California or whether Rabina just left him there, he wants to get out and hug a redwood. He puts down the window, breathes in, and can smell a river, hear it too.

Rabina walks toward the car. He never realized how cowboy-like her swagger is. Her pretty petite face remains a contradiction. She chomps on gum. She puts her sunglasses on, opens the car door that screeches long and painful, and she slams it shut as if to punish it for the noise. He looks up at her, feeling as if he was in high school and had a crush on the coolest girl.

"No luck," she says, turning on the ignition.

"Where are we?"

"The Russian River."

She drives slowly, eyeing vacancy signs, obviously being choosy.

"Got any more?" he asks.

"What?"

"*Gum*," he says, as if she were daft.

As she drives, she leans to get the pack from her back pocket. She hands it to him without looking.

"THIS IS A HATE FREE COMMUNITY," Sam reads the sign aloud.

"Looks like we'll just be missing the Russian River Massacre."

"Massacre?"

"It's a party." She grins, looks at him slyly.

"How can you joke with me like that, *all the time*?"

"Lighten up!"

"And I've got to take a leak," he says.

"Hold it," she snaps, playfully. And three minutes down the road, she pulls into a hotel lot, jumps out of the car, and heads for the manager door.

With his hands clasped in prayer between his legs, he sticks his head out of the window, looks up at the sky, so thankful to be derailed by Rabina.

In their room of two double beds, Sam falls asleep on top of the spread, as Rabina leaves for a run. She wakes him up a half hour later when she returns, and heavily shuts the room door.

"How was your run?" Sam asks in a hoarse voice.

"Good. Beautiful here, isn't it? But what would you know, locked up in here?" She grins, enters the bathroom, slamming that door shut too.

The minute she is behind it, his heart goes lonely. He sits up slowly, feeling lost. The hurry to get to the lighthouse is gone, as if his mother is stalling him. He pulls his wallet out of his pocket, amazed that he slept with it there in the car all night. The envelope for Greta is still in the other. He pulls that out, counts some money to reimburse Rabina for the room. He is comforted to hear the toilet flush. He waits for her to leave the bathroom, but he hears the shower go on, and he worries for his sanity. His cell phone rings, the number on the screen is Haley's, and he notes her impeccable timing.

"Haley, I'm so glad you called."

"How are you doing, Sam?"

"I'm okay. How about you?"

"I heard about Lamb's daughter," she says carefully. "It's so awful, baby. This has gotta be so painful."

"I don't know what to think, what to feel anymore."

"They've got a suspect, they haven't caught him yet, you knew that, right?"

Sam breathes in, holds it.

"You knew that, right?" she repeats. He exhales as if he might burst. "Joe told me yesterday. He's looking really haggard, Sam. But my guess is I don't look so hot myself, Joe even said so."

"I don't believe that."

"Believe it. And if Joe's telling the truth, his eyes aren't that good, so I must really be looking bad. I'm fucking up Sam. Big time."

He is silent, looking at the light under the crack of the bathroom door, listening to the shower water.

"Where are you? In that girl's house or at the hospital?"

"In a town called Guerneville. I'm back in California."

"You're coming home!"

"I'm stopping in San Diego first."

"Why you want to torture yourself for?"

"I just need to go. I never went to the spot, you know?"

"I'll go with you."

"No, Haley, it's okay. I'll see you when I get home."

"You're with Greta," she says, gritting her teeth, he can see her.

"Actually, no."

"You're alone?"

"No."

"Then who are you with?" Haley asks, failing to contain her anger.

"I'm with Greta's sister."

"*God.*" She huffs. "*God*, fuck you, Sam. You know that? You're nothing but a womanizer," Haley pronounces the words slowly and thickly with disgust, as if she had never before uttered any of its syllables.

Sam sits there, holding the phone, glad to be scolded.

"You're a shit. You are a *shit*!"

"Haley—"

"Don't. Don't you dare," she roars. She makes a revving up sound. "Why do I take this shit? I'm not taking it anymore. YOU HEAR ME?"

Out of the bathroom walks Rabina, nude, her hair dripping wet, she takes a corner of the towel and wipes annoyingly at her ear. She looks at Sam as if he were her cousin, her little brother, someone close but whom she was hoping would be out of the way for a spell, to give her a break.

"I do hear you," Sam says, with a pitiful tone. He looks up with big eyes at beautiful, golden, wet Rabina, and is surprised not to be turned on. Grateful is the only feeling he can get up at the moment.

Haley cries on the other end. He holds the phone to his ear, wanting to cry with her. Rabina strips off the other bedspread, plops back on the tight blanket, grabs the TV remote, and turns it on. Cutting down the volume is an afterthought as she surfs the morning news channels. She settles on one for a moment, the remote lying between her small, strawberry-pink nippled breasts.

Sam gets up and takes the phone into the bathroom. Haley's still crying, and it is as if he takes his heartache away with her own.

"Haley, we have separate beds. It's not what you think. She came along, and I didn't refuse the company. It's really that simple. Don't make it more than it is. Okay?"

"Fuck you," she cries.

"I love you. I really really do. And I'll see you when I get home."

"Don't bother, Sam. Just don't bother."

"I love you."

He waits for her to hang up, but she keeps on crying.

"I gotta go," he whispers. "I'm on roam. This is costing Joe a fortune. I owe him so much as it is."

"You're damn right," Haley spits. "Good-*bye*."

When he leaves the bathroom, Rabina is fast asleep on her back, head on two pillows, her chin looking uncomfortably wedged into her chest. Her titties look so kissable, suckable, her abdomen like a beautiful mound leading to a more beautiful mound. He stands there staring. Even though her head lies in such an awkward position, her face is as serene as a pre-Raphaelite painting. He slips the remote from her small, tough hand, covers her with his bedspread, and goes out for a long walk.

In the afternoon, they canoe together up the green river. It's wonderfully warm for October, people swim, dogs wade, and kayakers wave as they pass. Rabina is bossy with the oar. She sits behind him, steering. She grunts when he lets the boat swerve the wrong direction. He realizes that annoyance is one of her more comfortable emotions, and so he goes with it. That's when she speaks a little about her mother and how much of a mistake she'd made Rabina to be. She also speaks about her generous step-father. All of this between his choppy rowing, and her snappy corrections. He looks up at the houses along the river, wishing he could buy one, settle down with Haley, and make a new start. The more Rabina rambles, the more she drops her pronouns, like

Joe. He realizes how much she reminds him of Joe, comfortable in her skin, blunt but caring. When she snaps again at him, he thinks better of it. Maybe she doesn't remind him of anyone else at all. He turns around to look at her, and she grins at him with affection.

Over lunch, she takes a piece of bread from his salad plate, replacing it with five or six fries. When he asks her why she did that, she replies that he wasn't eating it but that he had scarfed down his rice. He tells her that the bread is worth more than a few fries. So she takes the half that almost touched her lips, bites it off, and puts it down, this time on his lunch plate. He folds his arms, scoots his chair an inch from the table. She daintily wiggles her fingers at the waiter to bring the check.

Without speaking, they walk down the street until they spot a pool table through a bar window. She points to it with her thumb and raises her brows twice like a saucy wink. He follows her in, and as they make change from the bartender, Sam realizes it's a leather bar, and how many gay couples, men and women, rather than buddies he's seen.

Rabina punches in the change, the balls drop down hard, and he likes the sound of it. She racks them up with gusto on the red felt tabletop.

"Wanna break?"

"Nah, you do it," he answers, standing back to watch. She looks good in her jeans as she bends over.

"So is your last name Bends too?" he asks, eyeing her ass.

"No, it's Alexander. I took my mother's maiden name." She breaks it hard, knocking in a stripe.

A hetero couple looks through the window at them.

"Bet we're bad for business," he says, as she practices her shot before knocking another in.

"What do you mean?" She straightens up, and rounds the table, without looking at him.

"Straight couples might come in here, drive away the leather boys."

She concentrates on her shot, hits but misses. He takes the stick from her, before she's ready to let go of it.

"Bartender seems bored too," Sam says, glancing at him before he sizes up the table.

"I *am* a lesbian, dumbass." Rabina puts herself in his line of vision. Sam stops where he is, stands the stick in front of him. His eyes getting bigger.

"Why'd you come onto me, then?" he spurts out.

"I felt like it."

"You play with just anybody?"

"No. I don't. I like you." She grins. "Not like that. I don't know what I was doing. I just felt like it."

"This about Greta?"

"No, not anymore."

"Oh, not any*more*."

"She told me everything you're going through. And, I don't know. I feel for you, is all."

"You pity me?"

"You feel anything like pity coming from me?"

"No."

"Well, then. Shoot."

Sam stands there for a while looking stupid, and then he chooses a solid to hit. The white ball goes in with it.

Rabina grabs it from the return, takes the stick from him, and chalks the end. She gazes at him knowingly; he seems to hear her tell him not to whine, though she says nothing. She then takes her aim at the green striped ball, smacks the orange striped into the left corner pocket.

"I'm hot tonight," she exclaims, and he stands there not knowing whether or not he wants to slap her.

25

Death's July

The body was found bright early morning in the dense evergreen shrub, lemonadeberry. Minute white hairs stood on end of the tough, leathery, wax-covered leaves, its rose-pink clusters in bloom. A Cabrillo Park ranger had spotted the long limbs, though the canopy of saltbrush partially hid the fleshy view on a steep slope off the Bayside Trail, just half a mile from the old lighthouse.

The body was nude, posed as if thrown down the hill, and badly scraped by chaparral. The left leg was bruised and blood blistered around fang marks of a rattlesnake, disturbed by the body's fall. Part of the scalp was removed: a three-inch-wide strip cut just behind the widow's peak to the main branch of the occipital artery at the back of the head. The larynx and jugular were slashed. The back was branded by an iron, in the form of the letters SL. Upon the medical examiner's determination, there was extensive genital abrasion and hemorrhage, as well as damage to the cervix.

Joe's missing person's report hadn't been official for forty-eight hours, so he wasn't called to identify the body for five days. Told he was lucky she was found, he lost his temper so hotly his vision blurred and tunneled. Because the police arrested Shawn Lamb within a week and a half of discovery, the body was retained for evidence and, after some complications, not released for burial until after two months. At first Lamb said he did not know a Julia Brown. When shown her picture he admitted he had met her as July, but maintained his innocence. He would not say if he knew who killed her or where, when indicted.

Ava was the first to talk to Joe about the tarot card reading that had warned July about Shawn Lamb. Yvonne Cook agreed he was an obvious psychopathic monster, and emphasized how she couldn't wait to get July out of the church parking lot where he'd stalked her. From this point on, anyone who had only met July jumped on the wagon that she had been well forewarned. Those closer chastised Joe for never noticing her stalker. On the evening of Sam's birthday, both Ava and Yvonne asked the fifteen-year-old directly if he would want to move in with them. Joe was furious, and started proceedings for adoption, which dragged on without end, he felt. Since Sam did not have his birth certificate, it was at first difficult to track down any record of a child born to Julia Brown of Memphis, Tennessee. When no transcripts for Julia Brown turned up at UCLA, Joe finally opened the mail he'd kept private: a rejection from UC San Diego and an acceptance from San Diego State University, both addressed to a Gwendolyn Purvis in care of Julia Brown. When Joe gave the adoption court this information, he was told they had already obtained the hospital birth certificate of Gwendolyn Purvis of Los Angeles and that the birth father, Wayland Griggs, as well as the deceased's mother, Mavis Maud Purvis, had been contacted. Even so, on the grounds of no previous contact or support, Joe was able to seek that the birth father's rights were terminated. Griggs did not contest, Mavis Purvis never answered, and Joe never asked how they stayed ahead of him on July's real identity.

"July often spoke of Memphis," Ava said to Joe upon the eve of Lamb's plea and sentencing. He sat glassy-eyed and frigid at the dining table beneath the officelike frames of sports heroes and political icons in the aquamarine room, where Ava and July spent so many Saturday afternoons with the tarot.

"She missed it a lot, you know. She said it was funny she could have lived in Tennessee so long and never visited Nashville. Just imagine it, our July singing country! In the car, she'd put on that country station, try and show me how it was related to the blues. She always told me she could play a mean blues song on the guitar, but she'd never do it. She'd ask me, when some song was on the line—'Now is this blues or is it country, Ava? What do you think!' She'd get so excited. The music drove me mad, but I loved to see her lit up so."

Joe knew July had gone to UCLA, but she had refused to discuss Memphis with him. And she'd never mentioned fantasies of singing, ever before. She certainly never played country in the house. Now he knew she'd been lying to him all that time, lying to them all, and covering up a past that shouldn't have been more complicated than a husband. Joe was there that night, after all, when she met Shawn Lamb. There was no use confusing the prosecutor with her false past. If there were even a hint of her meretricious ways, this would only give them reason to say she'd asked for it.

"Joe?"

"What?"

"You can't put it all on yourself." Ava's expression was so serious she appeared angry. "You're an honorable man. I didn't mean anything by Sam. Other than thinking, well, maybe he needed a woman in his life, you know, a mother figure. You're going to be a fine father, by him, anyone can see that. You already have been. Forgive me for asking." She had her hand on his back, caressing it in a small circular motion. Her face softened, still her miffed-doll features were intractable.

"She probably can't even play that guitar, she's such a liar," Joe spit out, and regretted it right after.

"Maybe she couldn't. And I know she lied to you about that monster, but I don't think they were having an affair, Joe. She might have toyed with the idea, but I don't think she went through with it. That's why he raped her."

Joe's back hunched with the punch to the gut. Ava rubbed him there, until he shook his head as if his skin crawled.

"Ava, would you please leave now?"

She stood up, her hand just at the top of his spine, the base of his neck. Her fingers did a swift ending massage of the knots. "It was in the cards, Joe," she said in a soft, lulling voice. "It was there in the cards for July to do something about. It's not your fault, you hear me? It's not your fault."

After Ava was gone for a long while, Joe got up to look for the guitar. He felt like destroying it, banging it against the wall into tiny pieces. He got so angry staring at it, dusty but arrogant in its corner, that his mouth was open; and like the water from his eyes, the drool escaped. Sam was asleep on the other side of the wall. So he put the guitar in the trunk of the car, promising himself he would sell it after court in the morning.

The semen collected from the victim's mouth swabs was identified as blood type A and PGM 2+1+, matching Shawn Lamb. The blood type and PGM of the semen on the vaginal swab did not match Shawn Lamb (or Joe), which lent some credence to Lamb's claim that there was another killer. That and the fact that the murder weapon was never found. Due to what could be only circumstantial evidence—the SL branded in July's skin, Lamb's semen in her mouth, and Yvonne Cook's statement that Lamb stalked her—the prosecutor didn't feel he could get a trial conviction of first-degree murder with special circumstances. He offered Lamb a deal, a plea bargain for second-degree murder. Lamb took it, pleaded guilty. He was sentenced eighteen years to life.

26

Of the Airwaves

Before they leave the Guerneville hotel room, Sam takes the bottle out of his bag in front of Rabina, spritzes his neck, and at both sides the air about him.

"Kinky." Rabina grins, as do her nostrils most unusually.

"What?"

"The perfume," she says, taking it from him. He feels violated, and wanting to be so. "Aliage," she reads, curling her lips with too much delight. "That's such an old brand." She brings the bottle up to her nose, smelling near the line of the silver cap. "Have you always been into women's perfume?"

Sam swallows, takes it from her, and looks at it. "It was my mother's."

"You've kept it all this time?" Her glee lessening.

"No one else has ever touched this bottle."

"Sorry."

"And it gives me a headache." He looks at her, his eyes huge with self-recognition and relief.

"Gives *me* a headache." Rabina grins again. "Smells *awful*. So cloying, like pine needle–scented bug spray, or something."

Sam narrows his eyes at her, his fingers wrapped around the bottle. "It was beautiful on my mother. Like marzipan. Like acres of green, and . . . *wild*flowers."

"Which wildflowers?"

Sam puts the bottle back in his bag, and zips it up noisily.

"You ever think it's the perfume making you sick all this time?"

"It's my mother, coming to me," he says, not looking at her. He finds the car keys on the bureau and stuffs them in his pocket. "You have the room card?"

"Right here." She picks up her own bag, then puts it back down on the bed. "How does your mother come to you?" she asks. "By the smell of her?"

"I don't want to talk about it."

Her eyes go fiery and Sam feels faint at the sight of them. As if July had entered Rabina's body, then changed her mind. He looks around the room for his mother, and startled, Rabina steps back.

"What's going on, Sam?"

"We need to just go." He touches his temples, and walks out the door.

Rabina picks up the bags. Sam goes straight to the car and sits at the steering wheel. He deeply breathes in fresh air, and takes the top down on the convertible. He plays with the steam of his breath as if it were smoke.

"Hurry up," Sam says to Rabina over breakfast in a coffeehouse the next day in San Diego.

She glares at him, then leisurely places a bite of almond croissant in her mouth, powdered sugar at the corners, he would like to wipe off. She wears a baseball cap, making her head appear all the smaller, like a peanut. Wishing she weren't so cute, Sam gathers up the trash on their small round table.

"What's gotten into you?" she asks.

"It's time to go, is all. I'm ready."

"Damn everything else." She shakes her head, still chewing, eyeing him from under the bill of her cap.

"I'm ready to go to Cabrillo Park."

"Okay. That's all you had to say."

Sam stands with his arms folded.

"I thought this was about last night." She looks up at him, fully, her nose so pert it snubs him.

"Under other circumstances, it would be."

"Look, I just thought it would make things less complicated on the road if I said I was gay. You seemed to think so when we first met, so I thought why not."

"As a matter of fact, I never thought so. But you chose to lie to me, then take it back while we're sleeping in the same bed?"

"I'm around guys all the time, you know, for my job. I'm one of them, I'm a bro. I didn't expect you to treat me the same way. You barely notice me."

"*What?*" he asks, irritated.

She stands up, taking her coffee with her.

"It's just a weird thing happening to me. Biological clock, I guess. I love my job, but I want more, I think."

"With *me?*"

"Don't flatter yourself."

"Who's the lucky guy or gal, then?"

"Are you still into my sister?"

"You're asking if I'm over Greta."

"Are you staying away from me out of allegiance to her?"

"It's over between me and her, period. Now let's go. The park opens in half an hour, that's when I'm supposed to be there."

"We couldn't be half an hour away."

"My mother will be there when the park opens."

Rabina doesn't look at him like he's crazy. Grateful he takes her by the hand, still sticky with croissant, and leads her to the car. It's disagreeably sunny, the warmth unnatural with the knot in his gut, the cold, hard wound he feels like an animal going off alone to die. The pain couldn't be fresher than if he were fifteen, and in those first few weeks of paralytic shock. All those years in between were numb in comparison. He'd walked through them just fine, and grown up without her.

Rabina chews gum, her elbow hanging out of the passenger window. Her shades are as disproportionately wide as a welder's safety glasses, and together with the cap, she looks like a sporty bug. As they drive up past the welcoming houses of Point Loma, some festive with pumpkins and cotton cobwebs for the coming holiday weekend of hallowed saints, Sam feels at once comforted and resentful, thinking of Rabina having thrown out his stolen medication for the migraines. She'd argued that this is what had given him the seizure in the first place, but as he passes the second to the last neighborhood street before the climb to the park, he gets a knife of pain in his temple. He wants to turn down the street, but doesn't feel sure that this is what he is supposed to do, as sure as he is that he should get to the lighthouse. Though he hadn't put on the perfume, he also hadn't taken a shower, his mother's scent musky and faint with sleep.

"Where is she buried?" Rabina asks, as they pass the veteran's cemetery diligently aligning both sides of the street. The western half on their right is a sprawling coastal view with bowing trees. She takes her shades off to look at their fairytale framing of frightful, uniform, white headstones dotting the green grass velvet against a bowl blue ocean and reflective glass sky.

Sam speeds up, holding his shoulders stiff, not intending to answer, not yet thinking about visiting his mother resting on the other side of town, which is not noted on tourist maps. She couldn't be resting anyway, he thinks. She hasn't left him alone since Lamb was let out of prison.

"It's beautiful," Rabina says. Sam looks at her as if she's kidding. She stares out the window at the barbed wire fence for the Space and Naval Warfare Systems Center, adding quickly, "Except for right here."

The park gate is just open up ahead, and Sam rushes it as if all 840 acres might disappear before he can find July. Rabina gives a comrade's smile to the ranger taking the fee. As she sees the lighthouse, she's in every bit as much of a hurry to explore it as Sam is to take the Bayside Trail. At the sign, she tells him she'll catch up with him on the trail. There they split up.

Sam makes his way down the path, locking his knees uncomfortably. His toes braise the front insides of his trainers. Soon, all he can feel is the ill fit of his shoes, the arches in the wrong place, the zipper too tight at the top. The sea breeze irritates him with gentleness against his face and neck. He should like to be pushed down against the grade of the old military defense road, knocked and scraped through the serrated sage scrub covering the slopes. Listening to the ripening speed of his own breath, he looks up at the sun spotting him on his way, and he wishes to burn underneath its rays until he is nothing but a fire scar on the landscape.

But there are no such marks of his mother on the terrain. He imagines Rabina flying above him in a DC-3, an Otter, or whatever else she prefers, the colorful streamers floating on the wind, as she stands at the door, ready to jump. With her jet eyes, she can find his mother's heat signature, her parachute ripples like a jellyfish, expanding into a mushroom cap, and she sails directly in her balloon for a skillful feet-together land. Mother and son, she could dig through to their hot spots, mop up, and carry them both in the pack out.

Sam stops in his tracks. He turns around and faces the top of the hill toward the old lighthouse, which he can't see. If he went a few yards down, he could just make out the new lighthouse at the tip of the peninsula, near the wastewater treatment plant.

"Rabina!" he calls, at once wanting her to hear him, and not. "RA-BI-NA!" he calls again, sounding rabid and desperate. He can see a father and son take their eyes away from the pay telescope on an observation point, a World War II bunker. They peer down at him. Sam turns around, veering off the path to scale the hill and fall, so his mother might catch him.

More likely to make the collar would be a ranger, he thinks, picking himself up, dusting off the seat of his brown denim pants. Near a rattlesnake warning he jumps to clear a bush, as if a northern red diamond—the one who bit his mother—hides there to prove the sign correct. As Sam carefully steps through a random circle of sage back to the trail, he is stopped in his tracks by a tall, hoary, fawn-colored man with short peppered kinks and a benevolent stare. This pitying, kindly look in the man's eyes is enough to split his head.

"Are you a snake charmer?" the man smiles, a dimple in his chin like a black hole.

"Excuse me?"

"One of those Deep South Pentecostal handlers?" the man laughs baritone and hard with a rasp.

"You see any snakes around here?" Sam asks, getting heated and dizzy. He stands purposefully on the ground, feet together, looks at his shoes, then back at the man, who eyes him seriously.

"Live around here?"

"No, do you?"

Peevish lines crosshatch between the man's brows, then he smoothes them in recognition.

"You're Gwen's boy," he says.

"I don't know any Gwen," Sam answers quickly, licking then biting his bottom lip.

"Well, you look just like her." The man gets closer, his paunch peeking out of his half-zipped hooded sweat jacket. Sam still stands firm, trying hard to listen to his mother, who seems to be trying to come in on the wrong frequency.

"You're mistaking me for somebody else," Sam says strongly in a high voice.

"What are you doing over here off the path?" he asks.

"What business is it of yours?" All of him so hot, his pits well up, his thighs sticky under his pants.

"You even *smell* just like her," he laughs again, the rasp wetter and thicker with phlegm. "July."

Everything goes quiet and slow in Sam's head—realization, actuality. Soft, and somnolent, it is the deadlock beat just before rage.

"Sam!" Rabina calls a few yards up the hill. He hears her but he can't see anything except the ending of his mother's life in front of his face.

"Who's that? Your girlfriend?" The old man's tongue makes a pit stop between his teeth, looking as if it could roll out like a rug to the ground before rounding his mouth and disappearing behind a smirk.

"Sam," Rabina calls again, getting closer with a dry, cutting voice. "I need to get home *now*. Let's go."

"Taking me for the spotted-face shitbox, son?" the man asks under his breath, intended for Sam's ears only. "Lamb's dead now, like your mother."

"Sam's neck muscles clench, blood squeezed to rush.

"So how'd you know I'd be here today?" The man leans closer to Sam. Rabina turns around and runs. "What's that bitch's problem?" he asks, pointing with his thumb.

Sam lunges for him, and the blow to his jaw feels like nothing but the taste of iron, there are no nerve endings to him now with his brain so wide awake and rushing. The old man is bigger and stronger in the crush, though not as quick to the kicking. Sam hears the long low grunt over his own breath, and the slam against his knee, but in the squeeze, he won't lose his grip on the wet, soft flesh. And it spits at him, then a splat, and the smell so loud now it feels as if his entire head is swelling up to a close. His fingers tight, raw, and stuck hard at the knuckles, not even the slam to his back can knock it out of Sam. He doesn't see Rabina until the shakes take him out and he lets the old man go rolling down the hill, howling.

27

Overcast

Not until Joe makes the turn off Highway 62 in Twentynine Palms does Sam's head surge with endorphins. At the sight of their very own majestic piece of Martian highlands in the distance, his heart comes all the way home with short-breathed overwhelm. Twilight infuses a faint purple halo to the northeast cavernous, rock mantle hillside of Joshua Tree National Park. He touches Joe's driving shoulder in acknowledgment of their luck, choice, or blessing. In the truck with superior suspension, it's a rich baby-buggy ride over bumps up the washboard road. But the pain in Sam's shin, ribs, neck, and lower back reverberates. Joe stops at the beginning of the driveway to pick up the two packages sitting at the leg of his slapdash metal design of a UPS box. As he opens the truck door letting in the crisp desert cold, the cactus wrens take flight from the edge of the house's solar-paneled dome roof.

Sam's crutches make parallel holes in the dirt up the walk. Once he reaches the paved path leading to the front door, he can't get used to the weighty stun under his arms. Accidentally kicking over a pile of PVC pipes, Joe takes long with the key in the locks, finally pushing open the entrance. The sight of his mother's documents, framed and hung salon style, all over the living room walls, astounds Sam.

"It's like a museum in here," he exclaims.

"Gotta whole lotta help from Zeke," Joe says, putting Sam's bag down and standing there proudly, looking around. "He found the framer, helped me put them up, everything. I wanted to surprise you."

"I see, I see," Sam says, looking around with his mouth open.

"They're in town, you know, his sister and the husband, everybody's been asking about you."

"Why didn't we do this long ago?"

"I don't know, son. Maybe she just wasn't ready."

Right foot raised in back, ankle in a cast, Sam stands silently in the middle of the room, his jaw still dropped but soft, his expression serene. The cat hisses to him from the hallway entrance.

"Come here, Charlene." Sam leans his crutches against a balding, plaid tweed chair. He claps for her. She leaps for the couch arm, waiting for him to pick her up. "How are you, my puss? I missed you." He limps for the cushion to plop down with the blue-eyed, tiny, fat tigress with feet, tail tip, and snout dipped in white.

"Could count the times on one hand you asked about that cat," Joe says, shaking his head, seeming frailer than Sam remembered.

From where he sits with Charlene, a calico muff in his arms, Sam studies the framed marriage certificates, deeds, and slave auction announcements, while Joe puts tea on.

"Abel was by here," Joe calls from the kitchen.

"Yeah?" Sam responds loudly, without turning his head. He strokes Charlene in meditation, the feel of her fur making him sleepy in caress. He hears Joe's exit out the back door, but not his return, and so jumps upon his approaching voice.

"He's moving, you know." Joe carries wood to the potbelly stove.

"Who?"

"A-bel," Joe enunciates, his already generous cheeks spreading.

"Where to?"

"Hell-A."

"When?"

"Next couple weeks, if I'm not mistaken."

Joe kneels at the red stone hearth, placing paper, twigs, and logs in the belly, lighting it in three places. He brushes off his hands making a welcoming, percussive sound. With eyes closed, Sam smiles, still stroking Charlene.

"He came by around the same time you were at the lighthouse, Sam." Joe turns to look at him with purpose.

"Guess he was tuned in."

"Guess so."

"But nothing's ever gonna surprise me anymore."

"Can drop you by Abel's tomorrow, if you like."

"I don't know, Joe, I'm kinda tired."

From where he sits, Joe pushes the footstool over to Sam, then crawls the two steps over to help him lift his ankle to rest.

"There's nothing like friends, son. Don't forget it. That girl Rabeen was sure good to you too."

"Ra-bi-na."

"Bina, yeah. She's your angel."

"She saved my life, yes, but Mom is my angel."

Joe gets up with the help of his hand on the stool. "I've got something for you," he says, looking down at Sam.

The kettle whistles, and he leaves the room to get it.

"Don't we have any coffee?" Sam calls after him.

"No."

Sam gazes at the fire, the gases seem to form one sheet of funhouse glass, reflecting the flames. Joe returns with two mugs held together by three fingers on one hand, the pot of tea in the other, which he places on the small square coffee table.

"What kind is it?"

"Chamomile."

"Ugh, that's tasteless, Joe."

"What you want, then?"

"Earl Grey, Irish Breakfast, something a little more punchy like that."

"Don't you want to get to sleep tonight?"

"Not really."

"What do you mean?"

"Still having nightmares." Charlene jumps off his lap and disappears from the room.

"You gonna let it go, son, or not? Thanks to you and that girl, the muthafucking bastard is in jail, and they gonna put him away for good. Now if this isn't the time for you to let it go, what the hell *is*, then?"

"There's still gotta be another trial, Joe."

"They're gonna put him away, you hear me, he's murdered *three* people!" Joe roars. "He steadies himself, then pours them both a cup of tea. "Drink it up," he says, firmly, his eyes cast downward, darting side to side.

Sam obeys him, first blowing across the surface, then slurping it down so fast he burns his tongue and throat, then burps. Joe gets up, and returns with an envelope.

"Have something for you," Joe says.

"What is this?"

"Court adoption papers."

"What are you giving this to me for?"

"Got all the proper names of your people. Your father there, might want to look him up."

"Why would I want to do that?"

"Why not, son?"

The fire snaps behind Joe's legs.

"He never wanted me in the first place. You're all the father I'll ever want."

"His name's Wayland Griggs, son. He's more than ten years

younger than me, you might wanna hold onto these papers. Never know when you might need to see him."

He hands the envelope to Sam, who throws it on the floor. "I'm not a child, Joe. You can't just decide on your own what's best for me."

"Offering you the choice and opportunity, Sam, that's it." Joe looks at the envelope on the floor, and leaves Sam in the room, alone by the fire. The next day when he wakes up in the near same position on the couch, it takes him some minutes to figure out where he is.

Sam doesn't visit Abel for two weeks. He waits to go and see his friend the day before his cast comes off and he's got his job back at the hospital. Joe drops him off out front. The house appears immaculate, either freshly painted or pressure cleaned, he can't be sure. Inside, the boxes are lined up in compulsive order. The dark circles under Abel's eyes are gone, his wicker white skin glows with sun, his silky dark hair almost touches his shoulders, and he sports the beginnings of a full, nappy beard. Abel embraces Sam, who stands firm on one leg and holds onto his crutches with his underarm. He hops inside much stronger, leans his crutches down, and awkwardly hugs Abel again, as if to start over.

"So, the hero finally shows, eh?" Abel says, looking him once over.

"'A hero ain't nothing but a sandwich.'"

"What do you know about it?" he laughs.

"You look good too, A. You off the meds?"

"Not really. Are you?"

"I took that shit for maybe a week, I told you."

"You told me in your dreams? I haven't spoken to you in months, man."

"Maybe one month, A."

"So, when's the arraignment?"

"Ask Joe, man, I'm not thinking about it."

"But talk about closure."

"Yeah, talk about it amongst yourselves."

"Hey Princess, if I heard right, it's you who was seeing double, it was you who was going a little crazy."

"But wasn't it all worth it?"

"I can't imagine, man."

Abel walks around the island that separates the kitchen from the rest of the room.

"Beer?" he asks, raising his brows like a cute delinquent.

"Got any juice?"

"OJ okay?"

"Good."

Abel opens the near-empty fridge, jiggles the quart carton, and makes a regretful face. "I got beer," he says. "But no OJ."

"That's fine, then."

Abel puts the empty carton back in the fridge. He takes out two beers, pops open the caps, letting them hit the floor, but doesn't bother to pick them up. Sam smiles as Abel hands him a bottle and sits down next to him.

"So why haven't you seen Haley yet?"

"How'd you know I haven't seen her?"

"I ran into her."

"At the club?"

Abel nods.

"Then you know, man."

"Know what? That you're still judging her?"

"No. I mean. Well, how'd she look?"

"She's still sexy as ever, but she's looked better, I guess. She misses you, man."

"I don't know, A. She sounds so haunted on the phone. I feel like I don't want to push her over the edge, you know?"

"Haunted?"

"Yeah."

"Well, aren't we all, Princess?"

"Maybe you are."

"I think I've got a lot of company across the planet. Aren't we all haunted by the life we think we should be leading?"

"Is that why you're going to your brother's, of all places?"

"His wife left him. We could help one another."

"That's a switch."

"Yes it is. You should consider that for yourself, one of these days."

"What?"

"A switch."

"To what?"

"A little reciprocity."

"You gonna give me shit the whole time I'm here, man? If so I can leave."

"Calm down."

"I am calm."

"I apologize, then. Shit, Princess, you've gotten even more touchy." Abel gulps down the beer, then looks at Sam, trying to make it up to him with his humble posture. Sam maintains the long silence. Finally, he slurps up his beer, as if all alone, then softens, looking at his friend.

"So what are you gonna do?" Sam asks.

"About what?"

"In LA. What are you going to do there?"

"There's a job at a center for the mentally disabled, not much pay in it, but I feel like I can help."

"I think you can too. I'm gonna miss you though."

"First thing I want to do is change the center's name," Abel says, straightening his back in a stretch.

"What is it?"

"Burbank Center for the Retarded."

"That's messed up, man."

"I'd say."

"They are retarded, though. I mean by definition, right?"

"A lot of people around them helping to retard them with their attitudes, I'd say."

"Okay. I won't argue with that. I've had my share of the hellish 'beloveds' of my patients."

"Bunch of selfish people, man, throwing themselves on the martyr's cross."

"Speaking of which, what's up with you and the church? When you left Greta's, it was certainly up in the air."

"I'm reclaiming the Jew in me."

Sam's mouth drops open. Then he nods his head slowly, with increasing fervor. "Well good for you, A. What happened?"

"I guess I got wise to the millenarian view, which can't come to pass without my extermination."

"Very dramatic."

"Is it not true?"

"Took you this long, A?"

"I never heard *you* talking about it."

"I hadn't spent two months with Greta Bends the Militant yet either."

"Yeah, well, it's certainly not *all* Christians. I'm not saying that. Would be absurd to think it's all their fault."

"No, it's not. But my mother might have blamed all spiritual belief that is organized."

"And that's your mother, maybe. What do you believe?"

"'Maybe?'"

"Do you really feel like you really know your mother, man? I mean, mine is still alive, and I certainly couldn't claim the same."

"I feel like I do know her now. I feel like I do, A."

"I thought she was going to church when she died, Sam, and wasn't she into tarot?"

"My mother had an open mind, man, and that's how I'm able to find her."

"So did you vote?"

"Are you kidding, A? What's the segue?"

"Do I look like I'm kidding? Hey man, while you were off on your vision quest, the rest of the world marched on."

"I had a lot on my mind, and they lost the election without my help."

"*Without your help* being the key words, Princess."

"Damn, Abel, give me a break, will you? I was out of my mind."

"You weren't out but a day."

"What all do you know about it?"

"Joe told me everything."

"Joe doesn't know everything."

"You planning on filling me in, then?"

"How does anyone *explain* channeling their dead mother? She was with me, I knew where to go, I knew where to find her, she told me how to find the monster."

"You heard her voice?"

"No, I didn't hear her voice. She was inside of me, or she *was* me, I just don't know how to explain it. I wasn't even really aware of what was guiding me, you know? I didn't know that I knew what I was doing. It was all too close."

"So what now?"

"The cast comes off tomorrow. I start work again in two weeks."

"What about Haley?"

"I love Haley."

"And?"

"I want to be worthy of her, at this point. She thinks I ran off with every woman I met."

"Didn't you? 'Cause I don't know what you call it."

"No girl was ever more important. I gotta find a way to show her."

"Then go see her, asshole. Isn't that the first step?"

Sam waits another week and a half before summoning the courage and stamina to see Haley. He had wanted to run to her so many times, even while still on the crutches, but felt too selfish. He didn't want to condemn her for dancing, and he didn't want to see it either. He'd rather take her away somewhere, to start over fresh.

Sam enters the club near the end of a girl's set, as she crouches on all fours. He tells himself, as he pays the new cashier and passes a familiar bouncer he ignores at the door, that if he can't stand the sight of Haley on stage, he has no business trying to be with her. Because of the long strawberry blond hair, he doesn't recognize at first that it's Haley up there. She's now on her stomach, rolling in writhes against the floor. She looks up at a guy, who pushes a bill toward her breasts, that she takes with her lips. Her sinewy arms move her back up to her feet, like a monkey. She grinds her hips, as she stands, the tattooed diamonds on the one leg making a psychedelic performance of their own. Her focus is potent but glazed on the next drunk who leans with a bill in his hand. She looks skinnier than before, and even with the makeup, under her eyes is blue and sunken.

Sam sits down two tables away from the stage, and the waitress takes his order at the same time that Haley's friend, Tish, notices him from across the room. She strides over, her short white skirt stretching with pleasure over her strong, tight thighs. She carries her head as if balancing a plate, her lavish mouth relaxed, self-satisfied.

Tish is just a shade or so lighter than his mother, he thinks, as she bends down to kiss him on the mouth. He looks into her eyes, and sees that she's really very close in color to him, and as he looks at her breasts spilling out of the sparkling pearl bra, the thought of sleeping with her seems incestuous to him. Almost as if their child would be inbred, though he knows this is absurd. She's the sister he never had. She sits down next to him, the smell of her delicious as fruit. The heat between them makes him uncomfortable, as he turns to look up at Haley making crass love to the pole.

"So I heard you've been through hell," Sam says, clearing his throat. The waitress puts down his whiskey in front of him.

"I could say the same for you," Tish says. Her far apart eyes slant downwards like a Marrakesh princess.

"I mean your roommate."

"I know what you mean."

"Cutting out her implants like that. Grim."

Tish shakes her head, then takes a sip of his drink. The music stops and the twelve or so men in the room start clapping. Tish joins in, and whistles loudly like a jock. Sam watches Haley leave the stage, and he imagines being with her, just the two of them somewhere else on the other side of the world.

"I'm glad you're back, you know," Tish says. Her face seems incapable of showing any extreme emotions. "But not if you're going to fuck with her anymore than she's fucking with herself."

"What's that mean?"

"What that means is," Tish stresses between her teeth with purpose, then seems to change her mind, "she needs you."

Sam looks for any details in Tish's eyes.

"So playboy?"

"I need her too."

"Then do it right this time."

Haley slinks toward them. Her hips sway widely in a clingy, glittering mini wrap skirt. Her hair is *Birth of Venus* long, he thinks, taking the new look of her all in. She gets that smile on her face Sam believes created just for him.

"You remembered the Leonids," she says in slow motion enthusiasm. Sam gets up to hold her tight. She feels tiny in his arms like he could wrap around her twice, still she towers over him in her high stilettos.

"The Leonids?" He holds her at the waist, looks into her face. As she opens her mouth, her breath smells acrid like smoke.

"The meteor showers tonight," she says, sleepily, but looking at all of him so thrilled she appears as if she could climb out through the top of her own head. "I tell you the parent comet is the Tempel-Tuttle? *Every* meteor shower should be a holiday, don't you think? All the kids should be let out of school, everyone should get up in the middle of the night to see them. Celebrations everywhere." She gestures with one arm that flops back down to the side of his ribs, which she caresses. "A national holiday, it should be, instead of stupid ones like Columbus Day, right?" She kisses him full on the mouth, looks him in the eye. "Did you see them last night?" she whispers.

"No, I didn't. But it will be great to see them with you." He kisses her on the chin. They rub noses, her makeup leaving a smudge on his that she lovingly wipes off with the tip of her index finger.

"So he's come to claim you," Tish says to Haley, taking her hand.

"I wouldn't say that, dude," she looks down at her friend. Tish smiles at her as happily as she can, but the arc of her mouth remains minor. She gets up to leave them, kissing Haley good-bye on the lips, Haley never letting go of Sam.

"Your hair couldn't have grown that fast," he says to her, running his fingers through the tangled, loose Botticelli curls.

"They're extensions."

"Really?" he looks at her incredulously.

"Come on," she puts her nose back on his, speaks softly into his mouth. "You think white girls don't get them too? What's

236

wrong with you?" He pulls his face back just far enough to look her in the eyes.

"What's wrong with *you* thinking you need them?"

"You met me with long hair, remember? I make more money that way. Should have never cut it." She lets her hand drop from his waist.

"Are you drunk?"

"I am not," she answers, indignantly.

"Let's get out of here, can we?"

"Absolutely. Nothing could keep me here now," she says, dramatically, then licks in one scoop the side of his face.

He follows Haley's car to her house in Pioneertown. Even at night entering the giant bedrock caves is like discovering a new dimension. They pass the late night crowd at Pappy and Harriet's saloon, the epicenter of the old town built for Western sets. Continuing up the winding road to less and less civilization, the chill in the air feels all the more vicious in the quiet desolation. It's never seemed like a place a woman should live by herself, but he has always admired Haley's preference for isolation.

He pulls around to the front of her shack, parks behind her just beyond the propane tank, and slips the bag of gifts out of the car. She doesn't seem to notice, as she gets out of hers.

"It's overcast," she announces, looking up at the sky and back at Sam with disappointment bordering hopefulness. "But the meteor storm's not supposed to peak until two tonight."

"Can we stay up that late?"

"That's barely four hours away." She opens her front door and turns on the light.

"You painted the walls!"

"Right after you left, but I prefer the black."

"This is much better, very warm and natural, adobe. Feels like we're in New Mexico, or something."

"What do you know about it?" she turns to him suspiciously.

"Nothing. But why couldn't we go there together sometime?"

She smiles, her eyes narrowing with charmed disbelief. "It's better, Sam."

"What do you mean?"

"You're not so preoccupied. The gloom and doom is lifted." She makes butterflies of her fingers, fluttering away from his forehead. Then she walks away from him, to take off her jacket. He follows, surprised by his insistence to be near her.

"I have some gifts for you," Sam says. He shies as he reaches for the bag of knickknacks he wasn't sure if he'd gotten for her or Sheba Moses. He pulls out the book first.

"Pablo Neruda," Haley says slowly with surprise. "Since when are you into poetry?"

"Is that the way to encourage a guy?"

"I've been writing poetry. Did you know that?"

"Yes."

"Another reason to quit dancing for good. As soon as I was back at the club, it dried up, I stopped just like that."

"You never told me much about your writing."

"I think I did, Sam. Yes, I did." She sighs. Out of the bag, he pulls the bottle and puts it in her hand.

"Cranberry *ketchup*?" She reads the label's ingredients. She turns on the table lamp with the bronze fringe shade. He looks around at how messy the place is, then closely at her face, her skin broken out. "Hmn. For all those gourmet meals I'm so famous for?"

"We could learn to cook together," Sam says. She puts the bottle down on the black vinyl trunk she uses for a coffee table. "Or we could just slop it on our burgers."

"Right," she answers jadedly. He can't help thinking that Tish has rubbed off on her energy wise, as it seems considerably lower. He opens up her hands, puts the palms together, and with her poised in an easy, vulnerable offering like that, her innocence resembles that of a saint. He empties out the bag of stones into her hands, two drop to the floor and neither of them bends to pick them up.

"From the beaches of Oregon?"

Sam nods, taking the best one. He wets his finger with his spit, rubs the gritty surface, revealing it's ephemeral gloss.

"Beautiful white stones," she says. "Was that girl with you when you found these?"

"I was alone. On my way up the coast. Abel joined me later."

"So where's the girl's sister now?"

"In Costa Rica. But she'll have to come back to testify."

"Did you fuck her?"

"I did not," he answers hotly. "And she saved my life."

"I don't really understand what happened, Sam."

"I don't want to talk about it."

"That's not fair. Here I am, happy for you that this has been resolved, finally. I've bore a lot of this pain with you, these past couple years."

"Okay."

"But if you don't want to talk about—"

"I fought him, but I almost lost my footing," he interrupts with a shaky, ashamed voice. "Rabina stepped in, nearly killed him, knocking him off the hill. Then she got help. They'd been looking for him. They had evidence that he'd killed Lamb at the border, then he'd killed Lamb's daughter, the same way he did my mother. So they locked him up. That simple, really."

"It's amazing, Sam, it really is," she nods, looking as if her own movement could hypnotize to sleep.

He is silent, looking at her strangely, then searching the floor.

"How did you know he'd be there at exactly that time?" she asks, delicately coming alive again.

"I didn't. I don't know how else to explain it. I just had to go there, right then. I was pulled."

"But why with that girl?"

"She *happened* to come with me. There was no great plan there, totally spontaneous."

"She's some kind of firefighter, isn't she? Super rescue girl, right?" she says with a mocking tone. "Is that what you need? Am I too weak for you?"

"Haley. *Please.*"

"I am weak."

"You can't be to have lasted this long with me."

"I'm weak," she nods again, raising her brows, and looking through his eyes.

"What's going on with you?" He studies her.

"A woman needs connection that lasts," she says with her hand, making a hula dancer's story in the air. "And you're off here, then you're off there."

"How can a man hunt and collect if he's home all day connecting? How would we survive?"

"Women can hunt and collect themselves, Sam. We just want love, is all. Don't be so selfish."

"Don't you think I needed time?"

"What happened to you is awful. Horrible. But that doesn't exempt you from caring."

"I never stopped."

"Look at Joe, you took on that rollercoaster. Don't take him for granted. Don't take *me* for granted."

"I don't," he snaps, then regrets it instantly. He takes her hands in his, kisses them, wondering if he should get down on his knees to convince her. "Some things end up working out."

"Well, this certainly did. Now you can get on with your life, as far as your mother is concerned."

"All this could work out too."

"This?"

"Not everybody splits up," Sam says.

"Oh, yes they do."

"Well you think what you're gonna think, and I'll do the same." He kisses her hands again, then lets go of her to cross his arms. "Tell me what you wanna do, Haley. I'll move in, take care of you. Quit your job, if it's not working for you."

"It's not working for *you*."

"Look at you. You're gonna tell me everything's just fine?"

Haley takes his face, licks him sweetly on the lips and in his ear. Her tongue tastes sharp, and as she makes her way down his body, she lashes him with it, taut like a weapon, and taking him in her mouth, using him until even the skin is swollen. She becomes so sloppy her teeth lacerate him until he pushes her head away, and joins her on the floor, where in theory they are hot enough to stay, but they soon get up with one another's help to fall into bed.

Haley grabs the clock to look closely at the time, two-thirty. Naked and pale, she jumps out of bed, Sam watching her frenzy. She pulls on her ugly wool-lined, rubber-soled, suede boots her neighbor once said in front of Sam were for contraception, and with her one winter coat of black shaved sheep, she runs outside to check the sky.

"Jesus, Sam. It's snowing," she says, stomping her boots at the door, and hopping back inside.

"You're kidding," Sam answers, snug under the covers, his ankles locked, eyes barely open.

"Lightly, anyway. Flurries. Shit. I really wanted to see the Leonids with you," she whines.

"We'll see them next time," he says smiling, eyes closed. "Kinda magical that it's snowing, huh," he mutters.

"So magical that you just can't wait to run out that door to see it."

Sam smiles again like a baby in his sleep, hears Haley shut the bathroom door, and he doesn't know how long she stays there since he's in REM before he can feel her joining him under the covers.

In the morning, Sam wakes to the soft light coolly glowing through the parted black velvet curtains. Though the gas wall heater is on, his nose and feet hurt with cold. Haley shows the thin, pallid skin of her back. She doesn't stir as he steps out of bed to run to the window. He is amazed to see the desert in disguise, covered in concentrated illumination of some seven inches of snow. The Joshua trees appear to sprout families of giant cater- pillars stretching their way out of the trunk, only to be caught frozen. The cabins and shacks in the distance look like Wyeth paintings of eastern farmland, caught in ferocious gusts of powdered sugar, the cacti like shocked and alien vegetation.

He turns the heater up and the radio on to hear that snow is expected through late afternoon, no plows in the county, the Pioneertown streets wouldn't be graded until after the main highway. The disc jockeys joke about the fact that people were forced to spend the night at Pappy and Harriet's saloon. In the tiny kitchen, Sam grinds the coffee, not caring if it wakes Haley, as he'd love to go out and make a snowman with her. He puts it in the percolator, and on the way to the toilet, sees with all that pronounced strawberry waved hair she still lies there like the marble *Venus di Milo*.

After he pisses, he looks in the mirror to splash his face with water, and there in the bowl are scraps of tinfoil, black, sooty, and streaked. Enraged that she could throw away eleven years of sobriety in one night—or even in the three months he's been gone—he goes roaring out to the bedroom to wake her up.

Yelling as he shakes her, she takes what seems like infinity to budge.

"God, let me sleep, Sam," she growls from the back of her throat.

Roughly, he sits her up, takes her face between his hands, squeezes her cheeks, makes her look at him.

"This isn't going to work," Sam says, slowly with definition. "I can't save you."

"Let go of my face," she hisses.

"Mistake, after mistake, after mistake, after mistake," he says trailing off. He gets up, shaking his head, returning to the view of the snow. "Just because I've made so many mistakes," he says to himself and the window, "doesn't mean I'll never get it right."

"I could say the same thing, Sam," she says from across the room to his back. She lets her hand drop heavily on the bed.

Sam remains at the window without looking at her. The wind has dropped and the flakes fall like infinite notes. There is wisdom to its quiet playful depth. Long diamonds melt off the roof. The house is alive with heat. He presses his face against the glass, and watches his breath of steam.

I am is what he could shout, running through the snow without shoes or coat, waiting to catch his death of cold. Instead, he stands there. After staring long enough, he finds himself all the more ready for the beauty ahead.

ACKNOWLEDGMENTS

Thank you for your time, help, and professional expertise: Kathy Belden, Lauren Black, Cory Bliesner, Tom Bodkin, Shawn Chapman Holley, Sakada, Chuck Sheley, Yumi Shioda, Alan Siporin, and Jerry Stahl.

Much gratitude, love, and affection to: Daniel Baxter, Cressida Connelly, Traci Lind, Karen Rinaldi, Erica, Laura, and Violet Teasley, and Imogen Teasley-Vlautin.

A NOTE ON THE AUTHOR

Lisa Teasley is the author of the award-winning story collection *Glow in the Dark* and the novels *Dive* and *Heat Signature*. She lives in Los Angeles.

A NOTE ON THE TYPE

The text of this book is set in Linotype Sabon, named after the type founder, Jacques Sabon. It was designed by Jan Tschichold and jointly developed by Linotype, Monotype and Stempel, in response to a need for a typeface to be available in identical form for mechanical hot metal composition and hand composition using foundry type.

Tschichold based his design for Sabon roman on a font engraved by Garamond, and Sabon italic on a font by Granjon. It was first used in 1966 and has proved an enduring modern classic.